KR Paul

Pantheon 3

RETURN OF APOLLO

Published in the United States of America by KRP Publishing

KRPPublishing.com

KRP Publishing eBook first edition – January 2025 ISBN-13 979-8-9898245-4-0

KRP Publishing first edition trade paperback – January 2025 ISBN-13 979-8-9898245-5-7

Library of Congress Control numer on file with publisher.

For those who have fallen and found the strength to rise again.

ONE

VALERIE "ATHENA" HALL
0854L/1254Z, 17 OCT

From her office in the depths of the downtown Limitless Logistics office, Val's eyes occasionally flicked to the CCTV video at the edge of her monitor. She was grinding through the day's paperwork, a military construction project known as a MILCON effort, for the 467th Logistical Group's new headquarters at Fort Belvoir, Virginia. The proposal was months late and already over budget. Val ground her teeth, anticipating the fight she would have with Missouri's senior Senator Maureen Mitchell and the Pantheon's grudging ally. Val sighed and irritably pushed her red-gold hair behind her shoulder again. Reading the report was far less stimulating than watching potential Pantheon candidates arrive for screening.

Just two months ago, when the Pantheon's extraordinary and highly secret gifts had been exposed on the greens of the National Mall, they had taken an aggressive and controversial step of opening the front doors to the public. In Mandy's first national address as "Hestia," she had welcomed anyone and everyone who thought they belonged in Limitless Logistics to show up to see if they possessed teleportation skills, called "Jumping" by the Pantheon. A week later, the first flock of candidates arrived and quick thinking on Val's part had weeded out the group of hopefuls, revealing Jafar and Rachel as having their vaunted power.

They had since adopted her method as their standard method of screening. A member of the so-called Pantheon, usually Damarcus, would greet the candidates with a firm handshake, telepathically impress Point Zero's image into their minds, then teleport to the location with an expectation those with the ability would follow. Like Jafar and Rachel, those who truly possessed the skill would know how to follow him. Those who didn't were gently but firmly escorted out by security.

Two months, Val thought.

They had a flood of people try to join them and had been forced to formalize the meeting and time. Today was the advertised in-processing day and Val hoped to find just one real candidate in the usual flock of wannabes.

Her eyes flicked to the monitor again.

In two months, only one other person had been able to follow Damarcus to the Jump room. Val wanted to groan just thinking of Braxton Chadwick Nelson's dubious tenure at Limitless Logistics. Chadwick, who hated his first name, was already twenty-nine, far older than even Val when she appeared. He admitted to being able to Jump for the past handful of years and to using his ability, plus his family's considerable wealth, to wander the world partying. He also admitted that his decade-long cocaine habit had impeded his ability to Jump on more than one occasion.

Val's jaw clenched. The little shit had been nothing but trouble since arriving, taking a stance of entitlement at every opportunity, even sneering at their considerable pay, which far exceeded anything Val had ever thought achievable in her life. To Chadwick and his family, it was a small addition to the interest from their considerable holdings.

The Limitless Logistics team had been working on getting him ready to be on missions, but so far, none of the Pantheon or their partner agencies had been willing to accept him for a full mission.

Val had nine active Pantheon members to cover two companies with distinctly different missions and she desperately needed more. Unfortunately, that meant she kept Chadwick on her books, despite his obvious flaws. Even if he was never truly useful, she wanted to keep the little party animal in check and keep him from making a bad name for them.

The newly reformed and rebranded Limitless Logistics held true to its roots and was the premier "just in time" logistics company, hauling humanitarian aid, organ transplants, or critical commercial and non-military cargo for those who could pay. The former Limitless Logistics had been split, chipping off the military personnel and cargo movements into Spartan Tactical. And overseeing it all was Valerie "Athena" Hall, CEO of Athena Strategic Enterprises, or the 467th Logistical Group, and her stalwart deputy, Damarcus Washington. She hated splitting apart Marco Martinez's hard work, but after being exposed in what had been dubbed the "Battle for D.C." the rebranding had been necessary.

Val's desperation for new members to fill two companies was enough to allow Chadwick to remain on the Limitless Logistics roster but it wasn't great enough to let him work alone yet. Jafar and Rachel, though slightly less new than Chadwick, had issues that limited the missions to which they could be assigned. She sighed, absent-mindedly running a hand through her red-gold hair, and let her gaze wander.

The monitor streamed the feeds from security cameras at the building's front door, lobby, and a small conference room that doubled as an in-processing or briefing room. She watched a few people loitering within camera range of the front door and checked her clock. They had six minutes until the designated screening time and Val didn't anticipate many of them heading inside for at least three more minutes.

Despite a media blitz designed to show Limitless Logistics and its personnel in a positive light, not everyone in America had bought their message. Many people were scared of their capabilities, even as they sought to join them. Val sighed and twirled her pen around her thumb.

From opposite sides of the screen, two men turned and started toward the door. Val watched as one opened the door and held it for the other, a charming smile on his face. She squinted. It was difficult to see from the CCTV cameras, but the man looked familiar and she squinted harder, trying to overcome the low resolution of the camera. As the front doors closed behind them, she saw others start walking toward the entryway.

Val clicked on the audio for the conference room, intending to listen to the welcoming brief. It didn't change much from week to week, but she did occasionally enjoy the startled exclamations as the week's briefer seemed to appear from thin air or Jumped abruptly away. Val checked the roster and saw that Damarcus was doing this week's briefing. She smiled. Her Deputy had an easy manner and calm smile that set even the most skittish applicants at ease.

Setting her paperwork aside, Val abandoned any pretense and focused on her screen. She counted five people in the room now and scrutinized their faces, looking for any sign that they might possess the natural ability to teleport from one location to another and weren't just there to sneak a peek inside the building.

One woman's face showed a slight smirk and Val dismissed her as a looky-loo, possibly a reporter from an obscure tabloid or social media "influencer" looking for the real inside scoop. It had happened at least twice so far and Val shook her head over the lengths folks would go to for their own fame.

Two men sat easily in the plush leather chairs at the conference table and Val mentally dismissed them as well; if they had the skill, they would look more nervous. Val searched the screen for the two she'd seen first enter the building. One, a dour-looking man, stood tensely near the door. Val squinted again and tried to find the one who had looked familiar as Damarcus Jumped into the room, but she could only see his shoulder, just out of the frame.

She chuckled as half the people reacted to his arrival. The woman's smirk wiped from her face as she stood from her chair, the dour man's frown deepened, and the two lounging at the conference table pushed back. The man who had been out of the frame stepped close and Val could see his face clearly for the first time.

Shock hit her like a frigid wave and she went rigid in her chair.

"Anna!" Val shouted to her secretary. "Anna, get the conference room on the line right now! Don't let Dee pass the Jump room location!"

Val watched in horror, strangely transfixed and unable to move, as Damarcus started his welcome speech, unaware of who sat in the room.

"Good morning and welcome to Limitless Logistics. I understand you are presenting yourself as candidate logistics officers?" He scanned their faces as they nodded. Just like shy middle schoolers on the first day of class, no one volunteered to speak.

Val could hear the phone on the conference room table ring as he spoke.

"Very well, then. I am Damarcus Washington. It's a pleasure to meet you all."

He walked from behind the lectern. "Now, if you are the kind of candidate we're seeking, you will be able to follow me."

Something in Val unfroze as he moved. She Jumped to the conference room, determined to intercept Damarcus before he could pass Point Zero's location, deep inside their facility. Despite her new resolve, she was too late to stop Damarcus from shaking hands with Apollo, an agent of Svoboda, the Russian terrorist version of their organization.

"Dee, that's Apollo!" Val shouted.

Apollo whipped around to regard her. His face was unreadable and in the moment, the only thing Val took in was his presence.

"They are coming. You have to evacuate your headquarters," Apollo said in barely accented but stilted English. "They are coming for you." He gave a slight bow of his head to her and Jumped away.

Damarcus looked at her questioningly, his warm brown eyes meeting her wide-open hazel. "Who?"

"One of Miller's Svoboda teammates from this spring," she told him. Val snatched the ringing phone. "Anna, flush the building," she said quickly and hung up.

"Oh, fuck. Val, oh God, Val. I didn't even realize!" Damarcus told her as his light brown face went pale.

Val shook her head and turned to the candidates. "Get out!" She turned back to Damarcus, "Dee, I'm arming up. Meet me in the Jump room."

Val Jumped to her office and grabbed the small handgun holstered under her desk. "Anna, flush everyone!" She yelled out into the outer office as she snapped the magazine into a Sig Sauer P380.

"Already on it, General Hall," Anna called back.

"Everyone, Anna," she said, thumbing the safety off. "Call Hank to warn him. We've been breached."

A breach by those who shared her ability to teleport was her nightmare. Once someone had the visual impression of a space, any space, they could teleport in and out at their will. The handshake Damarcus shared with Apollo had deliberately impressed the image of Point Zero, deeply embedded behind their security lines in his mind. The image was now available to anyone Apollo cared to share it with, including his Svoboda teammates.

Anna nodded once, head already pressing the little used red phone to her shoulder as Val Jumped into their Point Zero, the room specifically set aside for barrier-free teleportation departures and arrivals and unoriginally named the "Jump room." The tall, blond-haired, and blue-eyed man stood calmly in the middle of the room, clearly waiting for her. Val snapped her weapon up and pointed it at his chest.

"Why?" was all she could grind out. An alarm started blaring and Val heard Anna's calm voice call across the interphone system. Her finger twitched on the trigger and Val could feel the spring tension start to ride the hammer.

"All personnel, all personnel. Breach, breach, breach. Proceed to your stations, fallback Alpha."

"Do I scare you that much?" Apollo's voice was smooth with a hint of a guttural Russian accent.

Damarcus appeared beside Val. "The candidates are running scared. Alpha?"

Val nodded, her eyes still on Apollo. "Seems safest."

"He won't be pleased," Damarcus told her. "You know, Hank—"

"Don't!" Val cut him off sharply, seeing the look in Apollo's eyes.

Running footsteps sounded in the hall and Val flinched, strongly reminded of another occasion where she held a Svoboda member at gunpoint on Point Zero.

Val sneered at Apollo. "I killed him right here. You know that, right?"

Apollo flinched back. His eyes went hard and narrow. "We knew he was dead. I assumed it was at your hand. Now I know."

Val watched his jaw tighten and brought the tip of her gun up as he swallowed hard. Her pulse was hammering in her ears, but she mastered her breathing.

Breathe in for a four count, hold for a four count, exhale for a four count, she told herself.

"Why are you here, Apollo?" She closed one eye and centered the gun steadily between his eyes.

"Would you believe me if I told you it was because it was the only place I could be safe?" Apollo's posture was shockingly loose for someone who had a gun pointed at his chest.

"Nope," Val told him harshly. "Try again."

"They are coming for you. You are in danger and I do not want you to be harmed."

"Liar," Val snarled, finger slowly applying pressure to the trigger.

"No lie. They are coming."

"Who? Vmeste? The oligarchy's pets?" Damarcus asked.

"Worse, Svoboda and they want you dead." Apollo nodded to her once again, smiling sadly, and Jumped.

TWO

VALERIE "ATHENA" HALL

0903L/1303Z, 17 OCT

"Damn it!" Val yelled in frustration.

"Shit," Damarcus snapped. "I am so sorry, Val. I didn't recognize him."

"I know. I know, Dee. I almost didn't recognize him myself. It's too late now, he knows. We can't un-ring the bell. Get to your rally point and get your group out." Val yanked open the door to the Jump room and strode out, anger radiating from every inch of her toned frame.

Val, point Alpha? Murphy's mental voice resonated in her head. Personnel nodded to her as they jogged past on their way to their individual rally points, some eyeing the gun she held low as she strode down the hall.

Val inhaled slowly and let her anger flow. Her shoulders dropped and she let her mind reach out, gathering in the mental threads she came to associate with her team. *Yes, team. Point Alpha. Grab everyone and get accountability before you Jump. Someone tell Rachel if she hasn't already heard it from Anna on the interphone. See you in Hurlburt.*

There had been consternation from every member of the Pantheon when Val started pulling up Zeus's evacuation plans four months ago. They had bitched and whined that his plans were unnecessary and paranoid. Val had cheerfully ignored them all, updated the plans, and scheduled mandatory practices once a week for a month to Hurlburt Air Force Base in Florida. One of the few other organizations that knew they existed before they were exposed was stationed there and it was their safest location to use as an emergency Jump. Publicly, she said that if nothing else, it was good practice moving live people with whom you may not have had physical contact recently, a vital component to a safe personnel Jump.

"Besides, Jafar and Rachel could use the practice," she'd told them with a smile.

To Murphy "Ares" Hawkins and Amanda "Hestia" Squires, her two CEOs she told the full truth: While Miller Thompson had said he wouldn't have given up Limitless Logistics to *Svoboda* to protect Mandy, his daughter, she didn't fully trust him. Damarcus had backed her, but Murphy and Mandy had both grumbled and groused. Finally, Murphy told her that he would obey the lawful orders of his commanding officer and Mandy told her that Limitless Logistics would comply with the drills if leadership in their parent company, Athena Strategic Logistics, directed it.

Val swallowed the sense of satisfaction she had in completing the drills as she and Damarcus stalked the hall toward their departure points.

"See you in Hurlburt," Damarcus told her as he split at an intersection.

Val nodded. The holster she'd snagged from her desk and stuffed into a pocket was now safely attached to her fine grain leather dress belt. With a flick of the safety and a satisfying snap, she settled her gun into its holster.

"Anna, are we ready?" She called down the hall.

"All present, ma'am." Her face was as calm as ever as she held out a hand.

Val put both hands out and touched as many hands as possible, feeling the stress and fear that flooded along the touch. "It'll be okay, folks," she told them, keeping her voice placid.

Anna gave her hand a little squeeze of approval.

Val closed her eyes and Jumped them all.

The sudden loss of almost 3,000 calories that fueled the heavy Jump made Val stagger and drop to a knee. Hands grasped at her, flooding her with their fear, anxiety, and a sense of urgency. She batted them away ineffectually.

"I'm fine," she gasped and put a hand on the cool pavement of the hangar floor. The instant calorie debt pushed her down, robbing her of coordination and strength. She slowly toppled to the floor.

"Val!" Anna cried.

"Get Hank," she whispered.

A soft, wrinkled brown hand lightly clasped her wrist. "I've got you, girl. He knows and I can see the team now." Anna's voice was smooth and soothing, her touch an island of peace in the storm around them.

Val could hear the sound of other teams arriving. Voices filled the room and a sensation of minds buzzed around her.

"Well, hey there, Val," Hank's cheerful voice carried over the din. "Welcome back. Didn't think we'd be seeing you again quite so soon, but you're always welcome here."

Val watched him smile and nod at several people as he approached. People ebbed away from him like a tide, making a clear path. "*The kindest, scariest grandpa you'll ever meet*," Val had once called him to Mandy, well out of anyone's hearing. Hank was a man of average height, his brown hair graying at the temples, and he limped only slightly on his prosthetic foot, but he had a vitality and command presence that people reacted to, even if only subconsciously.

She smiled as she caught sight of an IV bag in his hand. "Thanks, Hank."

"Hey, give us a little space, will you?" Hank asked the folks around her in his usual kind but firm tone. "She just needs a bag then we'll be good. There's a big conference room down that hallway," he said to her group, pointing, "you may be more comfortable waiting there."

The press of bodies and minds ebbed as Hank squatted by Val's head. He worked quietly and quickly to set up her IV. Hank wore gloves as he worked so she didn't get the curious exchange of surface emotions and thoughts Pantheon members pulled from anyone they shared skin to skin contact with and for once, Val was grateful. She didn't speak as he hung the bag on top of his shoulder and sat next to her when he was done.

"Sorry, we don't usually get so many of you at once," Hank said and pointed at the bag dispensing precious calories to her. "But gravity is gravity and if I need to step away, I'll grab someone else to take the bag."

"Thanks, Hank," Val whispered.

"Level with me, Val, how bad is it?" Hank asked in a low tone.

"The main Limitless Logistics building has been breached by an adversary Jumper. I have no way to keep him out now that he knows, but I have no reason to believe he knows where we are now. You shouldn't be a target here."

Hank nodded once. "Good, I love this area. I'd hate to have to tell my girls we have to move again."

When Val started, he put a gentle hand on her clothed shoulder. "I'm teasing. It's okay. I'm glad your contingency plans worked."

"I'm glad we had them," Val told him.

"What now?"

"Now?" Val stared at the IV line and considered. "My immediate concern is to ensure we got everyone out. I'll execute a full accountability recall. Should be easy since no one should have left the hangar. Then establish communications with the Chairman of the Joint Chiefs and Senator Mitchell. They'll need to know all operations are paused for the immediate future." A wrinkle appeared as she furrowed her eyebrows.

Val shook her head, letting her red-gold hair fall out of her face, and met Hank's eyes.

"You've got this, Val. This Chairman may be new, but he seems to have a level head. It's not like he can fault you. Or fire you," Hank concluded with a small laugh.

She nodded. "Then we find a way to create a temporary base of operations. I'll need to send a team back to retrieve a minimum level of gear, but I can't guarantee there won't be a *Svoboda* team waiting for us when we go in." She shook her head again. "Stars above, Hank. We're ass deep in alligators this time. No working space, no gear, and no comms."

Hank clasped her shoulder lightly. "One step at a time, Val. Do your recall procedures. Reassure yourself that you have your people. Get to the mission once you know you have your people."

"One step at a time," she agreed. "Thank you, Hank. You're a good influence."

Val smiled at Hank and took in a deep breath. She closed her eyes as she exhaled.

Okay, team. Report back, in chronological joining order, with how many of your personnel you successfully Jumped, she told the group over their curious telepathy link that accompanied their teleportation skill. *Dee, get Rachel's count and report on her behalf.* Val frowned at the last part. Rachel had been with them for almost two months and the woman still couldn't let her barriers down enough to achieve telepathic communication with anyone in the Pantheon.

Wilson, I have my six.

James Lee and I have all four of mine.

Damarcus here with all six.

Val, I have all four of mine plus Kelly.

Mandy, five of five.

Murphy, five of six plus Zora.

There was a burst of frustration across the bond.

Chill folks, one of the nurses was out today. That's why it's five.

Rachel says she has her six, Damarcus told the link on Rachel's behalf.

Jafar al Rayyan and I have my one, Jafar told them, his voice formal.

Good work, thank you all. Tell your groups to get settled in and plan for at least one night here.

"Hank, is it okay if we stay the night?"

"My hangar is your hangar. Let me know what supplies we need to draw from on-base logistics." His mouth quirked in a little grin.

"Thanks, Hank. Will do." Val closed her eyes again. *Hank says they can accommodate us overnight here. Make a list of what you need. We have shelter, but let me know how many cots, sleeping bags, food requirements, and if we need any medical. Dee, you brought the backend logistics team. Have them consolidate the supply list and get it to Hank within the hour. Wilson, you have the cafeteria team and it sounds like only one shift's worth. Start them sourcing and setting up a large buffet meal for everyone. The Florida panhandle isn't ideal for good food, but,* her mental voice took on a humorous tone, *they do have a lot of it. I'm sure we can find catering, even if we pay out the nose for it. I'll have Anna and the admin team start getting the word out to our higher-ups.*

Val took in another deep breath and opened her eyes, taking in the now crowded hangar. *I don't know how long we'll be here, folks, so be ready to conduct operations out of here for a little while.*

THREE

RACHEL NG

0830L/1330Z, 17 OCT

Rachel Ng sat slumped against a crate, observing the hangar floor. Like the rest of the Pantheon, she had arrived moments earlier and was struggling to overcome the massive calorie debt she had incurred Jumping herself and six coworkers the 800 miles from Washington, DC, to Hurlburt Field, Florida.

Her brain spun trying to figure out the calorie math that Damarcus had taught her over the last two months. A calorie a mile was easy, but there was something about a "load factor"? She frowned, trying to remember how many additional calories it was per additional pounds of cargo. Either way, the folks she'd hauled had been average sized DC denizens, fit and dense and probably 200 pounds each? Load factored at 500 pounds? Or 400? Her head slumped to the side slightly as she considered losing just under 3,000 calories in an instant.

She had landed jarringly, several feet from where she had intended, and one of the people she had transported gave a yelp of pain as they bounced roughly off a hangar wall. Rachel had had just enough energy and concentration left to drag herself to the crate a few feet away and put it at her back, facing the open hangar. She had dropped in and out of consciousness, head lolling from side to side, as someone had placed IV nutrition in her arm and tucked the bag on top of the crate.

Half a bag of the company's custom-blended nutrients later, she had regained enough energy to watch the hangar with growing interest. Less than an hour earlier it had been a normal day, or what passed for normal working with this group. She had finished a workout and a massive breakfast, sitting alone by choice, when an alarm blared over the building's public address system. Rachel had sprinted to her assigned spot, dodging people as she went. When her booted feet came to a halt at her designated Jumping out point, the Contingency Leader had told her everyone was accounted for and Rachel held out a hand as she grit her teeth.

She hated the touch of others now more than ever. The invasive feeling that she was in someone else's mind put her on edge. Years spent forced into the world's oldest profession had left more than physical scars as it put her in contact with too many unsavory people. She never wanted to know what someone willing to engage with her was really thinking, afraid of what she would find, of shining a light on the dark corners.

But, the quick taps on her hand showed nothing more than light anxiety and fear. Not fear for themselves but for the group as a whole. Rachel had been surprised by how much the people with her cared for one another, for their collective safety. She had swallowed her own fear and Jumped them.

Now, she was amazed again as she watched the group recover from its abrupt displacement. She saw Carson, Wilson Armstrong's handler for the last decade, gently cradling Wilson's head on his lap as his unconscious form absorbed the bag of IV nutrients resting over Carson's shoulder. Carson appeared to be chatting amiably with a woman next to him, half his attention on the woman as he fussed with Wilson's IV line. A few yards away, Damarcus was struggling to sit up, helped by Ryan, his handler. They clasped hands and she was surprised to see Damarcus didn't wince at the touch.

Aware of her scrutiny, Damarcus turned to her. "How you holding up, Rachel?"

"Fine," she replied too quickly.

"Of course, you are, girl," he said with a smile.

Rachel studiously ignored his smile and approach.

"I didn't mean to imply you wouldn't be okay," he said with a slight frown. "I just wanted to check. To be certain, you know?"

"I'm fine, Damarcus."

"You can call me Dee."

Rachel regarded him quietly, her face expressionless.

"Or not, makes no difference to me. I'm going to check on Val and the others."

"I'm—" she hesitated. "I'm sorry, Dee. I shouldn't have snapped."

Damarcus's eyebrows rose in surprise.

"You all really care about each other, don't you?" she asked quietly.

"We do."

Rachel looked out at the group, the gentle, casual touches, the concern. "Why?"

"I've told you before, we're family here."

Rachel shrugged. *What was family anyway,* she wondered. *Just people who would screw you over and sell you out.*

Damarcus settled down next to her. Not too close, he'd learned the first week she was at Athena Strategic Logistics that she didn't want anyone too physically close to her, and she appreciated his thoughtfulness.

"Maybe we're more than family. Better," he said quietly. "Not shitty blood family, it's deeper," he told her and leaned his head against the crate. "I get it, girl. It's not like a foster family or a crew that gets pushed on you. We want you, but I think the last two months would have shown you that they're willing to wait for you to decide that you want them too."

Rachel looked out at the group again.

"Look at them," Damarcus said and gestured broadly to the group strewn across the hangar floor. "That's not forced. This isn't some soulless bureaucracy or corporation. Everyone here believes in the mission. In each other."

The murmur of voices drifted over her as she watched. Gentle hands on forearms, wrists, and elbows spoke of care and concern.

Earnest faces assessing a friend or coworker.

Rachel closed her eyes. Damarcus was right.

She felt herself relax. Relax for the first time that day. Relax for the first time in two months. For the first time, perhaps, since she was a teenager. Her shoulders sagged, her chin dropped to her chest, and as she took a deep breath in, her mind opened to the new family she had found.

I want to be wanted this way, she thought quietly.

Rachel? A quiet voice whispered across her mind.

Rachel bolted straight up, scraping her back along the box behind her. *Dee?* She asked tentatively.

Rachel! You did it, you broke the block! Damarcus's mental voice said jubilantly in her mind.

What? Surprise tinged her thought.

Rachel, you're speaking telepathically!

Rachel's eyes flew open and she looked at Damarcus and the huge grin on his face. He pushed himself up and put a hand out for her. Rachel hesitated for only a moment before placing her hand in his. He pulled her to her feet, a wave of pride and acceptance in his touch. She followed him across the hangar floor to where Val and Mandy lay next to each other.

Sit down, I want to see if you can reach them too, Damarcus told her gently.

Rachel gave him a look then settled down between the two.

"Eyes closed, open your mind again," his quiet voice still carried over the thrum of noise in the hangar. "We're your friends, your new family."

Rachel saw both Mandy and Val look at her before she squeezed her eyes shut. She let herself relax and felt something in her mind open.

Val? Mandy? Her mental voice felt so quiet.

Rach! Val's voice echoed across her mind.

Rachel! Mandy's tired voice followed Val's.

"Mandy, can you link us?" Val asked aloud.

Mandy's pale face and light blonde hair made her look ghost-like under the bright lights of the hangar, but she nodded. "I'm tired, but I think so. Hold on, it'll help." She reached out and took Val's hand. Damarcus crouched down at her shoulder and took her other hand.

Rachel watched with trepidation. Damarcus had explained that all Pantheon members, except her, had the ability to talk to each other telepathically now, but that Mandy was somehow able to link them all together.

"Relax again, Rachel," Damarcus told her.

Rachel closed her eyes and let her mind go. There was a wisp of sensation at the edge of her mind. Like the brush of a feather at the corner of her awareness.

We're here with you, Rachel, Val's voice told her.

I hear you! Rachel smiled.

The feeling was alien, but not uncomfortable. She felt other minds touching hers. Like the kind hands on forearms, wrists, and elbows that had spoken of care and concern among the personnel working for the Pantheon, the mental touch had the same feeling of care and love.

Rachel's eyebrows furrowed. *Love? Was this love? Surely not a romantic love. Or the twisted emotion her boyfriend-turned-pimp had claimed was love*, she thought, frowning. *This was different. It was acceptance. Pure, unabashed acceptance of her.*

Rachel's breath caught in her throat. She inhaled once and tried to let it out slowly but it came out in a sob. The feeling of fear and panic was quickly subsumed by the love and affection of the group. The sob that rose in her chest died.

She was finally home.

FOUR

VALERIE "ATHENA" HALL
0829L/1329Z, 20 OCT

"No, Maureen, we are still not operating at full capacity." Val was hunched over a secure phone in Hank's conference room. Stress made her body wire tight and she had one hand curled to her aching belly. Either the big emergency Jump or the inadequate food was making her feel ill.

"The President is getting worried, Valerie."

"Then the President needs to tell Congress to pay their damn bills!" Val rubbed her temples, annoyance written across her pinched face while she silently rejoiced that the communications team hadn't had the bandwidth to set up video conferencing in the hangar yet. "I'm sorry, Maureen, that was snappy. I didn't mean to imply that the President was personally responsible for the current fiscal delays which at this point I know are tied to the legislative, not executive, branch of the United States government."

"Watch it, girl." Maureen's voice held warning but was tinged with humor at being so neatly called out. "The Office of Personnel Management will ensure all your personnel bills will be covered for the year. And the House, Senate, and yes, even the President will get the budget approved in a timely enough manner to ensure you have all your usual support equipment available. Now, tell me how you're overcoming adversity."

"I understand that Senator Mitchell, but it has only been three days. Please understand that I am running distributed operations with an unsecured threat to my unit."

"You are a logistics company, Valerie, I would assume that all of your operations are distributed," Maureen Mitchell said with a smug tone Val was starting to associate with her odd sense of humor.

"Be that as it may, ma'am, it is adding friction to my operations."

"Explain."

"There are nearly 800 miles between here and our headquarters. While I am not allowing anyone to operate from our facility until the threat is neutralized, I am allowing the Pantheon members to travel back to their homes and families each night. The calorie load from a 1600-mile round trip each day is not unmanageable, but it is adding extra strain on our bodies."

"Then keep them at Hurlburt, easy."

"Ma'am, simply put, I don't have space. The two companies have taken every room on base and most of the close hotels. It is the—what did she call it?—'shoulder' of tourist season and hotels are still slammed full. I can make the support elements group up in rental cars and carpool each day, but it seemed more prudent to let the actual Jumpers rest comfortably in their own beds."

"You're willing to risk overloading a strategic national asset so they can sleep comfortably in their beds?"

"If it saves them from burning out on a mission that rises to the importance of a national crisis? Absolutely."

The silence that followed told Val that while Maureen didn't like it, she would stop fighting the issue.

"When will you be back in your headquarters?"

"When will you guarantee me the threat is neutralized?"

There was a huff on the line before Maureen answered. "Can you operate from anywhere else?"

Val pulled the headset away from her ear to stare at it incredulously for a moment. "Ma'am, I am."

"I mean here in the DC area," Maureen ground out.

"Certainly. I believe in my last MILCON meeting, I was told the military construction of a facility in Fort Belvoir would be ready in approximately six years."

"Valerie!" Maureen's voice was sharp as a whipcrack.

"Senator Mitchell, unless you can pull strings to get me a headquarters facility, fully furnished and with a full communications suite in the DC area or show me proof of death for our current threat, we cannot come back to the DC area." Val took a deep breath. "Maureen, his father worked in DC for decades. It's safe to assume he knows every safe house, clean room, and Point Zero in our inventory. I have one fallback location left; I'm not burning it out unless it's a critical need."

"I'll have my people get with yours. Have a list of requirements to my aide in the next hour, we'll come up with something."

"Thank you."

"How are your new members handling the change?"

Slightly taken aback, Val answered, "They're handling it well enough, I suppose. Jafar is about as even keeled as they come and took the emergency Jump in stride. Rachel is more high strung and the emergency Jump was rough for her, but it also seemed to grant her a breakthrough," Val said with a smile.

"Oh?"

"Nothing terribly interesting to note, just unlocking her full potential."

"And your third? Didn't you gain someone over the summer?"

"Yes, ma'am," Val said and was glad once again that her face wasn't visible. "Braxton Chadwick Nelson. He took it in stride as well, I suppose, but he is," Val paused, searching for the right word, "unreliable."

"Valerie, are you telling me you have a Pantheon member who is not under your full control? You're a military organization, order him to do what you need. Threaten to cut off his pay."

Val sighed. "Maureen it's not that simple and you know it. We were a military organization but I now have four fully civilian team members, I can't order them to do shit. He came to us when Mandy did her 'come all ye' speech and he seemed like he needed," she paused briefly, "guidance. And as for money ..." Val trailed off. She idly rubbed her temples.

"He's rich already, isn't he?" Maureen asked when the silence had stretched on too long. "With a name like 'Braxton Chadwick Nelson,' I'm guessing he's old money too. God, the little prick is probably a 'junior' to boot!" Maureen chortled.

"Worse, he's a 'third'! Braxton Chadwick Nelson the third."

"Oh, my dear sweet Lord in heaven," Maureen said. "He's a handful then."

"Maureen, I swear to you I think he's coked out half the time and there isn't much I can do about it."

"Cocaine?"

"He's twenty-nine. You know our members usually manifest their skills in the early twenties."

"Unless they have a significant grief," Maureen said gently.

"Yes. Unless, like me, they experience a loss so profound it inhibits their abilities. But," she sighed, "it would also seem that a drug and alcohol-fueled early adulthood will also inhibit the skill."

"And he admitted all this to you?"

"What am I going to do to him, Maureen? Throw him in jail? That's laughable!"

"Fair point. As soon as he sobered up, I supposed he'd teleport right out."

"Yes. He's ostensibly here to hone his skill and I need every Jumper I can get my hands on, but I'm starting to think he's not worth the effort. So, I have a bit of a loose cannon and I certainly can't have him out there making us look bad. Not when there are strong elements in power who want us registered like a draft."

"I know, Valerie. I'm," she paused and sighed, "doing my best."

"Thank you. I could drug test him to prove he's high but I can't court martial him or throw him in jail longer than it takes him to sober up. He's got enough family money that docking his pay is nothing." Val gave a derisive laugh. "I threatened it once and he kindly told me he made more passive income from the interest on his various investments in a week than we paid him in a month."

"Oh."

"Well, I think it was more along the lines of 'I'm rich, try me, bitch.' But you get the picture."

There was a slight pause before Maureen indignantly asked, "Then why for the love of Jesus did he ever bother coming to Limitless Logistics."

"Fame."

"Fuck."

Val pulled the headset away from her head again and stared at it in shock. "Yes, exactly. It's not enough for him just to be rich, he wants the fame too."

Silence stretched between the two women as they considered him.

"If he ever becomes a problem you can't manage, let me know," Maureen finally said quietly. "You know I'm good for it."

"Yes, ma'am," Va answered quietly.

"How are you holding up, Valerie?"

"Fine. This is a setback, but we're all working through it professionally," Val said smoothly.

"No, I asked how you were doing."

"I'm fine."

There was another pause. Val could feel an opportunity opening before her but ignored it.

"Is there anything else, Madam Senator?"

"No, General Hall. I'll make my report to the two Arms Committees and the National Security Counsel."

The barely audible hum of background static dropped as the secure line closed.

Val dropped the handset into its cradle and leaned back in her chair. From her corner of the hangar, she could see the team going about their daily operations, such as they were. Colonel Gardner and his team had set up a small multi-nodal communications point, or battle cab, in the corner with the limited communications equipment they had but it was nothing compared to her entire communications suite in the DC headquarters. Slapping the chair's arms, she pushed herself up to find Damarcus, who was hopefully working with Chadwick to refine his Jumping skills.

Val passed two handlers, Carson and Jesse, doing a gear layout for Wilson and Walker's scheduled haul that afternoon.

"Good morning, ma'am," Carson said formally.

"Good morning, gents. How goes the layout? Got everything you need?"

Carson gave her a stiff nod but she caught the look Jesse shot at him.

"Jesse?"

Jesse shot Carson another look and nodded in Val's direction. Carson smiled blandly.

Val looked at the pair and rolled her eyes.

"Just tell her, damn it," Jesse finally blurted out.

"Wilson destroyed another phone two days ago and I can't get an appropriate replacement before his Jump today."

"Are we out of the standard build?" Val asked, incredulous.

"No, ma'am, not at all," Jesse told her. "But the standard builds are all in the warehouse at HQ and we don't have the tools or supplies here to modify an off-the-shelf phone."

Val closed her eyes and let out a breath. "Get with the other handlers and figure out how many phones we think we'll go through in the next," she paused, considering, "let's say, month."

Jesse and Carson's faces fell at the mention of a month.

"Project any other perishable or expendable equipment we might need and get it to Mandy in the next hour. I'll get a team organized to do a grab by noon. Is that enough time for their mission this afternoon?"

"Yes, ma'am. But, is it really safe to go in there right now? I mean, with," Jesse winced, "him still out there?"

"No. It's absolutely not safe, but we don't have many options right now, do we?"

They both shook their heads and she strode off, still seeking Damarcus.

She wound her way across the hangar, deliberately avoiding the large painted "X" surrounded by blaze orange cones and flagging tape that designated their temporary Point Zero. Hank and his team normally had only a minimal white "X" as they all knew to leave the space open for an emergency or planned arrival but an unfortunate incident the first day led them to making Point Zero more visible.

The young admin clerk who had been thrown into a cargo container by the air James and Wilson displaced returning from a mission had suffered a compound tibia fracture and would be in the hospital for at least a few days until the threat of infection had passed.

Valerie finally found Damarcus and Chadwick in the hangar's small conference room, down a short hallway from the main hangar floor. She waited in the doorway, observing the lecture.

"No, Chadwick, you can't just use a photo. Man, we've been over this. Please tell me what you need for a clean Jump." Damarcus was leaning back in his aged leather chair at the conference room table but the stiff set of his shoulders and a slight edge to his voice told Val everything she needed to know about today's lesson with Chadwick.

"You need to know what the space looks like and where it is," Chadwick said.

"Do you need anything more than what it looks like?"

"Yes?"

Val saw Damarcus squint at Chadwick. He stared skeptically at Chadwick, blinking slowly, and clearly pondered what was had just said.

"Chadwick?" Damarcus asked.

"Yeah?"

"We talked about this less than an hour ago." Damarcus frowned, clearly unwilling to ask the next question. "How high are you right now?"

Chadwick laughed. A weirdly mirthful little chuckle. "Pretty fuckin' baked, man."

"Are you fucking serious?" Val spluttered from the door.

"Oh, heeeeeey, lady," Chadwick said.

"Damarcus, a word?" Val said. She shot Chadwick a disgusted look. "So," Val said as she shut the door between the conference room and hallway, "that as bad as I think?"

"Worse," Damarcus said with a groan. "I'm ready to give up my position as lead trainer because of that idiot."

"Dee, man."

"Val, he's that bad. I know I've only been the lead trainer since you showed up, but I've trained five people in the last ten months, given that we only get one new Pantheon member every four years, it's like having twenty years of experience as far as I'm concerned. And in my *twenty years* of experience, that man is a moron. Worse, he's a willful moron."

"Gods and stars above, Dee."

"That was a small example. I know you knew about the drugs and I also know there's not much you can do about it, but ..." Damarcus trailed off. "Val, he's high more often than he's sober and it's affecting both his Jumps and his ability to retain what I teach."

"Yes, I knew about the drugs. The fool told me to my face he was using and laughed when I said he can't do that here." Val frowned. "As I just told Maureen, he basically told me to pound sand when I threatened him with legal action or stopping his pay."

"Damn, you told Senator Mitchell already?"

"Of course. He's a loose cannon, a national security risk, I didn't think I could leave that out."

Damarcus winced. "How did she take it? Did she threaten you or our budget?"

Val gave a little laugh. "No, actually." She shook her head. "She may have made an offer for a more permanent solution for dealing with Mr. Braxton Chadwick Nelson the third. An offer I have politely declined and am only sharing with my second in command and no one else," she said giving him a significant glance.

"Understood."

They let an easy silence stretch as each considered their predicament.

"I think we need a leads' meeting," Val finally said. "There are more loose ends than I'm comfortable with right now."

"I'll get Mandy and Murphy in here. You clear out the garbage," Damarcus nodded toward the conference room door.

"Yeah. I guess he's my problem now. And hey, Dee?"

"Yes?"

"You know I appreciate you doing this? I know he's a tool, but I've got to get him some training or else he could hurt himself."

"Val, I love you like a sister, even if you're my boss now, but he may not be worth it."

With concern etched into her face, Val watched Damarcus walk away. He was the next most powerful Pantheon member after her. Strong and precise with a great recovery time. It made him the best suited to training because he could deal with many training Jumps in a short period. Mandy and Jafar both rivaled his accuracy but were still being trained themselves. Wilson was the next most accurate but lacked the stamina to conduct multiple Jumps in a single day. She shook her head, red-gold mane waving like the flap of a matador's cape. If Damarcus refused to train Chadwick, she'd be forced to take him on herself, time she didn't have right now. And Damarcus's comment that teaching Chadwick enough to keep himself alive might not be worth it? That was big trouble.

"Chadwick," Val opened the door to the conference room, "you're training is concluded for today."

"Yeah, cool," he said, not looking up from his phone.

"Chadwick, that means get out."

"Why?" he asked and leaned back in his chair, still clearly focused on his phone.

Val stalked to his chair, snatched him by the back of the collar and Jumped them to Point Zero out on the hangar floor. She released his collar and he dropped to the concrete floor with a chair no longer supporting his rump.

"Look here you spoiled little shit," Val addressed him, her temper flaring. "When anyone in this organization tells you to move your worthless ass out of the way, you move."

She turned and stomped back to the conference room.

"Val, you can't do stuff like that," Mandy told her, following closely behind.

"I'm sorry, Mandy, but he's being an ass."

"Sure, I don't disagree, but you are the head of this company and you can't go throwing your subordinates around when your famous temper flares!"

Val inhaled deeply and nodded. "You're right. I won't apologize to him, he's too fucking high right now to remember it, but it won't happen again."

Mandy nodded.

Damarcus returned with Murphy and gave his head a little shake. Val rolled her eyes and nodded, *Yeah I know, I fucked up.*

"Okay leads," Val said when they were all seated. "First off, I apologize for my lapse in professionalism. And yes, I've been suitably chastised for dumping Chadwick on his ass, it won't happen again."

"Too bad," Murphy muttered. "The man is bad news."

Val ignored him and went on. "I've been getting reports that we are in desperate need of some of our critical or proprietary equipment. Hank had some things on hand but the majority of it is back at headquarters."

"Cellphones?" Mandy asked.

"More IVs," Murphy countered. "And dog food."

"Doesn't the Hurlburt BX carry dog food?

"Not what Zora needs," Murphy said with a frown. "I can't take her with me if she's eating low quality stuff."

United States Marine Corps military working dog Zora had been Murphy's canine before he joined the Pantheon. He would never say that she had been "tactically acquired" as his companion now that he had a contract with Limitless Logistics. But the fact remained that the man who had ensured her transfer was dead and unable to speak on the nature of her transfer. Murphy was fiercely protective of her despite describing the Belgian Malinois as a "chainsaw on meth" and perfectly capable of defending herself.

"Okay, consider going solo until we can get that sorted. Sorry, she may have some kennel time in her future. But then yes to all of it and more," Val told them. "Look, I know we're missing things, but I need the consolidated list. Each company lead will confer with their teams and give me a full list by noon. We'll prioritize and build our team. I'm authorizing a Jump to headquarters at 1300 local. You'll have fifteen minutes to grab your part of the supply list and haul it back."

"But, Val—" Mandy started before Val cut her off.

"I know he's still out there; I know he can still get in." Val avoided Damarcus's eyes, aware the man had not stopped beating himself up yet. "But we don't have enough of several items that are considered minimum mission essential equipment. We have a priority two Jump this afternoon, and another one tomorrow morning, and we're on call at any time and we don't meet the minimum equipment list. I think the mission needs outweigh the risks if we're fast. We have to have it because currently I'm running a logistics company that is failing at logistics."

The room was quiet.

"You have thirty-five minutes to get me your lists and who will be going. One Pantheon, as many personnel as you need to go directly to an item's location and back to Point Zero for the Jump out."

Her statement was met with a round of nods.

Less than thirty minutes later, both Mandy and Murphy had returned with their list of requirements and who would best know where the equipment was kept.

"Good work you two. Dee, work with them to cross-reference the equipment, have a smooth list and who will get what in the next five minutes. I'll round up our expert personnel and we'll prep the Jump. Since Wilson and Walker are on this afternoon's Jump and Dee needs to finish training Rachel and Jafar, it looks like it's the three of us plus James for an armed milk run."

Murphy nodded once, clearly ready to go in guns blazing if needed. Mandy, on the other hand, swallowed hard and stared and Val blankly.

"Mandy?"

"You sure you need me, Val?"

"I'm not," Val admitted.

"You know me," she paused. "I'm not good with this." She waved a hand vaguely in the direction of the weapons locker Hank's team kept on hand for them.

"I do," Val said quietly. "But, when push comes to shove, you're going to be asked to take runs like it."

Mandy nodded.

"Tally up the weight of the gear we need. We aren't going to be able to do a logistic hold in DC, you know we don't have the time for it, but if we can get there and the weighted Jump back with three, I'll excuse you from the run. Okay?"

"Yeah," Mandy said quietly.

"Mandy, it's a risk already, and going with one fewer Jumper increases the risk. I hope you understand what you're asking of me. Of all of us."

"I do, it's just—"

"Mandy, you understand the risk or you don't."

Mandy's mouth pressed into a firm line. "I understand, Val."

When Val returned five minutes later with James and the rest of the retrieval team, the equipment list was complete.

"We can do it with three, Val," Mandy told her quietly. The tension in her shoulders matched the tension in Damarcus and Murphy as she handed Val the list.

Val looked at Murphy and Damarcus, searching for any hesitation. "You double-checked the math?"

Both men nodded silently but she could see from the set of their shoulders they were more than uneasy about it.

Val looked at Mandy once and made a decision. She nodded, "Okay. Jumpers you know who's going with you, tag up and get your weapons. We Jump in five."

FIVE

VALERIE "ATHENA" HALL

0959L/1459Z, 20 OCT

"Jump in three. Two. *One*." Val called out.

Murphy, James, and Val teleported their team to Point Zero in the DC headquarters. The team of six, bristling with weapons, landed safely on the other side with only a small rush of displaced air. Murphy dropped to a knee and pulled his side arm. Beside him, Joe, his ever-capable handler brought a shotgun up to his shoulder. James stood shoulder to shoulder with John and Mark, the two former handlers having the greatest knowledge of where gear was stashed throughout the building. Val stood alone across the landing area from them, holding only the lists of supplies.

"Team, here are your lists. James, you and John have communications equipment. Murphy and Joe, you have medical supplies. Do *not*," she emphasized, "forget the IVs and their associated lines."

"Of course, Val," Murphy said in a *how could I forget* voice as he grabbed his list.

"Mark, we've got the list of miscellaneous supplies." Mark took her list and hefted a bag to his shoulder.

"You have fifteen minutes to get your gear and get out. You do not need to depart from Point Zero, just let me know you're departing. If anyone sees anything, call it out immediately. In that case, do not bother to engage, just let us know and get back to the fallback immediately."

There was a round of nods before they broke for each of their respective searches.

You know going with only three is a huge risk, Murphy told her.

Val could feel the curious telepathic bridge form between herself, Murphy, and James. She was only slightly surprised it could form without the odd "Hestia link" they had been relying upon.

I do. It's why I asked Mandy to double-check the numbers and make the decision herself. I expected if you disagreed, you would have stopped her. Val told him in not quite a huff.

One pound, Val, Murphy chastised her, *one more pound and we'd be over the limit you set. As it is, if any of us get taken out, we can only get the team back. We'd have to leave the supplies.*

I didn't hear you voicing these concerns before we left, Val reminded him.

He's still sweet on Mandy and doesn't want to risk that, James chimed in.

Murphy didn't respond with words but Val and James both got the distinct impression of grinding teeth across their telepathic link.

Val chuckled as she and Mark made their way to the main supply room. "Sorry, Mark, James, and Murphy," she said and touched two fingers to her temple.

Mark smiled at the gesture. "Bickering?"

"Kinda." Val clapped one hand on his shoulder. "You doing okay?"

Mark nodded then paused, looking quickly down the intersecting hallway they had reached. With a nod, he moved forward. "I miss him, Val," Mark said quietly. "I was his handler for twenty-five of his thirty years. I should have seen Rich retire this year."

"I'm sorry, Mark. It's been a rough year." Val let out a hard breath. Mark had been the handler to Richard Dunn, one of the most senior Pantheon who had been lost alongside their leader, Marco Martnez, that summer during the Battle for D.C. "A really hard year."

Mark nodded again as they reached the headquarters' capacious storage room.

Val wanted to press him with more questions, but they needed to be silent as they opened the door, listening for any signs of Apollo or his team lying in ambush. She paused at the door, held up three fingers then with a nod gave a wordless countdown.

Three. Two. One.

She pushed the door open as quietly as she could, thankful for the dedicated Limitless Logistic facilities team that had kept the hinges squeak-free. Mark rushed past her, gun up at the ready, and paused inside the door. With an internal three count, Val eased past him, flanking the other side of the door.

"Thirty," she whispered to Mark and started counting down form thirty in her head. *We're inside the door*, she told Murphy and James, *nothing yet. I'm giving it a thirty count before we move in deeper.*

Roger, Murphy responded. *We're about five steps from Medical. Will report in a moment.*

I'm already ransacking the comms suite, James told them.

Val looked at Mark and they nodded in unison. The pair crept forward, guns low but ready, listening for any sound of movement. Val glanced at the sheet in Mark's hand. The supplies they needed were scattered throughout the supply area.

"I don't hear anything," she whispered. "Lead on, I'll be no more than an arm's length away."

Mark nodded and kept moving forward with a large type A3 bag looped over his wrist.

They had half their list when Murphy called across the link that he had his portion of the supplies. *Do you all need a hand down there?*

I'd ask Joe how well he knows the supply area, but he worked here for years before you came along. He probably knows it as well as Mark, Val told him. *Your carton is probably the heaviest. Send Joe this way and Jump your equipment back. I can bring Joe with me and Mark.*

You sure? Murphy asked just as James echoed the question.

Yeah, my load is the lightest, I can get him.

Okay, Murphy told her, but his words were threaded with

hesitation.

Help Dee with that nitwit, Chadwick, when you get back, Val told him. *Don't hurt him, but you know, put a little fear in him, Murph.*

She could feel vindictive mirth flow across the link. But "*Jumping in three*" was all he said.

Mark and Val's hands snapped to their guns at the sound of a door opening moments later. Val had to put her free hand on Mark's arm to lower it as she peered down the hallway.

"I think it's Joe," she whispered. "Murphy is done and sent Joe to help us grab the rest of the gear."

Mark nodded, tense.

"It's me," Joe called softly.

"Good, come take half this list," Mark told him and he appeared at the end of the row. Mark tore the paper in half and offered it to Joe who went in search of the items.

Val? James's mental voice was concerned.

Yeah, James? You see something? We got company?

No, but I think he's been here, James told her.

Yeah?

John says it looks like all our equipment is accounted for, nothing is missing, but it's definitely been moved around. Like someone was looking for something but didn't find it.

You think he was able to get into the network? Fear dropped heavily on Val. If he'd managed to get into their network, he'd know they were operating from the fallback location and where it was. If he'd gotten in, all of their fallback locations would have been compromised.

We aren't sure, James told her, a fear that echoed hers in his mental voice. *Neither of us knows enough about systems to check if it's been accessed in the last seventy-two hours. But the equipment has definitely been moved. What do you want to do?*

Get the last of it and go, Val told him. *I mean, if he was here we'd probably know by now. If he'd gotten into the system, we'd probably know by now as well. We'll just have to deal with it when we get back.*

Roger. Done in two minutes.

Val nodded to Mark. "They think the comms suite could be compromised. They're getting what they can, but we need to move it. I want to get out of here in the next few minutes. Joe," she called, "you've got two minutes then we gotta go, even if we don't have it all." She heard an acknowledgment from several stacks away.

We've got all our stuff, Val, James told her. *I'm Jumping.*

Good work, James. Clear the pad as soon as you can and report what you found to Dee. See ya in Florida.

"Thirty seconds, fellas!" she called to Joe. Beside her, Mark nodded.

"I've got everything on my half," he said.

"On my way," Joe called.

They rallied at the end of the long row of shelves, both men holding heavily laden bags.

"Everything?" Val asked briskly. Both men nodded. "Good. Jumping in three. Two. *One.*"

SIX

VALERIE "ATHENA" HALL

1014L/1514Z, 20 OCT

Val, Joe, Mark, and a pile of bagged equipment landed in the spray-painted Point Zero. James and two admin clerks were shuffling the last of his equipment outside the ring of blaze orange safety cones. Val dropped her bags outside the ring, effectively clearing it for Wilson and Walker's afternoon mission.

"Joe, get this to the comm team," she told him. At his nod and raised thumb, she set off in search of Damarcus. He and Wilson stood together near the conference room hallway, deep in conversation.

Damarcus was tense as he listened to Wilson, nodding sharply as she approached.

"Dee, you got the scoop?" Val asked.

"How confident is John that things were moved?" Damarcus asked her.

Wilson made a little noise of displeasure. "I know he's older, Dee but his memory is solid."

Val glanced between the two before answering, trying to read the tension that lay below the spoken conversation. "Sure. Very sure," she told him.

"Safe to assume Apollo has gone through our gear then," Darmarcus told her.

"Yeah, I'd say so." Val sighed. "Damn it."

Rachel and Jafar approached, and the group shuffled open slightly.

"We can't use it can we?" Wilson asked her.

"Not if it's been compromised," Val agreed.

"I still don't get why we can't just use normal phones," Rachel said and Jafar nodded.

"Ours are stuffed with extras, Rach," Damarcus told her. "I know we discussed this during training yesterday. Our phones double as trackers as well as running primarily on satellites. Since we Jump across time zones, we couldn't be leaving digital footprints of a phone moving across cell towers hundreds of miles apart."

"Yeah, but it's not like we're hiding that now," Rachel said with a little snort. "That cat is well out of the bag or we," she jerked a thumb at Jafar, "wouldn't be here."

"We also need phones that don't require a new sim card every time we cross continents."

"Yeah okay, that I get," Rachel told him. "But a satellite phone would work in a pinch."

Val's shoulders ached. They had been over this very argument the day before in the leadership meeting and the stress of it was being carried in her back. She wished either Mandy or Murphy had taken the time to brief the information to their teams. "Any commercial satellite phone puts us at risk because we don't know what other software is loaded. We use our phones which," she nodded to Damarcus, "are loaded with extras but also wiped of any superfluous or malicious code from the manufacturer or others."

"But we could—" Rachel started.

"The risk is too high, Rachel. End of story. We have to go with what we've got." Val caught Rachel's glare and heard her mutter something about *If I even get to go …* but ignored it. "Wilson and Walker are on a full mission this afternoon and we don't have time to hunt down satellite phones and reimage them to our specs. Walker, please tell the techs they have until your Jump to search for any malicious code that Apollo may or," she shook her head, "may not have left behind."

Rachel opened her mouth as if to speak again, but Damarcus

held up a hand and she snapped her jaw closed.

"Rachel, you are on a mission tomorrow. You and Dee are with Hank and his team for a full mission as well."

Rachel's face lit up.

Val held up a hand to stop her once again. "You showed you can connect enough for a Jump in full battle-rattle, so it's under Ares Tactical. Dee will shadow you. Consider this your first combat Jump."

Rachel smiled. "Thanks, Val. I won't fuck it up."

"Good. You all are dismissed, but Dee please stay."

The group dispersed, with Wilson walking briskly to the communications team. Damarcus stayed at her side, body still radiating tension.

"It's a beans and bullets run, Dee." Val told him quietly.

His shoulders dropped noticeably. "Thanks, Val. You had me worried for a sec."

"Yeah," she laughed, "I could tell. You okay, man?"

"I'm sorry, Val."

"It's not your fault, Dee. You know I don't blame you, right?"

He shook his head. "You should. I've seen him. It had been a few months, but I'd seen his face. I should have known who he was. And now this?" He gestured broadly to the packed hangar floor. "Hank is polite, but I can tell we'll wear out our welcome soon. He has other missions outside of us and we're in his way."

"I know."

"And we've got a problem with Chadwick. I don't know what to do with him. He won't listen to instructions. He's rarely any kind of sober. He takes off to do his own thing and I can't track him down."

"I know. I've talked with Maureen. She made … an interesting offer."

Damarcus laughed. "That woman is tougher than boiled leather."

"She's working on tracking down Apollo. Once he's off the map, we'll be back to normal ops. It'll be okay, Dee. We'll get through this."

"I know, Val. I'm glad one of us is keeping calm," he gave a light laugh.

Val chuckled and gave a small smile. "Yeah."

They parted and Val went about the business of running a logistics company with no base. Stress twisted her guts and a headache crept into her temples as she watched Walker and Wilson's mission from the minimal communications equipment in the makeshift battle cab, used to a robust suite that showed where Pantheon members were at all times when on a mission. She rubbed her abdomen as discreetly as she could but it provided no relief from the discomfort. They made the drop with no issues but there was an undeniable tension among the support staff about the manner in which the mission was forced to run.

"Ma'am, we have the bags prepped for Damarcus and Rachel tomorrow," Ryan told her toward the end of the day. "And the tech crew has been scanning all day without finding anything on the phones."

"I guess that's good to know, even with one mission having been completed already."

"Yes, ma'am."

"Thanks, Ryan, good work. You and Joe doing okay?"

"Yes. He's so calm about all of this, it doesn't seem to phase him. As long as he and Murphy get their workouts in, he's good."

"Good. Let me know if you need anything."

"Thanks, ma'am. You okay?" he asked after a moment's hesitation.

"Yeah, sure, fine," Val responded quickly, her tight smile in place.

Ryan gave her one searching look before he nodded. "Mmm-hmm, okay, but if you need to talk, let me know."

"I'm fine, Ryan," Val said with a sigh, "I'm doing my therapy despite all of this. But thank you. Get some rest. I'll see you tomorrow for Dee and Rachel's Jump."

Val swallowed hard and ignored the squirming in her guts. The red LED clock on the hangar wall told her that it was time to go if she wanted to get dinner with Brandon. She grabbed her phone and typed out a quick text to Brandon Powell, CIA Agent, and the man with whom she shared a tumultuous relationship.

I'm done for the day. Still on for dinner?

Sure. I'm home if you want to come over directly. He typed back after a moment.

Val pulled her ID card from the computer terminal and stuffed it in her pocket. With one deep breath to settle herself, she focused on the image of Brandon's living room and Jumped.

"Bran?" she called out.

"In the kitchen," he called back.

Val stood in his living room just taking in the familiar sights and smells of his apartment. The subtle lighting that illuminated his college football jersey. The small blanket on his couch she had brought over to cuddle under. The subtle smell of his cologne lingered under the smell of dinner being cooked. It wasn't quite the feeling of home, but it was a comfortable feeling.

Hands settled gently on her shoulders and she turned to hug Brandon. She sunk into his embrace, fully aware that he could feel her tension and stress with his curious empathic link.

"Long day?" he asked gently.

"It was …" she trailed off. "It's just, that there are so many decisions. And so many risks! Every decision has a risk. Everyone needs something. Nothing is smooth. I can't go five minutes without another crisis popping up." She looked up at him, face drawn and worried.

"Decision fatigue, huh?"

"Yes." Her shoulders sagged under his touch. "How did Marco do this?"

"Practice. Time. Experience."

Val could feel her temper flare. "I have experience!"

Brandon held his hands up. "I don't mean you're inexperienced or naïve. But Marco had weathered a hundred calamities. After a while, I'm sure he built a tolerance to them."

Her eyes narrowed but she nodded. "It's not my first crisis either, though."

"No. But it is your first while in charge."

Val gave him a hard stare. He looked back with calm. It broke her.

"I don't know what to do Brandon," she said with a sob. She started to speak again but the sob caught in her throat, choking her.

Brandon pulled her in close, holding the crying woman gently to his chest, letting her cry it out.

All the days' stress, the decisions, the risk, and the lives at stake overwhelmed her and she let it out. When the tears finally stopped, she wiped them with the back of her sleeve.

"I'm sorry. I should have gone home. Calmed down there."

"It's okay, Val. You know I'm here for you."

"My self-control feels so fragile. Like I'm moments away from exploding every second of the day."

"You need some time to calm down; find that peace you had this summer."

"I do. I need to get another therapy session or something. I need to get this team back home. I need—"

"Stop. Just stop, for now, Val. It's okay. Let's relax tonight."

"I want to, but I need to be—"

Brandon's right hand slid up to her neck, cupping the back of her head and pulling her into a deep kiss. The touch was calming, so calming, and she returned it with passion. Brandon chuckled against her lips.

"Let's skip dinner for now?"

She nodded and let him lead her to his bedroom.

SEVEN

RACHEL NG

0637L/1137Z, 21 OCT

"Alright team, suit up. We're Jumping out in thirty minutes," Hank's voice called across the crowded hangar.

Rachel watched him stride confidently to her spot on the floor and struggled to her feet. "Hello, Colonel Gardner," she said calmly.

"Ma'am, General Hall has cleared you for combat missions now. I understand you'd like to join us today?" Hank asked formally.

Rachel pursed her lips as she regarded him, unsure if his careful formality held a trace of mocking. But then, she suspected everyone was mocking or slighting her in some way. He showed absolutely no discomfort in the fact that Rachel topped him by several inches and stood regarding her plainly. For a man of unassuming height, he radiated the kind of confidence found only in truly powerful men; Rachel realized she actually liked that about him. Deciding he wasn't mocking her, she calmly answered, "Yes, please." Inside she wanted to wriggle with delight.

For two months she had been listed as falling directly under Valerie Hall. Not in Limitless Logistics and not in Spartan Tactical. She fell into an awkward in-between and had asked, almost begged, to be listed in Spartan Tactical. Sure, she understood the necessity of Limitless Logistics and knew the name was the most public face of the three companies, but she had no personal desire to be part of

Limitless Logistics' highly humanitarian mission. She wanted the fight. She wanted to kick down doors and wreck someone's world. She wanted to take all her anger and direct it somewhere safe, like at an enemy.

Which was probably why Val had never put her on the Spartan Tactical team. Rachel had guessed as much. Rachel's therapist had guessed as much. Damarcus had outright told her that her inability to link with anyone meant she didn't trust them and they, in turn, didn't feel they could trust her.

If Hank's polite and formal invitation was any indication, then her recent ability to link meant she was now in Spartan Tactical with General Murphy.

She slowed her long stride only slightly to keep pace with Hank as they walked to join the group of men leaning over a map covered table.

"What's the mission?" she asked Damarcus without preamble as she and Hank reached the table.

"Fairly simple," the uniformed man to Damarcus's left answered. "There's a team already down range prepping for an assault and we're their resupply."

Rachel's lip twisted in a grimace of irritation and the man whose nametag read "King," held up a mollifying hand.

"Whoa there, GI Jane, it gets better," he gave her a grin. "The team is deeply embedded in rough territory and moving constantly. We have a rendezvous point, but they aren't guaranteed to be there. So, you," he pointed to Damarcus and Rachel, "get to drop us in, and then we," his circling finger indicated the uniformed men around the table, "get to hang out while you do a logistics hold. Then it's a waiting game for the other team to arrive."

"Why a PJ team?" Damarcus asked, the low rumble his voice sending a shiver down Rachel's spine.

"Yeah, I know. Not really PJ-type work," King said with a shrug. "But we're briefed on your mission and if anyone takes fire, we can patch them up and return fire while waiting for you ladies to finish your snack and nap."

Rachel braced herself but was surprised to see Damarcus smile and laugh at King's verbal jab. With all of these hyper-masculine men, she was shocked not a single one was posturing or jockeying for prestige. Her eyes darted among the uniformed men and she saw that they all stood with the easy, confident lethality she'd seen in Colonel Gardner. It finally struck her, the difference between most of the men in her life and this group. Street toughs waved big guns to make up for small souls and small manhood. These men had the strength, skill, and willpower to be absolutely lethal, but the restraint to control it.

"Where?" Rachel asked.

"The coordinates plot out to a mountain range in Venezuela," King told her.

"What are they doing in Venezuela?" she asked, confused.

Silence stretched over the table and she saw one of the men glance at the full hangar.

Very carefully, Rachel opened a door in her mind. Reaching tentatively, afraid of rejection or rebuke, she touched the aura she came to associate with Damarcus. *Dee?* she asked quietly.

Can't say it out loud with so many people around. We can talk about it later if you really need to know, but it's a simple logistics mission. Plus guns. His mental voice held a hint of a smile that was reflected on his face.

"Fine. Less than thirty minutes?" she asked the group.

"Yes. Get your bag, and we'll sort out a gun for you. Then it will be about the right time to leave," King told her.

"Glock 19, if you have them, King," Rachel told the young man.

King's head tilted ever so slightly as he regarded her, but he nodded. "Sure thing, ma'am."

"It will be almost 1,500 miles carrying yourself, two men with guns, and a supply box. That's around 3,000 calories in an instant. You think you're ready for it?" Damarcus asked as they went to get their bags.

"Yeah Dee, I'm good. I did that on the emergency Jump with no problems. It's weird that the math works out the same for this."

He grabbed her wrist, halting her stride, and concern flowed across his touch. "Really? First combat Jump? No jitters?" He looked down at her wrist.

"No."

His eyes flicked back up to her face. "You really aren't nervous." He dropped her hand. "I don't know if you're brave or crazy."

"I've been through worse," she said bluntly. The brutal reality of her traumatic past electrified the connection and Damarcus dropped her hand.

Damarcus's stride faltered slightly. "Yeah, I guess so. Sorry." He stopped at his packed bag, squatting down to loosen the tie at its top. "You want me to lecture you about all the things we've gone over in training or do you feel comfortable with what you've learned?"

"I feel comfortable." Rachel gave him a smile. It was a genuine smile that put dimples on her cheeks and creases at the corner of her eyes. "After all, I had a good teacher."

Damarcus looked up at her and gave a small start. "I guess you did."

He looked at his pack, but Rachel could see the ghost of a smile on his lips. It struck her that in all the time he had been training her and complimenting her growth, she had never complimented him back. Inexplicably, she blushed. To cover it, she squatted down by her bag as well and wrenched the cord open.

Rachel proceeded to dump out her bag onto the hangar floor, scattering the meticulously packed contents in a heap. She pawed through the gear, picking out various pieces and placing them on the concrete behind her.

"You probably want to take the whole pack, Rachel," Damarcus told her.

"I'm picking out what I've used in training, Dee. And weren't you going to let me do this on my own?"

"I am, but as you've never done a combat Jump, maybe you'll take friendly advice."

"Friendly? Friends? Is that what we are?"

Yes, Rachel. I don't think you'd hear me now otherwise, he told her.

"Fine," she said aloud but it echoed to him telepathically as well. "What's the bare minimum I need?"

"Food and water. You have to have your IVs, lines, and physical consumables too. Otherwise, you won't be getting back easily."

She nodded and took them from the pile behind her, setting them beside the now empty bag. "Guns and ammunition next?"

"No. You can Jump out of most trouble, they're more of a security blanket than anything else. No, you need your first aid kit next. Can't Jump if you're bleeding out."

"Mandy did," she snapped back at him.

"Mandy Jumped a few feet and was in shock."

"Anyone who has been shot will be in shock. Also, Val Jumped from Eastern Europe to DC with a gunshot wound in the calf."

Damarcus shook his head, "Valerie Hall is an extraordinary human being who was put in an extraordinary situation. The rest of us might not have made it back, certainly not with our target." He gave her a level look. "In any case, you aren't Val. It's your first non-training Jump. I know we're calling it a combat mission, but it should be relatively benign. So, stick with the hierarchy of needs: food, water, first aid, and shelter."

"Why shelter? I can just Jump back."

"Girl, if you're out cold on a 'logistics hold,' you may not notice the heat or cold, but your fallback man will. Let the poor soul have a little shelter while they feed you and patch you up."

Rachel gave him a slight nod in acknowledgment and set a tarp, short poles, and 550 cord next to the first aid kit. "You really treat them like a team, don't you?" she asked quietly.

"Yes. We are a team, Hank's PJs and us. They aren't on the Limitless Logistics or Spartan Tactical rosters, but they are every bit as much a part of our team as any Jumper. We can't do what we do without them." Damarcus looked at her for a moment, considering. "You know I grew up in foster care, right?"

"Yes."

"Hard knock life and all that," he tried to smile but it was thin. "You learn to do a lot with nothing. I think you get that, right?"

"Yes," Rachel answered bluntly.

"Well, you live in the land of plenty now. You have money. If you need something, we can get it. Gear. Clothes. A personal trainer.

A private chef who not only grocery shops but actually cooks the dang meals because God knows you can't. We can get it." He smiled to soften the truth. "You don't have to rely on just your considerable wit. While I respect someone who can get by, and get out, on just their wit," he almost whispered, "if you're offered tools, take them."

Rachel stared at him, face blank. Inside, she smiled at the idea of having a personal shopper procuring her the latest designer fashions. Visions of unobtainable handbags and clothes waltz across her mind. She had heard of some "Madame Volaire" and her magnetic pull in Paris, but she hadn't trusted the connection to request her help.

"That includes the people. They want to take care of you and, shockingly, don't want anything in return but your respect."

Rachel nodded again but the ghost of a smile crossed her lips. She was beginning to appreciate the vehemence with which the so-called Pantheon held on to anyone they even remotely considered part of their team. Everyone was welcome, everyone had a part to play, and they genuinely valued both what someone could do for them as well as the person. For someone who ran with street crews, the idea that someone could be valued simply for being themselves was foreign to Rachel.

"I may request a special handbag or two," she said as calmly as she could.

Damarcus nodded once and she got the impression he was somehow disappointed in her. She wanted to reach across the distance between them. To somehow bridge the physical and emotional gap that she had built.

"You like purses?" His question was equally calm but the edges of her emotional connection with him felt fuzzy, like something was opening.

She ruthlessly slammed it shut.

"Name brands. Designer," she said. "I make so much money now, I should look like it."

She gave him a smile that lacked any of the warmth she felt and was disappointed in herself when his eyebrows shot up in surprise.

"New money always looks it," she said sharply.

"Just the look then?" Damarcus asked quietly.

Rachel nodded once and started repacking the whole kit.

They packed in silence until Hank came to get them.

"Jump in five, sir and ma'am."

"Thanks, Hank." Damarcus rose and held out a hand to Rachel.

She eyed him warily, seeking any ulterior motives, but grasped his hand lightly. Damarcus pulled her to her feet as a wave of emotion swept her: a tingle of nervous energy, attraction, and respect. The nerves were as understandable and as unremarkable as the attraction. Men found her attractive, that was all. But the respect surprised her. Never in her life had she felt like she had been respected as a person until she joined Limitless. Sure, people had respected some of her considerable talents, but no one had seen her as a human being and respected that. She was an asset. Disposable.

For the second time that day, Rachel blushed. A blush that deepened when she caught Damarcus's wink. Rachel hoisted her pack and settled it across her shoulders, keeping her face turned from Damarcus. There was no need for him to know he had an effect on her as well. She strode to the center of the hangar floor, weaving around the various Limitless Logistics personnel scattered across the space.

"Team One, with Damarcus. Team Two with Rachel. Tag up!" Hank's voice boomed across the room from his usual spot atop the platform. "Two minutes, teams!" He dropped down and stood with Damarcus and Rachel as the teams joined them. "I love mission days," he said with a boyish grin that was at odds with his grizzled hair and smile lines.

"We know, Hank," Damarcus assured him with a smile. "Going with us?"

Hank held out a hand for Damarcus to clasp. "You know it, Dee."

Damarcus grabbed his hand and pulled him in for a quick chest bump. "Glad to hear it, Hank. You'll Jump with me; I can heft one extra."

Rachel was aware of the men standing around her with looks of anticipation. "Uh, tag up?" she asked. She held her hand out and each man gave her a quick tap, no more than a brushing of their fingers across hers. She gave a mental sigh of relief when their mental signatures showed a verdant jungle and that they were more interested in how she would do on her first "real" Jump rather than wondering what she looked like naked.

They're professionals, Rach. Damarcus told her.

I know, Dee. But so was I. It's hard to unlearn that many years of skepticism. She glanced at him. *How did you know I was worried?*

You broadcast. Not to everyone, I don't think, he told her when she was startled. *But you send me some of your strong emotions when you aren't consciously suppressing them.*

Is that normal?

Damarcus gave a mental shrug. *Who knows? Six months ago we all knew that emotions and thoughts could* only *be received through touch. Then Val comes along and she can hear Mandy. Then Mr. Powell follows up with his empathic abilities this summer. Who knows what we can and can't do?*

Isn't he that CIA Agent? Rachel shot back.

Yeah. He and Val are, uh, close.

"Thirty seconds!" Hank bawled out to the group.

Deep breath, Rach, you've got this.

Rachel gave him a genuine smile again. *I know*, she said with a ring of confidence.

"In three. Two. *One!*"

Rachel inhaled, closed her eyes, and envisioned the Venezuelan jungle. On her exhale, she felt the horrible wrenching sensation she had come to associate with long range Jumps. Her eyes flew open but her vision blurred as she staggered forward. Hands caught her arms and pack, easing her to the ground as she batted feebly at them.

"It's okay, Rach. They're helping," Damarcus slurred from somewhere to her left.

"Dee?" Rachel's head lolled to one side as she tried to look at him.

"You're okay, Rach. Let them get a line in, it'll help."

She watched impassively, all the fight had gone out of her in an instant, as two uniformed men worked on Damarcus. One eased the pack off his shoulders as the other pushed his sleeve back and began scrubbing the crook of his arm with an alcohol swab. Rachel felt hands mirroring those actions on her. She picked her head up enough to look at the two men working to make her comfortable and place the IV.

"Quick pinch," the one at her arm told her. A sharp stab made her flinch, but she stayed seated. The man sat down at her feet and set the bag on his shoulder. "Easier than toting an IV pole with us," he told her with a quick smile.

Rachel nodded as blackness faded around her.

***

"Hey, Rach?" A gentle hand shook her shoulder. "Wake up. Nap time's over."

Rachel groaned as she pushed herself to a seated position. She dragged a hand through her chin-length black hair, brushing leaves and dirt from hair that was still pin straight in the humid jungle air.

Damarcus gave her a smile from where he sat across from her. Behind him, several uniformed men hunched over a map spread across the jungle floor. "They hacked our GPS coordinates while we did the logistics hold and updated the team. As briefed, the team is still moving but won't make a rendezvous here. They gave us a better spot to meet up with the supplies and we'll move out as soon as you're ready."

"This seems like a lot to drop off, what? Food? More ammo?" Rachel asked him.

"Beans and bullets, yes," Hank said from where he squatted by the map, having clearly heard their conversation. "We can transmit fresh intel through a satellite relay, but until you wonderful folks can figure out how to send snacks without sending all of us, this is how it's got to work." He gave a one shoulder shrug as if trekking through the jungle was of little impact to him.

Rachel decided that if he could be calm about the prospect of hiking through the unfamiliar jungle then she could put on her big girl panties and take it in stride as well. No need to mention that she, a lifelong city dweller, had only ever seen jungles in photos and movies. She gave Damarcus and Hank a nod before rising to shoulder her pack.

Not what you expected, is it? Damarcus asked in a quiet corner of her mind.

Am I that obvious? Rachel took a deep breath and smoothed her features into their usual cool imperious look.

Only to me. You're nervous now. You weren't before.

Rachel swallowed hard. *I don't like bugs, snakes, or spiders. I don't want to imagine how many of any of those are around me right now.*

Girl, are you seriously telling me you're nervous because you're afraid of bugs?

I'm also less than thrilled to go stomping through hilly terrain. I'm more fit now, but I'm not exactly you or Murphy, right? This is, she gave her head a little jerk toward the downslope, *pretty hilly terrain.*

Damarcus's eye tracked down the hill. *That's fair. If you need a break, tell me like this. I'll tell them I need the break if that would make you feel better.*

Rachel gave him a curious smile. *You'd really let them think you're tired?*

Why not? He gave a little shrug, barely raising the straps of his pack.

You aren't worried they'll see you as, she gave a tiny pause, *weak?*

Damarcus clamped a hand over his mouth to halt a laugh. *Rach, I can do something none of them can do. I could be a skinny stick and they would still respect me for my part in this team.* He gave her a mirthful look, but seeing the look on her face sobered him. *No, I'm not worried about being perceived as weak. And since I know you are, I am more than happy to request a halt on your behalf without calling you out.*

Rachel blinked once, struggling to hold her cool expression. *Thank you,* she told him simply. She finished shouldering her pack. Once it was settled, she nodded to Hank and the team.

"Move out," Hank said just loud enough for the group to hear.

The trek was not what Rachel expected. She had envisioned

them speed walking through rugged terrain, the fit men surrounding her strolling easily. Instead, they moved methodically. Two men led, scoping out the terrain as they went and quietly calling out any obstacles to the men carrying the supplies. Whenever obstructions made one man carrying the boxes impractical, another would automatically move to help him. Rachel was a bad judge of distance but would have guessed they didn't make it more than three or four miles in the first few hours.

This isn't so bad, she told Damarcus when they stopped to rest a second time without anyone having to request a halt.

Nope. They know their business and Hank knows the breaking point of men. Well, people, Damarcus said with a slight nod to her.

He cares for them, she stated.

Yes.

Rachel nodded again, considering. She slipped her bag from her shoulder, setting it at the edge of the rock that marked the downslope. The first stop had been several minutes and she wanted those precious moments without the weight on her back.

Are all military leaders like him? She asked Damarcus.

The good ones are, yes. Damarcus smiled at her. *Watch Val more closely. She gets mad, she gets flustered, but it's because she genuinely cares about us and wants to ensure we're taken care of. She gets really pissed anytime the government thinks they can push us over our capabilities. I haven't seen her get violent,* his mental voice gave a funny pause, *but I bet she'd crack some skulls if they really pushed at her.*

What is it?

What?

You hesitated.

Yes, I suppose I did.

Rachel gave him a level look that said he needed to come out with it already.

Hey, that's her story to tell. Powell had some things to say about her first mission to Paris, but you need to ask her about it, not me.

Did she beat someone up or something? Rachel asked incredulously.

Yeah, pretty much exactly that. Her target tried to assault her and she punched the hell out of him. Clawed out an eye too, I think.

Hot damn! I think I like her a little more now. Rachel told him. She leaned back to consider this new information about their boss, leaning back into her bag.

The bag, precariously perched on the edge of the rock, tumbled over the edge and began to fall downhill. "Shit!"

Rachel reached out, her hand outstretched toward the falling bag, and its fall arrested. She focused on it with every ounce of her being, unwilling to climb down the hill to retrieve it or worse, force one of the men to go fetch it for her. Rachel focused on the bag, her hand still outstretched, and watched it slowly slide back up the hill to her, leaving a line of scuffed dirt and leaves in its wake. Inhaling as she focused, it rose slowly before finally settling onto the rock in front of her, almost exactly in the same position it occupied before its fall.

Rachel exhaled, the sound harsh as it broke the silence that surrounded her. She turned around to see every man on the team staring at her.

"What?" Rachel's voice seemed loud in the silence.

Silence stretched across what should be an otherwise boisterous and lively jungle.

Damarcus stared at her wide-eyed. "Rachel, what did you just do?" he whispered.

"You all can't do this?" She took in his face. "Dee? The other Pantheon, they can't do this?" A shiver of fear rose in her.

"No, Rach, we can't use telekinesis."

Rachel's heart pounded. It would be gone, all gone. This team, family, she had finally found would be stripped away. She would be an outcast once more. Her heart pounded, fear rising in her throat choking her. "Am I going to get kicked out for this?" she whispered.

Damarcus rushed to her, embracing her, and for once, she didn't fight against a simple human touch. "No," he held her gently to her chest. *No, we wouldn't kick you out for this. We'll tell Val. Honestly, she might be excited to see a new talent.*

Please, Dee, don't let them send me back.

EIGHT

RACHEL NG

1148L/1548Z, 24 OCT

"I won't send you back, Rach," Damarcus told her with a quiet intensity.

Rachel nodded, fear still tightening her features.

"But we do have to tell Val." He grinned. "After we finish this mission."

Rachel nodded again and looked at Hank. "We good?"

"Ma'am, I'm good if you are. And if you can find a use for that new skill, I'd be mighty pleased."

"Yes, sir. I mean Hank. Colonel."

"Don't be flustered, ma'am. This is a good thing." Hank seemed to sense her inability to voice more because he turned to his team. "Break's over. Let's get these supplies to the other team. We've got less than two miles to go if Huber's GPS hack is correct."

"GPS shows it's locked on five satellites, that's as good as we're likely to get, sir."

Hank nodded. "Let's move out."

The supply teams hoisted their burdens with each man giving Rachel a curious glance. She had the same question: Could she carry the crates?

No, Rach, not now. Damarcus's mental voice told her.

Dee?

I know what you're thinking. I saw that look. We can mess with it later. But for right now, you have no idea what telekinesis does to your physical and mental state. We can't risk you being too tired or burned out to get your team home. I know you want to help them, but you can help them most by being ready to Jump when they need it.

Understood. Rachel lied but it didn't stop her from letting her mind wander as they slowly and carefully picked their way through the jungle.

An uneventful hour of hiking passed while Rachel considered the implications of her newfound skill. Her brain was exploding with possibilities and Damarcus had occasionally reached out to silently ask if she was okay.

Fine, Dee, I just keep thinking of new ways to use this!

"Echo Three, come in?" Huber whispered into his throat mic.

"Team, we'll halt here," Hank told them. "My dang toes are twitching."

The men with the crates dropped their burden while Damarcus and Rachel tore into their protein bars.

"How are your feet?" Hank asked her as Huber continued trying to raise the other team.

"No blisters, if that's what you're asking," Rachel told him quietly.

"Good. We're not far from the RZ now." His eyes darted to Huber.

Rachel fought the urge to reach out and grasp his hand, wanting to know what he was thinking. Hank must have seen the subtle shift in her hand because he extended his own hand, palm up, as a clear invitation. Rachel glanced quickly at Damarcus who nodded. She delicately placed her hand on Hank's.

Worry. Fear. Frustration.

Under his outwardly calm façade, Hank's mind was churning.

Rachel's eyes snapped up to Hank who gave her the barest of nods.

He's worried, Rachel told Damarcus.

I can tell, he told her.

How did you know?

I've worked with Hank for almost a decade, I know when he's stressed. If I had a guess, the other team is overdue. As things go, we should have gotten word they were approaching the RZ by now. Radio silence isn't the worst thing, but it means they're balled up by something. Hank will probably hold us here until he knows. No reason to walk into an ambush.

Ambush?

Sure. We're less than 400 meters from the RZ, you could probably see it if it weren't a jungle. What do you see from here east?

Rachel peered through the trees. *It slopes down, beyond that, not much.*

Good. I think the RZ is close to the saddle of this ridge, maybe just downhill from the ridgeline. It's in a bowl. Not a great position for the team and I'm not sure why they picked it, too easy to set up an ambush.

You think it's a setup?

Tough to say. The team sent the request via an encoded channel and it was authenticated. There weren't any tags to indicate it was sent under duress, so I can't say for sure they were forced to send it or that an adversary sent it, but it's strange.

Rachel flinched back with surprise. *You really think this is a trap?*

Damarcus gave a little shrug. *No, but Hank does and that's enough for me.*

Rachel settled back against her pack, discreetly reaching for the gun on her hip.

Easy, Rach. Give it time. Hank will run through all the protocols to establish how long the team has been—

"Contact, left!" Yates yelled as the sound of leaves and branches snapping exploded around them.

Rachel snapped her weapon from its holster, rolling to face the incoming fire. Her finger was riding the trigger when a hand landed on her shoulder.

Emergency Jump, back to Alpha now! Damarcus sent her as he ducked low. *Get your team out, I'll be a half-second behind.*

What about the other team?

"Cease fire, cease fire, Jump commencing!" Damarcus yelled.

GO! Damarcus's command thundered in her brain.

Rachel mentally sought her team, mind flicking across their signatures. As soon as she felt the last finger release from its trigger she Jumped.

Her team landed in a sprawled heap on the hangar floor, narrowly missing other personnel who had not anticipated their early return and were crossing near Point Zero. Rachel retained consciousness just long enough to see Damarcus and his team were the promised half second behind, landing relative to their positions in the Venezuelan jungle.

Rachel woke again on a cot set at the end of the taped-off Zero Point. Given the change in the team's reception of her, she was surprised to be alone with only her IV on a pole nearby. Groaning, she sat up.

Val must have caught her movement because Rachel watched her hurry over from where she was deep in conversation with Hank and his team. "Wait, sit back. You're only half done with that bag."

Rachel laid back as ordered, mainly because she lacked the strength to stay upright.

"What happened?"

"Hank says you were ambushed. Did he mention anything about his toes?" Val asked her.

"That's a weird question."

"Hank's got a sixth sense."

"He's like us?"

Val gave a quick smile and patted her hand, her mirth passing quickly at the touch. "No, nothing like that. He claims his missing toes twitch when he's about to get ambushed." She shrugged. "He's usually right too."

"Missing toes?" Rachel was thoroughly confused.

"You didn't notice that he's missing a whole foot?"

"What?"

"Yeah, he's an amputee. Refuses to leave the military until it's on his terms and gets a waiver to stay in every year."

"I just watched that man hike four miles through hills and jungle on a plastic foot?"

"It's carbon fiber and stainless steel these days, but yeah," Hank said as he came over. "How are you feeling, ma'am?"

"Recovering. What happened?"

"That's what we're trying to figure out. My team will take it, but it seems like someone knows enough about our operations to have lured us in." Hank looked to Val. "Think it's *Svoboda* or *Vmeste*?"

"With Apollo having been in our spaces, I can't throw that out," Val told him. Her face drew in concern.

"Means we're compromised," Hank said with a frown.

"And why hit us there if they know where we are right now?" Val frowned. "The oligarchy's little pets have just as much reason if not more, and more resources to hit our team in Venezuela. And they wouldn't have any idea where we are now."

"It's probably *Vmeste?*" Rachel asked.

"Seems most likely. I'm still worried," Val told her. "Hank, keep digging and see if our favorite friend at the Agency can lend a hand. Use our intel if you need to skirt the Title 10 and Title 50 rules," Val said, her face as serious as Rachel had ever seen it.

Hank nodded once and strode off.

Rachel caught the peculiar way she referred to her boyfriend, Mr. Brandon Powell, but didn't want to engage in her boss's personal life. "Did Hank tell you anything else about the trip?"

"He was vague and said it was Pantheon business, but I'd be interested. Are you willing to talk about it?"

Once again, Rachel was grateful for how Val seemed to always leave her options. She figured she needed to inform her boss, but Val had allowed her to decline until later. Trusting her, Rachel closed her eyes and mentally reached out for the pen tucked behind Val's ear. Gently, she withdrew it and held it level in front of Val's eyes.

Val gave a surprised grunt. "Stars above. You're doing this?"

"Yes." Rachel let the pen drop.

Val scrubbed her face with both hands. Rachel could see the purple rings under her eyes as she pulled her hands away. "This is cool and I need to address it when we get a moment, but until the current crisis is solved, I'm sorry, I just don't have the bandwidth.

Work with Dee, see what you can do without burning yourself out. Report any progress to me soon."

"Yes, ma'am."

"You can call me Val, Rachel." She rested her hand lightly on Rachel's. A feeling of pride and curiosity was foremost in her mind, but as the contact broke, Rachel could feel the turmoil and even fear that lurked below the surface.

NINE

RACHEL NG
1104L/1604L, 24 OCT

"Rachel, tell us what you were feeling?" Damarcus's voice was an ocean of calm in Rachel's inner turmoil.

Her last interaction with Val was unsettling, not because of what she said, but the feeling she left behind in Rachel's mind. Rachel wasn't sure if Val's uneasiness was from Rachel's new seeming ability or Val's own life. To Rachel, not knowing put her on edge.

"Fucking scared," Rachel said without thought. "I mean," she said and straightened in her seat, "I mean, I was concerned that my actions would force the team to expend extra energy to retrieve my bag."

Damarcus and Murphy both blinked, nearly in unison. Rachel wanted to laugh. Men. It's like they couldn't see the code switch between the woman and the Professional.

"You were," Damarcus seemed to consider her words, "concerned about how your actions impacted the team?"

"Or you were worried they'd be mad?" Murphy followed.

"Both," Rachel told them. "I didn't want to be a burden."

"That was enough to completely unlock a previously unknown telepathic skill?" Murphy asked, incredulously.

Damarcus shot him a filthy look. "It's not telepathy, it's telekinesis, and yeah, I can see it."

He gave Rachel a look that made her want to shiver in the best of ways. "Aren't emotional events the way we all unlock our skills?"

Their eyes all met briefly before each person looked away. Rachel took in a deep breath and upon exhaling, opened her mind to the two men before her. Emotions and turmoil surrounded each man like a cloud. A normal person might have held their hands out in comfort but Rachel could still barely tolerate being touched, let alone by people who would flood her with emotions.

Rachel huffed out a little breath. "I hate to play the 'who's got the worst trauma' game but who are the most emotional people in the Pantheon? Maybe I can teach them?"

"Val," Damarcus said immediately.

"Mandy," Murphy said a half second behind.

"Oh well no, I am not poking the bear!" She nearly laughed when each man's face showed they both thought the woman they named was "the bear."

"Maybe we can discuss tactics before we try opening up any fresh wounds in an attempt to teach," Murphy finally said.

Damarcus looked thoughtful for a moment before saying, "Well, it wouldn't work against anyone who can Jump, right? You try to grab them and they'd Jump away right?"

Rachel shrugged. "The bag can't Jump away, but ..." She focused on Damarcus again. She thought about lifting him from his seat, trying to make him slowly rise by the seat of his pants but nothing happened.

Damarcus clearly caught her look and smiled. As soon as she caught his handsome smile, she felt a little flutter in her belly. A lustful feeling raced through her and, embarrassingly, Damarcus started to rise.

"Fuck!" Damarcus said as he rose halfway out of the chair. "Put me back down and tell us how you did that."

"Emotion," she said quietly as he settled back into the chair.

Damarcus's eyebrows rose slightly but mercifully, he didn't ask which emotion.

"I felt sort of an opening? I think?"

"Was the opening feeling linked to that specific emotion? Or, if you keep practicing, do you think you'd be able to separate the emotions from the action?"

Rachel considered the question. A former hooker whose superpower was fueled by emotions? How fucking trite. Rachel frowned.

She looked at Murphy this time, keeping her mind blank, she focused on him and tuned out Damarcus. Feeling slightly ridiculous, she put her hand out, palm toward Murphy, and slowly rotated her hand, thinking of the motion lifting him from his seat. A feeling like a clasp coming undone snapped in her mind and Murphy slowly rose, just as Damarcus had.

"Yes!" She cried in triumph then watched Murphy thump back down into the seat. "Oh, sorry Murphy. I think losing concentration means I can't hold it."

"God, I think I was so shocked you really did it, I forgot to try and Jump out of it," Murphy said with a hesitant laugh. "Try it again."

Rachel, held her hand out again, palm to Murphy, and slowly rolled her wrist. The odd unclasping flicked in her mind and Murphy rose from the seat, drifting gently above the line of the table.

"Hold it, Rachel," Damarcus said in a whisper then nodded to Murphy.

Rachel's mind wrenched and Murphy Jumped to the other side of the conference table.

"Damn it, I had hoped I could hold him." She rubbed her temples, the odd wrenching feeling had left her with a slight headache. She saw Murphy and Damarcus exchange a glance but neither spoke. "Yeah?"

Damarcus gave a little cough. "I'm sure there are situations where being able to hold someone from teleporting would be useful, I admit that I am somewhat relieved that you can't hold one of us."

"Oh yeah, that would be, uh, weird."

"It would certainly alter our dynamics," Murphy agreed.

There was a long pause. Rachel wanted to open her mind and verify what they felt, but years in her former profession and years in an abusive household had taught her to read a person by how they walked, notice the set of their shoulders, and be ready to flee or fight at the sound of a door closed just barely too hard. One glance at each man's face told her all she needed to know: They had been scared. They had been scared of her and what she could have done to threaten their freedom of movement.

Rachel plastered a smile mask on her face. "Well, I guess it's good I can't. I'll keep practicing to see what I can and can't do. Is there anyone else who might be open to learning but, uh, less volatile than Val or Mandy?"

"Wilson," Murphy told her after a silent moment of consideration.

"Really? Isn't he … kind of old?" When Murphy and Damarcus both gave her a look she continued. "I mean, old dogs and new tricks, right? Isn't he the oldest member of the Pantheon?"

"Yes, Rachel, he is, but he's also going through some things right now." Damarcus told her before she could open her mouth. "That's for him to share, not me. But I think his current life situation might be enough emotional turmoil for … what did you call it? An opening? It might be enough for him to use that opening without being as on edge as Val or Mandy might be right now."

They found Wilson discussing an upcoming Jump with his handler, Carson, on the hangar floor.

"Excuse us, Carson," Damarcus interrupted them gently. "Wilson, may we steal you for a half hour?"

Wilson nodded to his handler. "You know what I need, Carson. I'll be back shortly."

"Sir," Rachel addressed Wilson formally, "I don't know what rumors have made it to you already but, well, I can use telekinesis, and I suspect I might be able to teach you."

Wilson looked at Murphy, his eyes narrowing slightly. "You taught the old man a new trick once and think you can do it again, Murphy?"

Rachel flinched at his words, but Damarcus's voice came to her mind, *He's teasing him, Rach.*

Thanks, Dee. He sounds mad.

Eh, maybe a little. When we learned we could access telepathy, it was Murphy who first reached Wilson. Found out more than he should have.

Oh!

"Yes, I think I can. I'm sorry, Wilson, but I think you're the prime candidate for this right now."

"Well, let's get on with it then," he told Rachel.

"Let's go to the conference room, it's more private," she told him.

Once in the room, Murphy closed the door.

"I'm sorry sir, but they've told me you may have something going on in your life that will help you access the emotional side of your brain." She held her hand up, palm out once again, and with the twist of her wrist, the conference phone on the table rose until it was at the end of its CAT 5 tether. She suppressed the smile she felt at how much easier it was with repetition.

"My God, young lady how did you do that?"

Rachel bristled at being called "young lady," but caught Damarcus's warning look. "Sir, my name is Rachel and would prefer to be referred to by my name." She harnessed the anger and threw her hand out, lifting the leather chair at the head of the table. "I do this by harnessing my emotions. There is a feeling in my mind, like it opens," she held up a closed fist and opened it like a flower in bloom while the chair hung in the air. As her fingers flattened out, she spun the chair around. "I'm able to lift objects."

"My apologies, Rachel." Wilson seemed genuine. "You remind me of someone is all."

She saw him look at Murphy and nod his acceptance.

"My daughter, Alicia, actually," Wilson told her. "Tell me what I should feel?"

"Think of something that brings you a strong emotion."

"Alicia," he all but whispered.

"Feel that emotion and focus on the object you want to move. Let your mind, uh, clear? Click? Open?" Rachel gave an exasperated shrug, frustrated by her own inability to describe it. "Look be mad, be sad, be giddy with joy and then focus, let your mind get really clear and you'll almost hear a click." She flicked the floating chair with a finger.

"Ah!" Wilson exclaimed and another chair rose. Shakily, but it rose to join the one beside Rachel's.

"Describe what you're doing. Tell me what you feel. Maybe we can find a better way to explain this," Rachel said.

Wilson's hand came up, mirroring Rachel, and the chair steadied. "I was thinking of my daughter Alicia. I was thinking about having to Jump home every night to check on her. She's going through chemotherapy right now and it's hell on her body. It's so hard to watch your child suffer like this." Wilson's voice dissipated as he fought the growing lump in his throat. His broadcasted emotion sent Rachel into a distant memory.

Rachel swallowed hard and tears formed in her eyes. Her chair dropped with a clang.

"Rachel?" Damarcus said, moving to her side. She saw his hands come up briefly and drop back down as if he wanted to hug her but thought better of it. "What's wrong?"

Tears coursed down her cheeks and she looked up at him. "My mother," she whispered.

"Chemo?"

Rachel shook her head. "She didn't make it."

"Oh God, I'm so sorry."

"I was fifteen," she whispered.

"That's so young. I—"

"My father kicked me out the day after the funeral. I don't know why, but he blamed me. Or said he couldn't stand to see my face. That I looked too much like her."

Words flooded out of Rachel. Years of pain and shame flowed out as she spoke.

"I ended up on the streets. He wouldn't let me in, even after a teacher called Child Protective Services on him. I—" Her tears caused her throat to close and she took a second to get a deep breath in. "I started stealing things and selling them to get by. I sold drugs. I sold everything." Rachel looked up at Damarcus again, meeting his eyes. "I didn't escape that until two months ago, Dee."

Damarcus raised his hand slowly, clearly telegraphing his intent and giving her the time to decide. "There is nothing I can say that will erase what happened to you, Rachel. But you're with us now.

You are family. You are Pantheon. You won't be thrown out."

Rachel nodded slowly and allowed him to embrace her. She cried on his shoulder and felt Murphy and Wilson reach out to pat her back. More importantly, she could feel their sympathy thrumming subtly in the back of her mind.

She had a home. She had family. She was determined to prove she was worth it.

TEN

VALERIE "ATHENA" HALL

0816L/1316Z, 27 OCT

Val squinted down at the map in front of her. The planning officer had been briefing her, Powell, and Mandy for the last fifteen minutes without getting to the point and only stern control over her annoyance was keeping her from snapping at the man. Since Major Kelly Ann Wilson had departed the strategic planning cell to be Val's new handler in Mandy's place, robbing it of half its manpower, the poor officer had been run ragged. This latest SNAFU wasn't helping the man either.

Val swallowed down her irritation and stared at the map again solemnly. Sometimes being in charge sucked. Like when she just wanted the chance to make one sarcastic and cutting remark.

Just once, she wanted to tell the man that the beloved Military Decision Making Process, known as MDMP, was nothing more than logic spelled out for kindergarteners.

It wasn't worth it though and she vowed to find the man a second planner to replace Kelly as soon as humanly possible.

"Kevin, just tell me how many calories, how many Jumpers, and how long the logistics hold is if needed," she ground out.

"Well, ma'am," he started, pushing his glasses up his nose where they had slipped down for the millionth time in an hour, "I know the math: a calorie per mile plus an additional calorie per 500 pounds of cargo. But, I need more details. How much cargo are you bringing back? I have a list but …" he stopped at her exasperated expression.

"You have all the details you will get, Kevin. Plan with an eighty percent solution, it's never getting any better than that."

The man fumbled his glasses once again. "Yes, ma'am."

Val swallowed down a sigh and suppressed the brief flash of apprehension she felt. Powell glanced at her and took a half step away. She glanced at Mandy who nodded and then leaned over to study the map and distances again. It was roughly 800 miles from Hurlburt Air Force Base, Florida to Washington, DC, which meant only 800 calories to them there. But Kevin was right, until they had a better idea how much they had to haul back, it was tough math. They certainly needed a logistics hold as soon as they arrived to prep for the return.

"Two Jumpers and at least forty minutes for saline-based nutrients," came a voice from behind and to her right.

It wasn't Kevin.

The hint of accent caused Val to whirl in place, her Sig Sauer P380 instantly snapping to the ready from its concealed holster. Powell's gun was up only a fraction of a second later. Beside her, Mandy staggered back a step.

"Apollo!" she snarled. "Breach, breach, breach!" Val shouted into the open hangar.

Around her, the support personnel hit the floor in anticipation of bullets flying. The Pantheon members who heard her shout sprinted to her location. Apollo, however, stood his ground, hands slightly raised, palms out, to show he meant them no harm.

"Where is *Svoboda*?" Val growled. She held one hand up to halt anyone from approaching any closer. Damarcus, Jafar, Rachel, Hank, and Murphy stopped a few paces from where Val held Apollo at gunpoint.

"They will not follow. They did not follow to DC, they will not follow here." Apollo's words were strained, as if he was pulling his English from the deepest recesses of his memory.

Something in the back of Val's mind remembered that a few

months back, he had an American accent, but his English was slow as if he had not spoken it in a long time. Her eyes narrowed.

"Why?" she asked simply.

"Because they do not know where I am. I left. I defect," he said in stilted English.

"Why now?"

"They are only killers. You help. You help people." He gestured toward Mandy. "She brings life itself to people in need. I do not wish to kill in cold blood. It was all I knew. It is not all I want to be."

Silence stretched between them.

"What do you want?"

"I want to get away from *Svoboda* first of all. I want to join you. And I want to end them."

"No," she snapped.

Powell laid his hand along her forearm, pushing her gun down and away from Apollo. "Hear him out, Val," Powell whispered. "He didn't come in shooting and clearly he could have."

Val glared up at him. "Bran," she hissed quietly.

"If you can hold him, he'll be a good source of intel." He glanced at Apollo. "And, if you'll believe it, he's telling the truth. As far as I can tell."

Val glanced at Apollo who was avidly watching their exchange. Mandy shuffled uneasily behind her and Val saw Murphy tense, leaning his weight onto the balls of his feet and ready to fight. Val shook her head and let the tip of her weapon lower slowly.

"If we agree to talk, we don't do it here," she gestured to her support personnel, still laying prone in case there was shooting. "You go to our location and we all go," she gestured to the Pantheon members in her immediate vicinity. "Hank? Powell? You in or out on this?"

"He came into my house," Hank growled, analogous to a shout of rage from any other man.

"In then. Powell?" she said, turning to him, gun still down.

"In," he said quietly. "I can frame questions for you. Or just listen."

For the first time, Val truly appreciated Powell's empathic gift that essentially made him a walking lie detector. "In then," she told him.

Val turned back to Apollo. "Walk slowly to me, hands out, and I will give you the point. You will Jump there within five seconds or I will assume you don't intend to follow." She glanced at her team around her. "Mount Charleston, the tri-trail merge off of Trail Canyon," she told them. "Murphy and Dee, hang back fifteen seconds just in case he tries anything funny. Hank, tag up."

Apollo and Hank both approached, eyeing each other warily. She pictured a sparsely wooded trail, the crunch of gravel across dirt, the crisp winds at higher elevations, and the tang of pine scented air. Each man tapped her hand briefly.

"On the count of three," she told Apollo, staring him down. She holstered her gun and took Powell's hand. She didn't need to touch him to know his mental feel for Jumping, but the brief touch gave her courage. "One. Two. Three."

On "three," she made the Jump. Her feet crunched onto the rocky dirt where multiple trails merged and she staggered. For the second time in ten days, she burned a massive calorie load with no prep, 1,700 calories in a single Jump. Hands caught her as her vision dimmed.

Sorry folks, I didn't really think that through, she said widely to her team as they appeared around her.

It's okay, Val. That was definitely what I would consider an emergency Jump, came Damarcus's reply. Near Rachel, Jafar also staggered to one knee.

Val took in a deep breath and tried to focus her vision as it swam. In front of her was a huge bristlecone pine the stood twisted and gnarled by wind, weather, and age. Somewhere in the back of her mind, she remembered someone telling her they could live to be thousands of years old. The tree certainly looked like it had withstood the test of time and would outlive them all by centuries.

Damarcus and Murphy's arrival a moment later brought her awareness back and she saw that Apollo had followed, true to his word.

ELEVEN

VALERIE "ATHENA" HALL

0621L/1321Z, 27 OCT

The Pantheon team closed around Apollo, forming a loose ring. Not that it would hold him, but it subtly reinforced that he was not part of their group. Powell stepped closer to Val but she could see from his wire-tight posture and the way his eyes darted around the trail, he was feeling the stress and anxiety radiating off her.

"Dee, the team?" Val asked quietly. A sharp, chilly wind cut at her, grounding her in the moment.

"Packing gear and prepping to be pulled back if this goes sideways. They're rattled," he told her.

"I'm sure my guys are too, Val," Hank told her.

Val nodded. "I know, I'm so sorry, Hank. I exposed your team to a terrible risk."

Hank nodded, jaw clenched closed over everything she suspected he wanted to say, but he didn't speak again.

"Val, are you sure about this?" Damarcus asked. "I don't think this is right."

"I know, Dee, but what else can I do? I can't kill him in cold blood. Other than follow us, he hasn't done anything else," she whispered to him.

"Okay, Val. I'll follow your lead."

"Alright, Apollo. You said you want out of *Svoboda*, to destroy them, and to join us. Why?"

"They are evil," he said simply.

"Yes." Val agreed. She reached out for Powell's hand and squeezed it once. He squeezed back twice, his subtle signal that someone was being truthful.

"So?"

"They are a threat to you. To Russia. To America. To the stability of geopolitical dynamics," Apollo said slowly as if winnowing each word from the depths of his memory, his dark blond brows furrowed in concentration.

Two squeezes.

"What's in it for you?" Val asked.

"Vengeance."

Powell gave no squeezes and Val rolled her wrist in an 'out with it' gesture. When he didn't speak, she told him, "Be more specific. On who? Why? What did they do to you? What did they take from you?"

"My life, my lover, and any chance at having my family." His eyes darted around the circle once.

Val wondered if he was trying to convince all of them or if there were specific people he felt he needed to convince. Powell squeezed her hand twice again.

Powell indicated he's being truthful. It may not be the whole truth, but what do you all think? Val asked the group.

End him now, before he causes us more trouble. Even if he is trying to escape Svoboda, *I bet they want him and I don't want them stumbling on us looking for him,* Damarcus said bitterly.

No. No. We cannot take his life. He is a threat, yes, but simply being a threat is not enough, Jafar countered.

You didn't see him in Orsha this spring. He's not one of us. He never was and never will be, Damarcus replied.

And you cannot trust someone who isn't wholly American? Jafar spat back heatedly.

I'm with Jafar, Murphy told them. *He's an adversary but he's not currently hostile. No need to get blood on our hands just yet.*

Mandy? Rachel? Val asked.

End him, was Rachel's response.

Val looked to Mandy who was studying him intently.

I hold him responsible for my father, Mandy said. *End him.*

Val rocked back and a ripple of shock went through the link at Mandy's harsh pronouncement.

I'm asking Powell and Hank. They're part of this now too, Val said.

"Powell, Hank. We're determining if he's worth it or," she said quietly, "if he should be removed from the equation." She eyed Apollo to see if he would bolt or if she was vague enough that his broken English would be insufficient to catch her meaning.

Hank shook his head. "I can take a life in combat, but this isn't it, Val."

"That's three for and three against. Powell?"

He looked at Apollo, face impassive, but the touch of his hand was a frenzied feeling that Val came to associate with him focusing his skills intensely.

"He's afraid but hopeful. I don't think he means you harm," Powell said carefully. "That doesn't mean he won't still cause you harm."

"Where do you stand though, Powell?" Damarcus asked.

"With Val, as always," he said. "Three for and three against, Val. My vote lies with you and you're the tiebreaker."

The entire group's focus shifted to her. Val took a deep, considering breath. He was a threat and it was clear he knew more about the Pantheon and its operations than he should. The idea of burning through every backup location they had weighed on her. The risk he presented was enormous, but she couldn't kill him in cold blood.

The weight of five other minds in the link pressed upon her as heavily as Hank and Powell's hard stares. She closed her eyes.

"He lives. For now." Val opened her eyes again to see the relief on Apollo's face. He knew what they were deciding and, curiously, had not immediately fled.

"Tell us more," she commanded.

TWELVE

VALERIE "ATHENA" HALL
0626L/1326Z, 27 OCT

"I was not always in *Svoboda*," Apollo told her. "I was American, once. My father, he was American, and my mother was a Soviet. I do not think you care about that right now."

"Nope. Start with *Svoboda*. Where are they? What are they doing? And why are you getting away from them?" Val told him.

"*Svoboda* is gone. Almost gone. After you killed Miller Thompson, Pyotr assumed full control of them. He is evil."

"I recall," Val remarked dryly.

Apollo nodded. "Only Pyotr, Alexei, and Yuri live. Iosif is dead. Pyotr has control of them. He hates *Vmeste*. He hates the oligarchs. He wants to destroy both. For the last six months, he increases the number of murders, the assassinations. I grew uneasy. This does not sit well with me. I tell Pyotr we are pushing too hard; we will be caught. He tells me it is okay, he has a plan. There is no plan."

Powell squeezed Val's hand twice. She gestured for Apollo to continue.

Apollo's face hardened. "I tell Pyotr I want to leave. That I want out. He says okay. Next day, my lover is dead. In Russia, they did not accept my lover as American's would see accept him. Iosif killed him and left him where I can see. It was a double warning but I killed Iosif and left. I know the offices in Washington, DC,

Miller Thompson told me long before he died. Gave me the images, feelings. He knew I will not be safe if he ever dies and wants to give me protection."

Val felt two more squeezes. She opened her mouth to speak but a single long, hard squeeze stopped her. One glance at Powell showed her a subtle shake of his head. She let Apollo continue.

"I leave Russia, hide where *Svoboda* cannot find me and plan a way to come to you safely." Apollo looks at Mandy, "You say on television that you welcome all with your abilities to Limitless Logistics." He enunciated the word carefully. "I come to see if that is true. I have your abilities. I am on your side."

Val felt two more squeezes. "You do have the abilities," she acknowledged carefully. "But whether you are on our side is yet to be seen."

"Yes. But I did not come in shooting and I could have. I did not Jump directly into the Washington, DC, office, even though it would have been easy. I came through the front door as any other applicant. Please, let that earn me some trust."

Val saw Murphy and Jafar nodded while Mandy's face was mutinous. Val's brow furrowed; she had never seen her friend look so dire. She realized Mandy really did blame *Svoboda* for luring Miller away. She shook her head and focused on Apollo again.

"Why did Miller give you the images of our office's interior? Why did he think you were at extra risk, other than being the only other American on the team?"

"No father wants his child to face that kind of risk," Apollo said simply.

There was a brief moment of silence across the remote mountain trail before the full meaning of his words sunk in.

Then, the emotional blast wave of his words could be felt throughout the group.

Several cries of "liar!" and "lies!" echoed across the surrounding hills. Mandy took a staggering step back, her dour face now contorted with rage before Hank had to restrain her when she lunged, shrieking at Apollo. Val could feel the mental link Mandy had held for them drop.

"Bran?" Val asked Powell over the commotion.

Powell shook his head, mouth set in a frown. "He's conflicted, I can't tell."

Val bobbed her chin once and gathered their signatures, pulling them into her own mind to reestablish the link.

"Shut up, you lot!" Val shouted into the chaos, echoing it with a mental shove across their link for good measure.

Hank pulled Mandy to his chest, his arms wrapping over hers to keep her from lunging at Apollo again. Damarcus stepped halfway in front of her as well, but his face said he was unsure if he really wanted to stop her. Jafar, Rachel, and Murphy resumed their spots in the circle.

Val stepped forward, holding out a hand. "Take my hand and say that again. Prove it."

Apollo took her hand without hesitation. "My name is John Elias Thompson, I am the son of Miller Thompson and his," he hesitated only briefly, "mistress I believe is the right word. Lover? Not wife. Girl … friend, maybe?" He waved a hand toward Mandy. "Her mother was his wife after, but Miller loved my mother first."

Images of a dark-haired and kind-faced woman flowed across their touch. Sporadic images of Miller Thompson flashed through. Val felt and saw the day Apollo's mother died as well; her face was gaunt and her head was covered in a soft wrap, an antiseptic feel permeated the memory. She could see the day Miller brought him to *Svoboda* as well.

"Your mother was a lovely woman, Apollo," Val told him quietly. "Your father was a bastard, but he was Miller Thompson," she said loud enough for the group to hear.

A feeling of relief washed across her, emanating from Apollo.

"You believe me?" he asked hopefully.

"I believe Miller was your father. The rest?" She shrugged. "That remains to be seen. Now, you harm my people, I'll kill you the same as I did him." A flash of rage spilled over and she squeezed his hand. "Feel this truth, Apollo. Miller was crazy at the end," she allowed her memories of his end shoot through their touch. She showed how he held a gun to his own daughter's head and spewed illogical nonsense. "Your father was untrustworthy and violent. You have to earn our trust. You lose it and you die. Do you understand?"

Apollo's jaw tightened. "Yes," he ground out.

"Powell, Murphy," she snapped, still staring Apollo down. "Stay here and interrogate him."

Murphy shot Powell a look she couldn't fathom but nodded.

"If he tries anything?" Powell asked. His tone was bland, as if asking about tomorrow's weather but she understood his unspoken question.

Val's eyes snapped to him, just as hard as they had been on Apollo. "Everything short of grievous bodily harm." Her mouth twisted in a disgusted scowl. "Get in his head if you have to, Powell."

She hated asking him to do it. She hated that he could manipulate like he did. He had promised not to manipulate her again, but she had nagging suspicions that he wasn't being above board with their interactions.

Powell's head gave a quick jerk of acknowledgement.

"Team, fall back. Prep to move back to the primary site," Val told them.

Without the standard countdown, they disappeared as one, leaving Apollo in the hands of Murphy and Powell.

THIRTEEN

MURPHY "ARES" HAWKINS

0647L/1347Z, 27 OCT

The City of Sin was known for hot dry temperatures lingering well into October, but the tri-trail crossing on Mt. Charleston lay a mile above sea level and the early morning breeze nipped at the three men's cheeks. Murphy pulled up the collar of his polo and turned his back to the wind. He considered the information he needed from Apollo and how to get it from him. Murphy knew Powell would act as a walking lie detector, so it was a matter of constructing questions that would have answers Powell could verify.

Step one: Baseline his answers.

Murphy nodded at Powell. "Ready?"

Powell nodded and took Apollo's hand.

"First, Apollo, tell me your full name."

"My name is John Elias Thompson."

Powell nodded.

"What year is it?"

"2016."

Another nod.

"Tell me the sky is yellow."

"The sky is blue," Apollo said, confusion evident in his furrowed golden brows.

Murphy shook his head. "No. I need you to speak a lie." Out of the corner of his eye, he saw a smirk of acknowledgment on Powell's face. Of course, a CIA spook would know how to frame questions on a lie detector.

"The sky is yellow," Apollo said flatly and Powell shook his head.

"When did you come to the United States?"

"Which time?"

Murphy crossed his arms over his chest. "You're a Russian, when did you come here to learn our culture?"

"I am not a Russian. I was born a Soviet," he said with a sardonic grin and Powell nodded reluctantly, "when the Soviet Union lived." Apollo gave a shrug that conveyed his indifference over the rise and fall of an empire. "But my father was an American, so I hold an American citizenship."

Murphy's jaw dropped and he glanced at Powell who nodded with a frown. Fuck.

"When and where were you born, Apollo."

"My father teleported my laboring mother to Detroit, Michigan where I was born in a US hospital on the fifth of August, 1986."

"Shit, you are legally an American citizen." Murphy glanced at Powell again. "You gonna have an issue interrogating a US citizen? You intel spooky guys always have an opinion."

Powell gave a harsh bark of laughter. "Keep going Murphy, I'll tell you when he lies."

Murphy nodded side to side a few times, loosening his shoulders, as he considered his next questions. "Did you grow up here? I mean America, in general, not Las Vegas specifically."

"No. I grew up in the USSR until just before the fall. My father knew it was coming and got my mother out. We returned to the US until 1994." His face darkened and pulled into a grimace.

Murphy glanced at Powell again who nodded, but his eyes were narrowed. He wished he had Powell's talent, that he could do this on his own. This secondhand bullshit was like pulling information through a sieve and he questioned Powell's motivations. Murphy groaned with frustration.

"Why in the hell did Miller Thompson date? Marry? Either way, father a child with a Soviet woman?"

"You know this answer." Apollo shook his head. "Your leader, Zeus, murdered his friend in cold blood because he had been seen near the Soviets in Grenada."

"How the fuck is that relevant?" Murphy exclaimed.

Powell shot Murphy a look. "He's not—" Powell started and cut himself off. "He's not lying, but it's not clean."

Murphy considered it. The human mind is a fickle thing, especially when dragging memories out.

"Damn it. I don't think it's his memory, Murphy." Powell told him. He seemed reluctant to speak. "That's why it's not clear. He's telling you what he's been told, not what he directly knows."

"My father showed me his memories. He has shown me enough times that they are in my memory now too."

"He's angry," Powell said dryly. "But are *you* angry or was your father 'mad'?"

"Both," Apollo said bluntly.

Murphy didn't miss Powell's unsubtle insinuation and grabbed Apollo's other hand. "Show me," he commanded.

Murphy's mind whirled as his hand touched Apollo's and he understood what Powell had meant. He could feel Apollo's anger, but it was a cold anger, the frozen, stale anger of decades gone by. Murphy realized it had somehow been transferred to Apollo; he didn't feel it naturally. Murphy could feel the echo of a warm, humid breeze across his face, a sharp contrast to the biting wind on Mt. Charleston in the here and now.

The scene in his mind showed perfect, turquoise waters and a small sandy beach rimmed with lush tropical vegetation. The warm breeze across his face dried the heavy sweat dripping down his brow and into his eyes. No. Not his eyes. Murphy shook his head.

"This is Miller?" Murphy asked.

"Yes. He told me he supported American Operation. Urgent Fury?"

The scene that flowed across their joined hands looked picture perfect, but a deep and biting fatigue overlaid everything. His heart thudded against blood like sludge from dehydration, a feeling Murphy knew all too well himself; however, the acid burn of depletion sang in his veins. In short, without nutrition soon, Miller would die. The scene wavered and Murphy realized Miller had fallen to his rump and was now digging an IV into his own arm.

"No fallback man?" Murphy whispered.

"Fallback man?"

"You know, the guy who hooks your IV up and covers you while you recover?"

"No." That cold and stale anger reached a simmer for a moment before dropping into cold fury.

Murphy almost recoiled at Apollo's emotional torrent but gripped his hand tighter. Time in the scene seemed to skip forward and Miller was staggering to his feet.

"*I'm here, Zeus,*" Miller called out in the past.

A tall, broad-chested man in green fatigues came into Miller's view. Murphy realized with a start that it was Morgan "Zeus" Ward, Pantheon's founder. Murphy had never met the man, having only seen his portrait in the halls at Limitless Logistics' headquarters. The portrait, a commemoration to a lost leader, had only captured a man fading into his golden years, not the robust bull of a man in front of Miller.

"*Fowler's gone off somewhere and he's not at the RZ,*" Zeus said shortly. "*Bastard's probably gone back without us.*"

"*Sir, he knew the plan. You know he wouldn't have gone off without us.*"

"*Don't tell me what I know, boy. Shut up and pass me a bag.*" Zeus snatched at Miller's rucksack, taking a bag of fluids and jabbing the IV into his own arm without bothering to swab the spot clean.

Miller's view showed him quietly letting his superior get his calories in but the feeling that flowed from Apollo was worry and a hint of disgust. The disgust was odd, extending beyond just disgust for his current attitude to something bigger.

"*Sir, Mike is here somewhere, I just know it. If he had a bad Jump, he might be injured. These have been brutal—*"

"*Don't you nag at me too!*" Zeus said, cutting him off. "*I get enough of this from her.*"

Something in the way Zeus said "her" made Murphy believe he meant his wife, Ada "Hera" Ward and Limitless Logistic's cofounder. Oddly, Apollo didn't have the same spark of recognition.

"We didn't have enough time to plan before those bureaucrats had us in here," Zeus grumbled.

Murphy felt Miller swallow down frustration. *"Sir, my bag is done and I have one spare. I'd like permission to go search Mike's landing point for him."*

"Fine. Fine. Let me finish and I'll go with you."

Miller nodded, pleased. There was an almost filial level of respect that Murphy could feel from Miller with respect to Zeus. The scene seemed to skip forward in time again, as if Miller hadn't given Apollo the full memory. The scene now showed Miller and Zeus walking through the jungle as Zeus ranted about "the damn Soviets."

"Can't trust Commies, boy. They don't care about what we care about. They'll take everything you have and swear they're giving it to your neighbor in need but at the end of the day, you're both starving."

Murphy could feel Miller nodding along with Zeus's rant, but in his mind, he didn't agree. Miller felt the Communist ideals were misplaced but it didn't need to be met with the level of vitriol Zeus seemed to harbor.

"Once you get in bed with the commies, they'll have you on their hooks forever. You're compromised. They'll always try to take more."

The two burst through the tree line into a small clearing and Zeus gave an angry shout. In the clearing, several men attended another prone man and Murphy could feel Miller's spike of concern, but beside him, he could see Zeus looked apoplectic. His face was bright red and veins throbbed in his neck and at his temples. A caricature of an angry man.

Murphy took a mental step back and realized the perspective was heavily filtered through Miller's own perception and then Apollo's mind as well. He glanced at Powell who shook his head.

"I only feel the emotions, I don't see what you see, Murph."

Murphy nodded. "Keep it to facts, Apollo."

"I do keep to facts. I give this to you exactly as my father gave it to me."

Powell nodded. Murphy realized that it was enough that Apollo believed what he said was truth and if Miller had somehow managed to manipulate his own memories before passing them to his son, Apollo's perspective might still "feel" truthful. Murphy gave a grunt and slapped a big grain of salt on everything he was receiving.

"Continue," Murphy told him sharply.

Apollo's face hardened and annoyance flared across their touch, but the scene restarted. Zeus strode angrily to the group of men. He was shouting and the men returned unintelligible answers. Miller registered a flare of recognition between the language and uniform that these were Soviet soldiers. He felt a flash of fear as he realized the prone man was his coworker and missing teammate, Michael Fowler.

Murphy watched through Miller's eyes as Zeus drew his weapon and pointed it at the Soviet soldiers. They scattered back and held their hands up in defensive gestures.

"*Goddamn commie lover. What in the hell, Fowler!*" Zeus screamed down at the man.

Miller could see the man was barely conscious, an IV deftly inserted in his arm.

"*Zeus!*" Miller shouted over him. "*He didn't do this. They must have found him like this. They tried to save him.*"

"*Oh, are you some goddamn commie sympathizer now too, boy?*" Zeus whirled to face Miller; gun now trained on him.

"*No, Zeus, it's just—*" Miller held his hands up, trying to placate the man. "*I mean. Look at him. Look at him, Zeus! He is passed the fuck out. Do you think he's in any state to insert that IV?*"

"*He didn't have to accept help from them. He's a damn traitor. Fucking commies have been plaguing this country my entire life and I'll be damned if I let them plague my organization.*"

"*He would have died without accepting their help. Probably wasn't even coherent enough to deny it. Zeus, look at him! Just look at him!*" Miller gestured to the man, who struggled to sit up.

"*Could have died? He should have died rather than accept their help. Better dead than red.*" With no additional warning, Zeus put a round between Michael Fowler's eyes.

Murphy released Apollo's hand. "Jesus Christ."

"He went slightly mad after that," Apollo said bluntly.

"No fucking kidding." Murphy scrubbed his cold cheeks again, almost startled to be back in his own body in the blowing cold and dry air of Mt. Charleston. "Miller, he looked up to Zeus?"

"Yes, he said—"

"Hand," Powell said and took Apollo's hand again.

Murphy took Apollo's hand as well.

Rather than answering, Apollo gave him more flashes of Miller's memories. Miller as a young man, excited and nervous about meeting Zeus and Hera. Miller and Zeus sitting silently in bloodied uniforms as they shared a beer at a bar made of a plywood slab in a tropical jungle, Zeus putting a fatherly hand on his shoulder and Miller feeling bittersweet pride in his work and the approval of his mentor. Zeus's good-natured ribbing of Miller for being in his late twenties and still a bachelor with Miller shooting back that if he didn't work so hard maybe he could find a good woman.

"He did find one. Not long after Grenada," Apollo told them quietly.

"Your mother?"

Apollo smiled and scenes of the dark-haired and kind-faced woman flowed from his hand to Murphy's while Powell simply read his emotions. Unlike Miller's memories, which had a stale quality to them, the emotions were full and robust, and the scenes were colorful. Murphy saw moments in what appeared to be a small, austere apartment in Soviet Russia. Scenes with Miller lovingly holding his mother in another apartment's more lavish kitchen.

"Wait, you lived in America too?"

"Yes. As I said," Apollo met Murphy's eyes. "When the fall seemed imminent, my father came and got us both and put us in an apartment in Detroit. I went to an American school for two years before we went back."

As he said the last part, anger spiked across the touch.

"Watch it, Apollo," Powell told him. "Val might be all for a fair vote, but I'll end you here and now."

"Chill, Powell. I don't think it's us he's mad at."

"No. My father met Amanda's mother. And when he did, we were discarded. I spent the next decade in the new Russian republic, struggling as the former Soviets rebuilt themselves."

Bitter anger flowed across the touch.

"He abandoned you," Murphy said bluntly.

"Yes. He sent us back. He knew what it was like after the Soviet Union fell apart, and he still sent us back. He threatened my mother any time she said she wanted to return to the US or she asked for help. He came occasionally, sometimes with gifts even, but he was dedicated to his American family now. He had his white picket fence American dream, what did he need with his Soviet whore and bastard?"

Murphy absorbed that pronouncement like a blow to his own chest. His own family was complicated. He hadn't seen his father in a pair of decades and he kept only the most tenuous contact with his mother knowing that if she ever because aware of how much money he made now, she would make his life hell with emotional blackmail and outright begging.

He took a deep breath, catching Apollo doing the same. Murphy gave him a quick nod of understanding.

"Wait, you spoke English, as a child? But now, you seem to struggle."

Apollo chuckled. "Speaking English in Russia was," he considered a moment, "frowned on. So no, after not speaking English for a decade, it faded from my mind."

Murphy eyed Powell who gave a noncommittal gesture.

"When did he pull you into *Svoboda*?"

"Eight years ago. I lost my mother a decade ago and was a bit wild. My father had difficulty finding me on occasion but always tracked me down. One of the times? I will show you."

The scene Murphy saw showed the perspective moving quickly down a narrow alleyway. Occasionally Apollo's perspective would turn to glance behind him, showing that he was running from Miller.

Apollo turned abruptly into an alley blocked by a high chain-linked fence topped with razor wire.

"*You're coming back with me, John,*" Miller called to him in Russian.

"*I do not want to go with you! I live here. This is my life, not some American family who has never met me. How will your wife,*" he sneered, "*feel when you bring home your bastard?*" His fingers quested along the chain link fence, pushing and prodding, seeking a hole.

Murphy could feel the resentment, the disappointment in Apollo's words. He had been thrown aside for a new family and hated the idea that he could be transplanted on a whim.

"*And you'll what? Keep living on the streets as someone's boy toy?*" Miller walked slowly, deliberately toward Apollo.

Murphy felt the quick snap of fear at being outed by his father.

"*Like you would want someone like me in your home?*" He snapped. His fingers moved more desperately, knowing what Miller could do. If he could get his hands on him, it was over and he'd be in America in a blink with no possible way to return to his home.

"*You're my son and I accept who you are. You could be more, but I'll take what I can get.*"

Apollo laughed harshly that this man could claim to accept him yet had kept him at arm's length almost his entire life.

"*Forget me. I am nothing to you. I have nothing you want.*" He looked at the other side of the alleyway, just beyond reach, feeling the creeping dread as his whole life would be taken away in a moment as Miller stalked closer. He closed his eyes, envisioning making it over the wall unscathed and running back to his life. He wanted nothing, *nothing* more in life, than to be away from Miller and on the other side of that fence right now.

The vision was shattered by the sound of Miller's wild laughter.

Murphy saw the perspective change and Apollo was on the other side of the fence, having Jumped for the first time. A breath caught in Murphy's throat unexpectedly. This was a moment every Pantheon member knew and the trauma of their first Jump was like a knife slipped gently between the ribs. It was so quiet yet the pain and blood flowed almost immediately.

"*Oh son, you are just like me,*" Miller said between chuckles. "*And you have so much more that I need than you ever thought.*"

Apollo released Murphy's hand with a last wash of regret flowing across the touch.

"You didn't want this either, did you?" Murphy asked quietly.

Apollo looked at him, face unreadable. "No."

Powell's face looked sour.

"Powell?"

"It's not true," he said. When Apollo glared at him, he continued, "It's not completely true."

Apollo shook his head. "I did not want this, but I do not hate it now that I have this. I did not want to go with my father, but my mother had died not long before that memory. I had no," he thought for a moment, "reason to stay. I was lost. I didn't want to go with him, but he gave me purpose. Direction."

"*Svoboda.*"

"Yes," he acknowledged. His shoulders were held tight as he recalled. "I did not love it, but I did not hate it."

Powell nodded.

"I watched him fall apart. His mind. When I was young, he—"

"Don't tell me. Show me."

Once again, Apollo reached out and took Murphy's hand. He didn't show a single distinct scene this time. Murphy caught flashes of Miller's face: calm, angry, stern, angry, stern, twisted in violence, stern, angry. With each flash, the perspective on it shifted up, as if Apollo's line of sight was moving upwards. He was growing, Murphy realized with a start. The early, calm scenes were from Apollo's childhood. The perspective shifted suddenly to an eye-to-eye perspective. From that point on, it was only fear, anger, and violence. Murphy shut down his own memory of meeting his father one last time in his adult years; it was just short of violence too.

The perspective shifted again and the image got the cold, stale feeling of Miller's memory, not Apollo's. It showed Zeus Ward, Limitless Logistics' founder, as an old man. Zeus lay in a soft, lonely, and darkened bed, face illuminated by moonlight but a hand was clearly on his neck.

"No," Apollo whispered.

Murphy felt the memory starting to be ripped back, as if Apollo was trying to close a mental door. "Hold him, Powell."

Powell's face twisted into a snarl and Murphy felt as if threads of steel wound their way across the bond, holding it. Apollo's eyes widened in fear.

"I'm leaving, Zeus. I'm retiring," Miller gave a bitter laugh. *"And you won't know where I'm going. I want you to feel fear, the fear I've lived with for years. I want to see your hands shake and the sweat on your brow."*

Beneath Miller's hand, Zeus squirmed. He seemed too weak to push the man off, too weak to even Jump away. Perhaps even fearful Miller could follow him if he did Jump.

"I'm leaving and I'm doing the one thing you always feared I would: I'm going to Russia." He smiled at Zeus's gasp of anger. *"And I'm telling you because I want you to fear for what remains of your miserable, bitter life. I want you to fear what happens to you. I will get my revenge and it will break you. It will take everything you've built. And I'm telling you so that you get to live broken in every way a man can be broken, powerless to stop me."* The memory stopped abruptly.

"When was this?" Murphy whispered.

"2012," Apollo told him, unable to meet his eyes.

"You knew he was set on exacting revenge on us? Even then?"

"No. He wanted revenge on Zeus," Apollo answered quickly then looked at Powell to confirm his truthfulness.

Powell nodded and Murphy frowned. He let the statement bounce around his mind, considering all its implications.

"Miller left as a man with trauma only to return as a mad man." Murphy shook his head. "You knew the power Miller held, what he could do, and how it could be used for bad?"

"Yes. When one of us," his mind flashed several of the Pantheon's faces and three unfamiliar men he assumed were *Svoboda*, "goes bad, there is only one way to stop them."

Murphy got a quick, stomach-turning image of a man laying

face up in a pool of blood and lumpy brain matter, like scrambled eggs tinged pink. His empty right eye socket showed the bullet's entry point. Murphy's hand twisted in Apollo's grip.

"That is Iosif. He killed my lover to get to me, so I killed him."

Apollo delivered this news simply, quietly, but even without the skin-to-skin contact that shared a person's thoughts and emotions, Murphy could feel the utter hatred Apollo held for Iosif. Murphy's eye snapped to Powell who nodded very slowly. *True.* Murphy frowned at the strange hint of a smile, just barely tugging at Powell's lips.

"He was wild, and as a Jumper, he couldn't be controlled," Powell said. "There was only one way to end it."

"I'm sorry for your loss. May her memory be a blessing," Murphy said over Powell and glared at him.

"His memory," Apollo corrected, "and memories of him bring me joy and sadness every day. I had no love for *Svoboda*. I had no real love for my father. And," he sighed, "perhaps you will kill me for this, I have no real love for the Pantheon, but you can help me end Pyotr and what is left of *Svoboda*."

Powell nodded and Murphy sighed. He released Apollo's hand.

"What am I going to do with you, Apollo? Jesus."

"We do not have to be friends," Apollo said with quiet dignity, "but we do not have to be enemies. We can work together against *Svoboda*. They will continue attacks in my nation. They will attack within your nation. Their attacks could de-stabilize," he strung the work out oddly, clearly working hard to ensure he said it correctly, "both nations. What happens to the world when Russia and the US are not stable?"

"War," Murphy answered.

"Yes. None of us want that."

Powell nodded one last time and released Apollo's hand. "No, we need to keep things stable."

FOURTEEN

MURPHY "ARES" HAWKINS

0832L/1432Z, 27 OCT

"Give us a five-minute lead to announce you're coming back with us," Murphy told Apollo. "I'd hate for them to put a bullet in your skull for showing up unannounced again."

Apollo nodded his understanding.

"On three, Powell. One, two, three." On the last number, Murphy snagged Powell's hand, dragging him along.

They reappeared in a sunny parking lot. Powell squinted in the late October sun, watching what appeared to be wetsuits drying in the breeze.

"Where?" Powell asked sharply.

"High Springs, Florida. We're only a few hundred miles from Hurlburt, so the Jump over won't be hard. But no one would think to come here. Well," he gave a surprisingly shy smile, "Kelly Anne might know. This is cave diving central in the US and I grew up a few streets over. It's, uh, how I knew about her weird hobby."

Powell gave him a faintly disapproving stare. "And now you seem to know much more about this weird hobby."

Murphy glared back. "Just say it, Powell."

"You're fucking her now." Not a question, but a statement. "What about Mandy?"

"Yes. And what about Mandy?" his question was voiced with

more than a hint of frustration. He struggled against the calorie drain and Powell's questions. "She pushed me away. So, no, Powell, if you're asking, I don't feel bad about it."

"You Pantheon folks really like dipping your pens in the company ink, don't you?"

"Oh, that's real fuckin' rich coming from the guy fucking my boss. You wanna get into *that,* Powell?" Murphy exploded. "You wanna dig deep into how I still think you're manipulating her and she doesn't even know it?"

Powell's hand shot up to Murphy's throat but Murphy snagged his wrist and twisted hard enough to start hearing tendons creak before releasing his hand.

"Don't start with me," Powell growled and rubbed his wrist.

"Then don't start with me, you lying psychopath. Oh, don't for one second think I'm letting your bullshit slide."

"White knight much, Murphy?"

"Fuck you."

"Your dance card happens to be full right now, so I'll pass on your generous offer," he said sarcastically.

The two glared angrily at one another as dark wetsuits flapped behind them. Murphy realized Powell was baiting him deliberately. He pushed his awareness out, seeking any additional influence but found none. It didn't mean Powell wasn't manipulating him, it just meant he was sticking to words.

"I like you less and less every day," Murphy spat.

"Likewise."

Each shuffled a half step back, willing to let their anger subside. They both silently acknowledged that in a physical fight, it would be an even match but Murphy's ability to simply teleport out of Powell's grasp left him at a disadvantage.

"He's a threat," Powell said bluntly.

"Yes, but he might be worth the risk. Or at least, the risk of keeping that enemy close is less than the risk of leaving *Svoboda* operating unchecked."

"I don't agree."

"You had an option to voice your opinion, we'd have ended him right there on the mountain."

Powell looked at him, something dark and almost hateful lurking in his eyes. Murphy inhaled sharply. He knew Powell had a certain moral flexibility, but this was new.

"I was willing to follow Val's lead. To give her the choice. But he's unstable and too great a risk to her."

"*Us.*" Murphy watched him closely. "I think you mean us, Powell."

"Yeah, to Limitless," Powell said quietly. Outwardly, he appeared calm but Murphy could see him subtly rubbing his hands on his pant legs and a light sweat form on his forehead he might not be able to attribute to the sudden Florida sun.

Murphy let his face relax, slipping into the quiet blankness that Powell showed so often, trying to cover the sudden churn he felt inside. "What do you propose, Mr. Powell?"

Powell looked quickly down at his watch as he drew his gun. "There's about one minute left. If you can Jump in behind him, I can end this all right now."

"You realize, if we end him right now, we lose a valuable intelligence asset?" Murphy said, voice completely and carefully devoid of emotion. Inside, his belly churned sickly.

"Yes, but we have other options. Tick, tock, Murphy."

Murphy tilted his chin up slightly, looking down at Powell. He let a few more seconds tick by before speaking again. "Was it this easy to direct men to kill Major Parker too?"

Whatever Powell had expected him to ask, that wasn't it. "I am protecting her, you asshole!" Powell exploded on Murphy, taking an aggressive step forward. "Not that you'd know, fuck boy. You flit from one woman to another at the drop of a hat. What would you know about need? Or building a life together?"

"A life built on lies? On murder, Powell?" Murphy shook his head. "I am not working with you anymore, Powell. I can't trust you. None of us can."

"I just want her to be safe."

"No, Powell, you just want to be in control." He grabbed Powell's free hand. "Holster it, we're going back."

Powell looked down at his hand and then slammed his gun into its holster. Murphy realized Powell hadn't even noticed he had drawn the weapon as they Jumped.

Murphy released Powell's hand the moment they reached the temporary Point Zero at Hurlburt.

"Apollo is coming in, at our invitation," Murphy shouted before he took a short, staggering step sideways, and swore. Powell's hands went under his armpits and he eased Murphy to the floor.

"You didn't eat," he said bluntly.

"You didn't give me much of a chance," Murphy slurred as his vision dimmed.

"A little help over here," Powell shouted as Murphy passed out.

***

When Murphy awoke, he was surrounded by Apollo, Powell, Val, and Damarcus.

"Glad to see no one shot you while I was out, Apollo," Murphy said. "And before you nag at me, Val, yes, I know I did 'stupid Marine shit' by not eating before Jumping back, but this asshole prevented it," he said and pointed at Powell.

Powell half lurched up from his seat on the pallet marking out Point Zero. Val put a hand on his arm and he sat back down, glaring at Murphy. Murphy shot him the bird from his spot on the floor.

"Boys, do you want to pull your pee-pees out and measure them or do you want to give me your risk assessment?" Val asked.

"He's an unacceptable risk, Val," Powell said before Murphy could speak again.

"Mr. Powell has a dim view of anyone he deems a threat," Murphy said carefully, staring Powell down. "But I assess Apollo to be worth the risk."

"Thank you," Apollo said quietly.

"But let there be no misunderstanding," Murphy continued, "he is a risk. He may not be against us, but I won't guarantee that he's with us either. Enemy of my enemy kinda thing."

Val nodded, considering. "Can't trust him but we can work with him?"

"Trust is earned. Work with him long enough and maybe we can," Murphy said with a little shrug.

"Is he stable?"

"Yes. More stable than Miller, if that's what you want to know." Murphy swallowed down the revulsion he felt at the memories he'd seen. "But his perspective of us is skewed through Miller's perception. It's an added layer of risk. That said, he knows *Svoboda* better than anyone else right now. If anyone can help us get ahead of them, it's him."

"Fine. I get balancing risk. I just can't handle a loose cannon right now," Val said with a little flick of her hand.

Murphy's eyes caught Powell and he frowned. He opened his mouth to speak but was cut off.

"You have one loose cannon already," Powell said, his hand going to Val's. "Mr. Nelson doesn't seem to exist in the same reality as the rest of the Pantheon."

Val nodded absently, her eyes slightly unfocused. "True, but it's chemically induced rather than a mental health issue."

"Nevertheless, do you truly need another loose cannon right now? You know there is only one way to reel in a rogue."

Val seemed to snap out of her reverie and her head whipped to face Powell. "And what are you suggesting, Brandon?"

He put both hands up defensively. "Nothing, I'm expressing concern that you have a lot on your plate right now and it's stressing you out."

"Damarcus, you're my deputy, what's your opinion?"

"If we can get useful intelligence, actionable intelligence," he corrected, "the risk is worth it."

"Speaking my language," Val said with a smile. "Okay, that's three of our four leads in agreement."

Murphy suddenly realized the leadership team was incomplete. "Wait, what about Mandy?"

He was met with silence. Murphy looked to Val, who looked away, then to Damarcus who shook his head.

"Val?"

"She didn't come back from Mt. Charleston." Her voice was almost calm, devoid of emotion.

"She's AWOL?" Murphy asked her but she wouldn't look at him.

"It would seem so," Damarcus said.

"You can't go AWOL when you aren't in the military, Dee," Val countered. She looked down at Murphy finally. "She is temporarily indisposed. We know what her vote would be anyway. She was damn clear about that," Val said quietly.

"We can't assume her vote," Damarcus told Val.

Murphy nodded. "I'm with Val, she made her choice pretty clear. It's three leads against one, Apollo is an asset but acknowledged as high risk."

"Done," Val said with finality.

"Dee, execute the move. We're going back to DC."

FIFTEEN

VALERIE "ATHENA" HALL
0842L/1442Z, 27 OCT

"Pack it all, Dee. We're going home." Val told Damarcus as soon as she broke away from Murphy. "We have more than we started with given our pick-ups from inside and the Herculean effort the team went through to get equipment from the local area. Local-ish, anyway."

"Hank and his boys helped the team get it staged. I'll have lift rosters out within the hour." He laughed. "Obviously, Murphy will get shifted to light duty lifts only until he's had a break. Expect to have it all out within the next forty-eight hours."

"Got teams to receive on the HQ end?" Val asked. She knew they had the capacity to receive their fresh set of extra gear but having folks to receive, catalog, and store was another matter entirely. Military logistics, as she had experienced it, was damnably hard.

"Already called in. We hired a mix of our folks on retainer and one large commercial moving company. As far as they know, they're helping a new multinational shipping company establish their DC headquarters."

"Great work, Dee! I know we don't need as many covers as we used to need, but good work ensuring some operational security."

He nodded his thanks. "You sure about him?" Damarcus asked, looking to where Apollo stood. He was near where Rachel, Wilson, and Jafar formed a loose semicircle, but not part of the little trio.

"Dee, we can 'what if' into eternity. At some point, I have to make the call." She looked up at her deputy, longer serving in the organization than she, and wondered if he resented her elevation. "If things go south, you are welcome to say a big, fat 'I told you so' if you desire," Val said bluntly but softened it with a smile.

"You're more like Marco than you want to admit, Val. He'd have said the same." Damarcus gave her a sad grin. "And I only got to tell him 'I told you so' once."

"Oh yeah?" Val asked with a snort. Marco, rest his soul, was as stubborn and pigheaded as her, but he was also a kind father figure and mentor to her.

"He was worried you were a spy, if you recall."

"I do," she said blandly.

"I told him to have faith in you, you'd come into your own."

Val gave a light laugh. "So, I did. Marco Xavier Martinez, you were a real one and a good bonus dad," she said by way of blessing. She hugged Damarcus. "You're a good big brother, you know that?"

Damarcus gave a quick squeeze and smiled down at her which quickly faded to concern. "Yeah, but we have one last little sister to round up."

"Mandy needs time to get over the shock." Val swallowed hard. "Maybe we all do. But it cuts deeper for her. *Tio* Marco is gone and now it's like Miller got one last punch in from beyond the grave. Bastard. I'd shoot him again if I knew where his body was."

They were silent for a moment as they stood taking in the buzzing hustle of activity around them. She was glad Damarcus declined her tacit invite to tell her more about Miller's final resting place.

"Ask Hank to send Mandy to DC if she reappears at Hurlburt after we leave," she said finally.

He nodded and Val watched as he strode off, clipboard in hand, to Commander Emilia Sartori, a new hire from the US Navy. They'd found her in the parking lot of the Hurlburt BX, oddly enough, discussing finance with an Air Force Major. Damarcus said he had listened in for the thirty-second walk to the Limitless-leased company car and decided to hire her on the spot. While he said she seemed a little jaded with her Navy career, she had the kind of analytical mind he needed on their planning team. Two security checks and an interview later, Commander Sartori had taken Kelly's position on the planning team now that Kelly had taken over officially as Val's handler.

"Apollo," Val said sharply.

He stood from where he had sat near Point Zero. "Valerie Hall."

She eyed him, truly taking him in. Her eyes noted he was as fit as when she'd first seen him in Oshra. He was Miller Thompson's golden-haired son and as well muscled as his Greek god namesake. Lean, with a boxer's muscles, he still looked every inch like an American "boy next door" but now his face was drawn with fatigue. He had crow's feet, beyond what his age might allow, and dark purpling circles under his eyes that rivaled what Val saw in her own mirror. He'd Jumped to Nevada and back as they had; he had to be worn down.

She looked again and saw a tightness in his eyes as well, the strain of feelings held tightly in check flattening his mouth to a thin line. Val realized he was worn down by more than fatigue, he was carrying the burden of grief with him every moment. Val, who had lost her fiancé before joining the Pantheon, knew more than anyone the terrible weight the loss of a lover laid across your heart. In that moment, she felt a spark of kinship for Apollo.

"Did you choose 'Apollo' or did Miller choose it for you?" she finally asked.

Apollo's expression changed. He hadn't expected that to be her first question. "He chose it," he said softly.

"Apollo," she mused. "God of music. Do you know Greek mythology?"

Apollo gave a little shake of his head. "Some. Not so much. We do not cover it as I assume American schools cover it."

"Apollo was the god of music, but he was the god of prophecy, healing, and truth." She thought, digging deep into her Greek mythology.

Apollo listened politely but didn't answer. Val wondered if his English was good enough to follow this very specific train of thought.

"Apollo was seen as someone who helped the other gods ward off evil. Like the Pantheon of antiquity, you've brought a warning to my Pantheon. I've been shown enough truth from you to believe what you say."

Apollo looked relieved. "He had a sister too, yes? Artemis."

Val smiled, glad to know he understood. "Yes. We don't have an Artemis yet. We do have a Hestia, although she refuses to use the name."

"The original Apollo was a son of Zeus. In this life, my father killed Zeus."

"I suppose the parallels fall apart in the real world eventually." She gave a little shrug. "I want to believe you will help us avoid disaster and stop *Svoboda*. If you do, there's a place for you in this Pantheon. If you want it."

The thin line of his mouth slackened with shock. He stared at her, blinked, and recomposed himself. He gave the scantest shake of his head, but for some reason, Val didn't believe it was a denial so much as a deliberation.

"Consider it." Val left him then to go handle her team and ensure Damarcus's relocation plan went smoothly.

Things did not, in fact, go smoothly.

SIXTEEN

VALERIE "ATHENA" HALL

1349L/1849Z, 27 OCT

By afternoon, the lift roster Damarcus had carefully crafted, even around Murphy's recovery time, had to be reworked when Chadwick showed up for his first heavy haul Jump hungover from the night before.

Damarcus had allowed the Jump despite his reservations because it didn't have live cargo, only several pallets of equipment. James had called only minutes after his arrival because the lingering effects of alcohol and probably more had caused him to miss his landing area by more than ten feet, both vertically and laterally. The displaced air and misplaced cargo on his arrival had thrown a stevedore into another large crate, giving the man a deep laceration and suspected concussion. The cargo container had also broken open once it hit the floor, spreading loose ammunition across the storage floor, bullets rolling around like lost ball bearings.

"Damarcus, he is as high as a goddamned kite still, how could you let him Jump?" James shouted into the phone. Val and Murphy, having shifted their assigned loads plus Powell earlier in the day, were in the main staging area when the accident happened. Murphy had missed the concussive pressure wave of the large load only because he had been behind the container he had just shifted.

"Jim, I'm sorry. I knew he was looking rough, but he seemed sober enough here at Hurlburt," Damarcus told him, clearly exasperated. James looked at Val and Murphy who shrugged. Chadwick hadn't come in yet when their assigned lift came up, he must have staggered in late as usual.

"Hey asshole," James shouted to Chadwick across the cluttered bay, "did you snort a whole damn line before your Jump or what?"

Chadwick gave a vague smile and thumbs up from where he lay sprawled on the floor.

"Okay, geez, Jim, get him into the clinic," Val told him with a deep sigh. "Not in the same area as the guy he hurt, for the love of everything holy. See if Nurse Sarah knows how to run a safe detox for him and if not, get an expert on contract fast. That man is a damn addict and can't see what it's doing to his life. Dee, go work the schedule and we'll get a new plan shortly." Val dropped her head into her hands.

"What the actual fuck is wrong with this guy?" Murphy asked. "Val, we can't keep him on the roster. He's gotta go."

"I know, but go where? He's been with us for what? A month? He knows our inner workings," Val said. "We can't just release him into the wild."

"I mean, there are protocols for this sort of thing. Maybe he just politely overdoses on his shit and the problem solves itself," Damarcus said from the speaker.

"Damarcus! You did not just say that!" Val scolded him but deep down, she realized it solved a whole host of problems. She suppressed the feeling before even a whiff of it could leak to the group.

"We can't control him, Val," Murphy swore with all the creativity of a United States Marine for a moment before getting back on track. "The only thing that seems to affect him is a boat load of cocaine and a bottle of cognac. Hell, he's got so much money, we can't even withhold that and expect it to impact him!"

"Brandon?" Val called to Powell who had been lingering nearby as always, having overheard the call.

Powell eyed Murphy then turned his attention to Val. "Yeah?"

Val inhaled. "I know you heard all that." When he nodded, she continued. "What do you think?"

"Val, I don't think he's the right person to ask," Murphy protested but Val held up a hand to silence him.

Powell ignored Murphy's glare and answered. "Do you want to hear what I would do or what I think you are willing to do?"

"Jesus fucking Christ, Powell!" Murphy growled.

"Murphy! Can you chill on the blasphemy for a second?" Val shook her head as Murphy settled back. "No murder, Brandon. Obviously." A slight twitch in her red-gold eyebrow told them all she still held Major Parker's death against Powell, regardless of her personal feelings.

"Fine, I'll do it your way. Keep him drugged." When Val looked like she'd interrupt he pushed onwards. "Balance the uppers and a sedative. Heck, he's probably enough of an addict that he'll go into withdrawal if you don't keep feeding him the hair of the dog right now."

Powell's face twisted with disgust. Val reached for his hand but he pulled it back, shaking his head at her. Val realized he must not want her to see what he was really thinking about Chadwick. Given what they were discussing, maybe it was for the best.

"I heard you ask Nurse Sarah to get an expert, but you need to keep him under at least until we finish the transfer back to DC You can build a better plan then." Powell concluded.

"Murphy? Dee? Thoughts?"

"If holding someone under sedation worked, why didn't Zeus do that with Miller? Why didn't Marco?" Murphy asked.

"Because it's not a long-term solution," Damarcus told him. "It's a stopgap at best."

"There's only one way to deal with a rogue," Val said, frowning. "Marco told me about 'certain protocols' one of the first times we talked." She shook her head. "He didn't elaborate but he was clear enough."

"There's nothing in our procedural manuals, Val," Damarcus, voice sharp.

"Of course not, Dee. Marco and even Zeus were smart enough not to write down a plan for how they take care of a rogue."

"We're not killing him," Murphy said emphatically, holding Powell's gaze.

"No, we're not," Val agreed.

"We can't," Damarcus said finally, as if he had needed a moment's consideration.

Val looked to Murphy who shook his head. She looked at Powell who looked away, crossing his arms so she couldn't take his hand. She finally looked at Damarcus who shook his head as well.

"Okay, I can't believe I'm even saying this, but I need cocaine and alcohol," Val said as she massaged her temples.

"Do not say another word, Val, you are all still military members. I'll take care of this," Powell said and finally took her hand.

Calm flowed through the touch. Val exhaled forcefully, letting the tension drop out of her.

"Dee, Murphy, rework the schedule. Bring it to me in an hour. I'm going to the C-suite to call Maureen. Powell, walk with me."

The group broke up. Val and Powell walked hand in hand to her office.

"I know you have to go dive into disaster mitigation but come to dinner with me tonight."

"You know this is going to take the rest of my day."

"I don't care. We'll eat at midnight if we have to," he said with a smile.

Val smiled back, basking in his calming presence. "Okay."

Powell kissed her forehead and left her. She didn't ask where he was going or what he was doing, but she knew the problem with Chadwick would be stabilized, at least for the time being.

SEVENTEEN

VALERIE "ATHENA" HALL
1649L/2149Z, 27 OCT

"No, Maureen, you know how it goes. You settled down one issue just for another one to rear its ugly head."

"Mr. Nelson?"

"How did you know?" Val asked dryly.

"Girl, I have been in politics long enough to see what happens to a lot of those old money children."

"Well, I have definitely confirmed his cocaine use but now he's doubled down with alcohol. The bastard injured one of the laborers we keep on retainer. Thank goodness, someone," she drawled, "ensured my budget stayed high because I will be paying through the nose for both his medical care and to keep it quiet."

"I won't always be able to save you or your budget, Valerie."

Val gave her a hum of acknowledgment.

"I mean it. I've been on the SASC long enough and there are rumblings of something afoot up top," Maureen told her.

"Are you going to make me drag it out of you or will you just tell me, Maureen? I'm tired and I don't feel like political guessing games today."

There was a sigh on the line. "Child, you are so refreshingly blunt and direct, I think it's why I like you."

"I could read your upper thoughts if I was there and touching your hand," Val reminded her.

"True."

"So?"

"Ha! Fine. The Secretary of State has been caught with his pants down," Maureen said with the air of two old church friends spreading gossip.

"You don't say? It's always bottles, wallets, and zippers, isn't it?"

"You have bottles, we have wallets, and I'm dealing with zippers so yes, nearly always." Maureen gave a huff of laughter. "Any who, the old man is fit to be fired. You know the current leadership," she said and Val knew she meant the President, "he won't stand a dishonest man in his Cabinet. Despite the fact that all of us politicians are dishonest!" Maureen let more than a hint of her Missouri drawl come through.

Val could almost see Maureen sitting in her office, readers hanging from their gold chain, as she dished the latest hot gossip. Maureen had once said that the chair of the Senate Armed Services Committee and a recipient of CIA and FBI briefings, she was in the information business. Today Val truly believed her.

"And?" Val asked with a smile, already as sure where the conversation was going even if she didn't receive a skin-to-skin contact to confirm it.

"Well, as it would be, there is a certain Senator from Missouri who had a surprisingly excellent track record in International Relations and, as a widow who has never remarried, no zipper issues of note."

"Well then an early congratulations Madam Secretary," Val said with genuine joy. "I do wish you were remaining in your current position though. The last event has been rough," she knew that word of Chadwick's antics would get out eventually now that Limitless Logistics was a publicly known company.

"Tell me, what happened exactly."

"You really want to know the technical details of a lift?"

There was a quick chuckle across the secured line. "No, I suppose it's enough to know you need money and you're executing mitigation plans."

There was a pause while Val considered how she was going to handle a Jumper that couldn't be controlled.

"In your experience, do these old money types ever sober up?" she asked quietly.

"No." The answer was cold and blunt.

Val waited to see if Maureen would elaborate. "No? That's it?"

"No, Valerie. They don't. He's rich. He has access to all the drugs and alcohol or whatever other vices he wants with almost no consequences. And you said he has a trust fund? Good luck convincing his parents or other rich relatives to break that trust, if they even legally can. You can send him to rehab but he'll leave. Most rich boys like this simply bribe their way out but in your case, he would simply Jump out as soon as the detox feels too hard for his pampered ass. Given what you've already said, it will be rough for him." She sighed. "Simply stated: no, he will not change."

Val groaned and dropped her head into her hand.

"Marco had contingency plans, go look into them," Maureen said briskly.

"Maureen, I—"

"No. Do not say anything else, even on a secured line."

"Fine."

"Now tell me about your other rogue Jumper. The Russian."

"That's what's wild, Maureen, I don't think he is. Technically, he was born to an American father on US soil. Undoubtedly, he has a very American birth certificate from his very American hospital. He may have Russian sympathies from living there, but I think he is legally a US citizen." Val deliberately declined to say who Apollo's American father was; she didn't need that fight as well.

"Hell," Maureen swore. "I thought you said this issue was settling down?"

"Well, compared to thinking we had a breach in our headquarters, this seems minor."

"Minor," Maureen scoffed.

Val's eyebrows rose and she looked at the phone. "You're going to take a Cabinet-level position because someone couldn't keep it in their pants. I have a man who is technically a US citizen with US sympathies and can do what I do. You tell me what's minor today."

There was a long pause on the line before Val continued like she hadn't just snapped at a soon-to-be member of the US Cabinet. Val felt the weight of all four stars her position levied on her as she waited for Maureen to reply. When she didn't, Val took it as a concession and carried on.

"The team collectively interrogated him, our way, and I feel comfortable returning to our headquarters now. I had Murphy and Powell do a more in-depth interrogation as well and they indicate while he may not be fully on our side, he is firmly against *Svoboda* and willing to help us take them down. We believe he also provided credible intelligence that shows they will attempt a destabilizing attack on US soil in the near future."

"How near?"

Val shook her head, "I don't know. We were working so hard to get that piece of intelligence, that was all we could pull."

"No target, no timeline, and no threat vector? Weren't you an intelligence officer? That's shoddy work, Valerie."

"Well, Maureen," she said heatedly, "if you'd like to find a way to hold him down while you torture the information out of him, you go right ahead. I have three companies to run and one of my CEOs is AWOL, so I'm stretched a little thin right now!"

"Amanda is gone? Why on God's green Earth? She was the most sane of the lot of you."

"Some of the information Apollo gave us was personally difficult to hear, it would seem she needs her space for a moment."

"Ahh, he must have talked about you killing her father."

"Their father," Val blurted out.

The line was suddenly silent and Val cursed herself.

"Sweet Mary and Joseph, Valerie. You people don't do things by halves do you?"

"Maureen, I'm tired. I'll send Murphy and Powell to brief you on everything tomorrow if you need more."

"Of course I do."

"Okay. I'll have Murphy taken off the lift rotation for an hour tomorrow. Don't waste our time with 'delayed meetings' or other crap. I'm serious about being in the middle of a huge lift getting everything back, I don't have time to fuck around."

"Watch you tone girl, you're still speaking to a United States Congresswoman."

"And soon-to-be Cabinet member but you are speaking to a four-star general and the CEO of the nation's most precious logistics asset."

The line was quiet once again.

"Marco trained you well, Valerie. Have a good evening, I'll see General Hawkins and Mr. Powell tomorrow."

Val dropped the handset back on its cradle and sighed deeply.

EIGHTEEN

VALERIE "ATHENA" HALL

2027L/0027Z, 27 OCT

Val broke her own rules and Jumped straight from her office to her apartment as soon as she had reviewed and approved Damarcus's new lift schedule. She had one night free until her next haul and wanted to spend it with Powell.

She dashed around her apartment, looking for "date night" clothes as she punched out a text to Powell.

Hey, dork. Done and home. Changing now. Still wanna meet up?

Val was pretty sure he'd say yes, despite the hour, and started applying makeup as she waited.

Absolutely, I need to see you. Dinner? Dessert?

Please! I'm starting.

Val didn't see a response for a moment and checked her phone again.

Starving! Not starting. Stupid phone.

OK, glad to hear it. I couldn't tell if you meant you were starting dinner without me. :)

Seeing Brandon Powell, CIA agent, use a smiley face emoji made her giggle.

Nah. Just trying to get makeup on and text at the same time.

You're gorgeous, come as you are.

Thanks, but I want a little war paint if I'm going out in public.

You have the body of a bikini model and the face of an angel. You're fine.

Val laughed and finished applying mascara. *Charmer! Where do you want to meet?* She typed out as she hunted down the mate to the red high heel beside her bed that clashed violently with her red hair.

Archives Metro? We can walk to Capital Grill?

They still open? A quick glance at the clock told her she was working later hours than even the most hardened DC denizen.

We may be a-holes popping in as the kitchen is closing but we could still grab a crème brulée and a Stoli Doli.

Deal. See you in 15?

Yes.

Val set her phone down and dug under her bed for the missing red heel.

Within minutes she was dressed for her date. Somehow, through the magic of makeup, she'd erased the dark circle of fatigue from under her eyes and looked like she'd woken from a light nap rather than having worked a heavy cargo lift for the last day and a half. The ultra-expensive leave-in conditioner in her hair gave it a shine and luster that masked the brittle quality it had from too many days of functioning on a calorie deficit.

In short, she had a thin veneer of health and beauty over her fatigue and the lingering pain in her belly that had plagued her since their hasty departure.

Val Jumped into the Archives Metro station in a discreet nook under the escalator. Glancing to ensure no one had noticed her arrival, she took the escalator to the street level. She yawned as she walked toward Pennsylvania Avenue. She and Damarcus had worked hard to ensure the whole team was fed and had their IVs but with their entire operation in transit, they weren't working on their optimal setup and Val knew she was well behind her calorie intake for the day. The cumulative fatigue and hunger dragged on her as she came to a halt a few feet from the curb, yawing again.

"Hello gorgeous," Powell called to her.

He stepped out from where he'd been leaning against a low concrete retaining wall. Val took a moment to admire him. He was tall, athletic, and leaner than when she had met him that spring. She idly wondered if he'd been trying to lose weight to blend in with the Pantheon member's ultra-lean physique. She looked at him more closely. Powell smiled then, transforming his face into the vital and magnetic man she knew.

Powell offered his arm and they strolled slowly toward the restaurant he'd chosen. Val smiled warmly, suppressing the drag of calorie debt and lack of sleep. Her fatigue could wait.

"Hey dork," she said, grinning up at him.

"I'd ask how the rest of your day went, but that would leave you open to ask me about mine. And I don't think you want to know."

Val gave a light laugh, "No. No, I do not."

The hostess looked slightly dismayed to see them walking in less than a half hour before closing but sat them quickly. She must have felt a little vindictive toward them or sympathetic toward an overworked kitchen because she sat them at a table almost dead center in the room rather than a cozier and quieter booth. The table, set with a crisp white tablecloth, was stylish but exposed to every conversation in the room. The elegant Art Deco chandelier should have given off a warm, subtle glow but somehow felt like the single overhead light of an interrogation room.

Powell must have caught her small frown and asked, "Is this okay?"

"Yeah, it's fine. Just ..."

Beside them, an elegantly dressed but loud woman was apparently chiding a group of lobbyists about a matter affecting Puerto Rico. Val wasn't trying to listen in as the queenly woman held court beside her, however their proximity and her volume made it hard to ignore.

Val gave Powell a thin smile. Fatigue tugged at every fiber of her being, making her patience thin but she was sure he meant it to be a romantic date. She wanted so badly to keep her famed temper in check, but they were surrounded by Washington power brokers, even this late at night, and it killed the mood.

A harried waiter offered them menus and Powell immediately ordered two of their signature Stoli Doli drinks. Val gave him a more genuine smile as the waiter went to get their pineapple-laden drinks.

"Ah, there's my Val," he said with a genuine smile of his own. "It's been a long day, for both of us, I know. A long day away from you."

He reached across the table to take her hand. Val felt a thrill of lust as he rubbed his thumb across the back of her hand.

"Yeah, but this is the best part of a long day," she told him with a smile.

"Seeing you, feeling your immense power makes mine better."

Val frowned slightly. "Power?"

"I do love those days where work lets me see you. It brightens up my whole day," he said with an easy smile.

Val nodded. Before she could ask any more questions, the waiter returned with their drinks.

"Would you like something from the menu?"

"Crème brulée, please," Powell said and handed his menu back.

"I'm so sorry, I know we talked about just getting dessert, but the café at work still isn't back on its feet and I'm starving," Val told him. She turned to the waiter. "Could I please get the tuna tartare, the lobster bisque, Parmesan truffle fries, and the glazed Brussels sprouts?"

"Yes, ma'am. Sir?"

Powell's lips pressed briefly into a thin line. "Just the crème brulée for me, please. That's all for her."

The waiter's professional façade slipped momentarily as he goggled at Val, but the mask slammed back into place quickly and he gave a nod before departing.

"I'm sorry, Bran, I'm starving. I'll cover the check."

"No, it's fine."

"Please, I insist. We agreed on here because it was just drinks and dessert. Now I'm racking up a huge bill on you."

"It's fine," he snapped. When her face pulled into a frown he raised a placating hand. "I'm sorry. Long day."

Val nodded but the air between them quivered with tension.

Powell held out his hand, palm up, silently asking for her touch. Val looked away for a second before placing her hand on his. The pressure that had built between them melted away slowly as they held hands quietly and sipped their drinks.

"I know it's only been a few months, but sometimes I feel like I've known you forever," Powell said, finally breaking the silence at their table.

"It does seem like we've attached at the hip, doesn't it?"

"It does. I like it, I" he was interrupted by the waiter arriving with a small mountain of food. Their table was delicately rearranged to hold all of Val's plates, some hanging precariously off the edge. The elegant lady at the table beside them paused her conversation long enough to give Val an evaluating look before nodding with a wry smile.

"Oh, this looks amazing!" Val said enthusiastically. "Do you want some of the tuna? It's divine," she said around a small bite.

"No thank you," Powell said. He looked down at his crème brulée and his mouth went into a firm line again before slipping back into a pleasant mask.

They ate in near silence, broken only by the conversations around them and Val's moans of delight over her food. With only one small dessert, Powell spent most of his time quietly sipping his drink and watching Val.

"Bite?" she asked, offering a spoonful of glazed Brussels sprouts.

"No, thank you," he murmured.

When the waiter returned to check on them midway through Val inhaling an adequate but overpriced meal, Powell ordered them drinks again.

"Wait, no more Stoli Dolis for me. Could I get a glass of cabernet sauvignon?" Val asked.

Powell looked up at her sharply.

"What? The Stoli Dolis are too sweet for all this," she gestured at the soup and parmesan fries.

"Right away, ma'am," the waiter said.

"What?" she asked him again when he stayed silent.

"Nothing. This is just, uh, not going how I'd planned." He let out a little huffy sigh.

Val tilted her head and raised an eyebrow. "Oh? Because things with me always go as planned. Come on, Bran. Lighten up. It's a quick meal after a long day. After this, we can go back to my place and relax."

Powell sighed and reached into his pocket. Val gasped when he placed a small Tiffany blue box on the table.

"I had hoped to make this a little more special, but you have this unexpected way about you. A way that seems to derail everything in my life."

Val stared at him in shock.

"In only the best of ways, I assure you," he said with a grin. "I was planning on being a divorced bachelor for the rest of my life, enjoying travel with my unique career, and settling comfortably into my solitude. And then this woman comes along. This extraordinary woman with incredible talents. Who turns my entire life and part of my career upside down. I find myself doing the most wild things for her. I find myself in Paris trying to stay sober enough to fight a paunchy Russian only to find this woman taking him down harder than I could." He gave a light laugh and raised his glass to her.

Val raised her glass in return but frowned slightly. Being assaulted by Leon Orlov and then blinding the man wasn't something she joked about or took lightly.

"You bring so many good things into my life and I appreciate that. I appreciate you." He reached out and took her hand, thumb rubbing slowly along the back of it as his other hand fumbled the box open. "Valerie Hall, will you marry me?"

Inside the classic blue box was an enormous diamond ring. Val briefly searched her mind for a report that the Hope Diamond had been liberated from its display a few blocks west of them. The rock was perched in a gold setting on a gold band that looked far too thin to support it.

Taking her silence as a yes, Powell withdrew the ring and started to slip it on her ring finger. It caught slightly on her knuckle, but he pushed firmly and it settled snugly against her hand.

He held up her hand, curling her fingers to let her look at the small ice skating rink now occupying her ring finger. "Well?" he asked, with an almost breathless smile.

"Uhh. Yes," she finally said.

Powell bounced to his feet and swept her up as well. "She said yes!" he declared loudly to the room at large.

A few people clapped as he swung her in a tight circle. Val thought she saw a camera flash and she glanced around, uncomfortable with the public display.

"I think we should get our check and take this to go," she whispered in his ear as he set her down.

Powell's smile turned lustful. "That sounds like a great plan." He waved the waiter over and in moments, they were back on Pennsylvania Avenue, laden with the boxed remains of Val's dinner.

"Your place or mine?" she asked quietly.

"Yours, it has the better bed," he said quickly.

Val didn't need to touch his hand again to take them both back. They landed in the cleared space in her front entryway. She stalked to the kitchen, heels clacking loudly on the floor. Depositing the to-go boxes on her countertop, she whirled to face Powell.

"What in the hell was that, Brandon?" She said, her temper finally allowed to come to the fore.

"What?" He looked stunned.

"That! That," she waved an angry hand, the golden ring reflecting the dim lights of her kitchen, "display!"

"I wanted to have a romantic dinner. I wanted to show you I cared. I wanted it to be romantic."

"I've been working eighteen-hour days for the last few weeks and today we didn't even have the right nutritional support. I'm exhausted. You took me to a powerbroker's wet dream for dessert, got upset when I ordered the food I *needed*," she stressed the word, "and proposed in front of a gaggle of strangers. How was *that* supposed to be romantic?"

"I'm sorry, Val, I know you like good food and drinks. I thought you'd enjoy that." His shoulders were tight with tension and rejection. "Are you saying you don't want to marry me?"

"I'm not saying no," she said. "But, I'm not really sure I'm saying yes either."

Powell's shoulders slumped and she caught a flash of anger he wasn't quick enough to hide.

"Bran, I love you. I do. And I do see a future together, but this was so unexpected. I'm sorry." She sighed. "Look, let's just go to bed. We'll talk about it after we've had some sleep."

Powell nodded but didn't speak.

NINETEEN

VALERIE "ATHENA" HALL

0832L/1332Z, 28 OCT

The next morning, after a passionate, but restrained evening, Val kissed Powell goodbye.

"I have another day of long-haul cargo movement, Powell," Val said, hoping he would catch her underlying meaning: *I'll be tired as hell tonight, no more bullshit.*

"Yeah okay, babe," he said distractedly while slipping a shirt on. "I've got meetings at State today. I'll be back around dinner time."

Val looked at him, but he seemed to be avoiding her eyes.

"Back?" Val's voice was cold. "You mean, done."

"What?"

"You said 'back' like you're just going to show up at my place."

"Yes?" he asked, confused.

There was a moment of silence as Val waited for him to process things. Surely, he recognized he didn't live in her apartment, he had his own space, and he wouldn't just assume he was always welcome to come and go from her space. After all, he'd been strict that while she had the "key" to his place, she could Jump in and out of any place she'd seen, she was not allowed to simply pop in uninvited. How could he expect he would be given free rein in her place without accepting the same in his? She hadn't even *given* him a key yet.

Powell stared at her as he put on his pants. "Val, we're engaged, why wouldn't I just come over?"

Val stared at him, head cocked to the side, not believing what she just heard. "We aren't."

Powell pointed at the ring, still perched on her finger. "You're wearing my ring."

"Your ring is sized wrong. I'm an eight and this is, what? An industry standard seven? You didn't even have it sized," she said with a disappointed huff. "Either way, I can't take it off right now because it's too small! Jesus, I know I'm slender now but how skinny do you think I am?" she muttered the last part under her breath.

"You don't want to marry me?"

"I'm not sure, Bran."

"But," he faltered as he slipped on a sock. "But last night?"

"What about last night?"

"Yeah, you said you weren't sure last night, but we made love."

Val stared at him. Brandon Powell. Human lie detector. A man who could feel emotions couldn't feel how conflicted she was. She watched him finish putting on shoes, seemingly oblivious to her emotions.

Deliberately oblivious.

"Brandon. What happened?" she asked. Her voice was calm, neutral. Even if they couldn't feel her emotions, anyone who truly knew Val knew that was the human equivalent of a snake's tail rattling a warning.

"Nothing. It's fine. I need to go."

"Bran."

"I'll be at State today."

"Brandon." She reached for his hand but he took a step back.

"I'll see you sometime tonight."

"Brandon Powell." Val's voice was sharp as a whip crack.

At the sound of his given name on her lips, he paused, hand on her doorknob. His shoulders slumped and he let his hand drop.

"Nothing has happened, Val. Why are you pushing me?" He turned and looked at her. The complete lack of emotion on his face scared her. "Nothing happened, Val. You're overreacting. I'll be back tonight after work."

He left without another word.

Val dressed briskly, consumed with curiosity at why Powell would be seemingly railroading her into a marriage. They'd been together less than a year. Sure, she had money now. The average Pantheon member cleared roughly a half million dollars per year. They made more money than ninety percent of the American working population and were guaranteed a tidy military pension upon retirement even if they didn't save their vast income. But, she supposed, by Washington, DC, standards, they were small fries. Val didn't know what a CIA agent was paid, but she assumed it was enough to keep them from turning against their own government and that her pay wasn't a driving factor in the proposal.

If money wasn't the driving factor and love wasn't the driving factor, Val was scared to find out what was.

Val found herself Jumping from the fat to the fire when she appeared in the CEO's office to the sound of a verbal altercation just beyond her door.

"He's a liar! This man needs to be thrown out, killed off, and never able to enter our spaces again!"

Val could hear Mandy's shrill yell through her thick wooden door. She wrenched the door open to find Mandy had finally returned.

Returned and was being restrained by Anna and Kelly as she tried to escalate her verbal attack to a physical one.

"Amanda, I will not force a relationship on you if you do not want one. We are strangers, after all. But we are blood, whether you like that or not." Apollo's voice was calm, measured, and had only the faintest trace of his accent:

"Blood is nothing. You're a *Svoboda* criminal," Mandy spat. "You followed a mad man. A crazy man who claimed to be my blood and still betrayed everything we had in the end."

"Amanda, I am sorry our father hurt you, truly I am. But, he was a broken man and there was only so much I could or would do to control him. In the end, our choices are our own. I chose to stay with an organization I thought was helping, but I also chose to leave them when I realized what they were really doing." He held out his hand, inviting her to touch him and verify his words. When she recoiled with a shudder, he continued, "I swear to you, I am here to help your organization stop my former organization."

They both seemed to realize then that Val was watching them. Mandy took a half step back, Anna and Kelly releasing their grip on her. She freed herself but settled hard onto her cane as their hands came off.

"Valerie Hall," Apollo said with a nod of acknowledgment. "I would beg a moment of your time. I wish to discuss *Svoboda* with you."

Before Val could acknowledge him, Mandy jumped in. "Val, no. Don't listen to his lies. I'm sorry, I need to talk to you about leaving and … and …" she stuttered to a stop, clearly staring at the engagement ring on her left hand.

Val shifted her hand to hide the ring but not before Kelly and Anna spotted it as well.

"Oh my God, Val!" Kelly squealed and rushed to hug her.

"Kels," Val said warningly and took a step back to avoid the hug. Her eyes met with Anna's and she silently pleaded for help.

"Did this happen while I was gone?" Mandy whispered. Lost and hurt, her shoulders slumped and she looked suddenly childlike.

"Ladies, General Hall has a very busy schedule today," Anna broke in briskly. "I'll have to ask everyone to work with me to get on her calendar."

"Val?" Mandy asked quietly.

"Sort of? It was last night." Val held up a hand to forestall further questions. "I'm sorry, Mandy, your apology will have to wait, I need more intel from Apollo right now."

Mandy looked hurt and mutinous, rage starting to twist her face.

Val took a step back, shocked by the sudden twist in her friend's character. "Talk to Anna, we'll have time later."

Mandy gave her an angry look but stepped back and allowed Kelly to pull her out of the front office.

Apollo watched silently as they left before giving Val a small nod. "Thank you."

"You'd better come in," Val told him. "Anna, get Damarcus up here. Have him bring one of our intel folks if he's got one to spare.

Tell him he can come in directly; he doesn't need to knock."

"Yes, ma'am."

"Come on, Apollo." They settled in Val's office, Apollo sitting quietly across the desk from her. "Do you want to be called 'Apollo'? I realized, we never really gave you an option."

"Apollo is good."

Val wanted to ask what his family called him but realized he might not appreciate being asked by the person who killed his father. She nodded. "Very well."

Damarcus appeared behind him and sat with a brief nod to them both. "Sorry, none of the nerds were available, and we don't have time for any of the three letter agencies to send someone."

"It's okay, Dee. Apollo wants to give us more intel on *Svoboda* and their plans. We'll take notes and give it to my fellow nerds when we're done," she said with a smile. "Go ahead, Apollo."

"What did Miller Thompson tell you about *Svoboda*? Their purpose?"

Val let out a little huff of breath. "What did he say or what do I believe?"

"That is a fair question. What do you think you understand?"

"Based on what Miller said and what I saw, *Svoboda* claims to be freedom fighters of some type. They seemed to think they could counter *Vmeste*, the government's group, and control the Russian oligarchy." She squinted off into the middle distance for a moment before continuing. "The way Miller spoke, he thought he was in charge. He seemed to indicate he brought them tactics from Limitless Logistics, like the IVs, and this put him in a special place with them. That said, I think Miller only *thought* he was in charge. I would estimate with high confidence that Pyotr was the real power in *Svoboda*, using Miller as a conduit for contacts in America."

Apollo nodded along with her comments, a hint of a smile gracing his lips at her observation about Miller and Pyotr. "You are astute."

"I was in the thick of it for a moment there."

"Yes, you were." Apollo inclined his head to her briefly. "Miller, despite his claims and delusions of grandeur, was not ever in charge of *Svoboda*. It was Pyotr. Always Pyotr." Apollo's mouth went tight with anger.

"What was Pyotr's original goal?" Val asked. "I suspect what Miller believed to be *Svoboda*'s goals and what Pyotr believed to be your goals are completely different." She shook her head and looked at Damarcus. "If, in his twisted little head, he truly believed his own bullshit, it explains why he 'felt' truthful when Marco and I talked to him."

Damarcus shook his head. "Probably. Too late now. What does Pyotr want, Apollo?"

"Pyotr does not want to take down oligarchs. Or if he does, it is only for a larger goal: anarchy. At his heart, Pyotr is a violent anarchist who believes strength is power and those who have our skills are inherently destined for greatness."

"Oh, great, a classic realist and a narcissist. That's just great," Val groaned.

"Realistic?" Apollo asked, confusion written on his face.

"No, 'classic realism,' really. It's, uh," she thought for a moment, considering how to explain the nuances of international relations theory to someone with a middling command of the English language. "There's an old Greek historian dude, uhh, Thucydides, who studied the original realists and said, 'The strong do what they can and the weak suffer what they must.' I think Pyotr would agree with that statement."

"Thucydides, it's a trap!" Damarcus said with a laugh as Apollo looked confused.

Val laughed. "Yeah, yeah, Dee, I know! All those classes Marco made me take are making me a weird little nerd. Sorry, Apollo. You got a wild nexus of nerdery there."

Apollo nodded. "You are correct, Pyotr would agree with Thucydides. And I agree with the Mon Calamari, this is all a trap."

Val's jaw dropped open. "Did? Did you just …"

"You forget that I spent many years in America before going back to Russia. I have seen *Star Wars*." It was Apollo's turn to laugh at them.

"Okay, this moment of levity aside, if Pyotr is an anarchist at heart and just wants to watch the world burn," she gave a half smile when Apollo nodded to her reference, "what is he planning?"

"He wants to take down both the Russian and American governments."

"No easy task for, what, three men now?"

"Yes. Only Pyotr, Alexei, and Yuri remain. But even with only three, they are lethal, tough to catch, and likely to succeed now. My father may have been a useful idiot, but for a time he was keeping Pyotr's bloodier ambitions in check."

"Miller? Miller Thompson was keeping them in check?"

"Yes. While he did give them the technology they did not have before and teach them tactics to be more effective, he also had a way of talking Pyotr off the ledge."

Val squinted at Apollo, considering the words he said. "Apollo, I know you loved your father, but I find it hard to believe he was the mitigating force."

"Believe. Do not believe. It does not matter to me. The facts are facts. With Miller gone, Pyotr is unhinged, running rampant, and the number of murders they are committing each week is increasing."

"Can you give examples?"

"You do not truly believe all the people who fell out of windows really fell through a window, do you?"

Damarcus dropped his head and sighed. "The English word is 'defenestration' and yes, we are aware it is one of the Russian elite's favorite tactics. You're saying they're mimicking him?"

"Of course. If you want to destabilize a government, first you must sow doubts amongst the elites against their own leaders. The Vladivostok explosion this summer was their work too. The leadership of *Vmeste* wanted a meeting with all agents. Pyotr found out and ..." he shrugged as he trailed off.

"Killed by an all-call," Val said quietly.

"There are only a small number of *Vmeste* agents remaining now. The oligarchs have lost their transportation and are losing their peers. Things are very shaky at the top."

"*Vmeste* was their main source of power and movement aside from money. Teleportation at the beck and call of the Russian government and the oligarchs, just gone." Val shook her head. "And here? In the US?"

Apollo shook his head again. "They want to destabilize as well but I was not part of their planning. I was preparing to run by then. I know they want a large target. Something or someone close to international politics. But I do not know beyond that."

They were silent for a moment as they pondered the implications of three rogue Jumpers hellbent on making a splash in international politics.

"Thank you, Apollo. It's not much, but we'll get the intel team on it and see what they can come up with." Val nodded to Damarcus. "Dee, I know you're still organizing the return, but take him down to the intel folks and get them working on possible targets. Get me an update by close of business."

"You got it, Val," he said. "Tag." He held a hand out for Apollo.

Apollo cocked his head slightly in question but tapped Damarcus's outstretched hand. "Ah, yes. You pass locations by touch."

"You don't?"

"No. We," he seemed to hesitate, "did not trust one another enough to risk exposing information. We used recent photographs for site surveys."

Val and Damarcus both made faces at his statement.

"Didn't that make the Jumps more difficult? We always go on the cleanest visuals we can get."

"Yes. But you forget, we do not trust as you trust."

Damarcus nodded and Val sighed.

"Speaking of trust, I need to go calm Mandy down." She glanced down at her left hand.

"And you know you're going to tell me about that later too, right?" Damarcus told her.

Val shot him a look.

"Girl, after Mandy, I am your oldest and closest friend here. I know you'll tell me when you're ready. I also don't need to touch your hand to see how conflicted you are. It's all over your face." He shook his head. "Good luck."

"Thanks, Dee. Good luck to you both as well."

As soon as they departed Val rose from her seat and squared her shoulders. Pulling her door open with slightly more force than necessary, she walked into her front office.

"Anna, you are a saint, you know that right?"

"General Hall, I have worked with more general officers and politicians than I can count. I also have survived two teenage daughters and now their daughters. While Ms. Squires's outburst was loud, hers was nowhere near the worst temper tantrum I've seen," Anna told her with a slight smile.

Val burst out laughing and squeezed Anna's shoulder. Anna was unflappable and Val didn't know what she would do when the iron lady chose to take her well-earned retirement.

"Where is she now?"

"I offered to schedule her for later this morning, but she declined." Anna gave a small frown. "If I had a guess, she is just outside the door, waiting to pounce on you."

Val gave her a quick nod and strode to the door. She opened her mind, searching for Mandy's signature, and was surprised to see the connection was still closed. She steeled herself and walked through the door.

"Val!" Mandy all but cried.

Val put a hand up quickly to stop Mandy from grabbing her arm. Mandy took a quick step back.

"Amanda Squires, if you want a moment of time with the CEO of Athena Strategic Logistics, you will make an appointment through Anna like everyone else. Especially when you need to explain to your boss while you have been AWOL for the last twenty-four hours." A cold fury that had lodged in Val's heart the day prior radiated from her eyes and had Mandy kept their connection open, she would have frozen from Val's cool anger.

"And what if I don't want to talk to General Valerie 'Athena' Hall, vaunted leader of the Pantheon? What if I just want to talk to my friend, Val?"

"I'm not the one who closed our connection, Mandy," Val said coldly.

Mandy glared at Val for a moment before the connection

suddenly flared to life.

Pain.

Fear.

Rejection.

Anger.

Betrayal.

The mélange of emotions washed over Val and a sob caught in her throat. She snatched Mandy's arm and Jumped them to the Limitless Logistics cafeteria.

"This is going to take a moment. We'd better get food and caffeine." She surveyed the cafeteria, which was emptier than usual while they worked to re-open the full café following their abrupt departure. Val had endured a long conversation with her head chef over spoiled meat and restocking perishable food. Vast quantities of high-quality food were hard to get on short notice and even pushing a small mountain of money at the man and his team wasn't sufficient.

Mandy looked at her, mouth open.

"You wanna talk or not, Mandy?" Val released her arm. "I've been behind on calories for days, I'm emotionally drained from the last week, and I'm hangry. You want this conversation? Then I need food."

They walked the cafeteria line silently, speaking only to politely request food from the short list of available items cafeteria staff had available. Tension simmered across their link.

"Where were you?" Val finally asked as they set both of their trays down in a quiet corner of the dining room.

"Bozeman," Mandy told her as she ripped open multiple sugar packets and dumped them in her coffee. She took a sip and made a face. "Instant."

"Montana?"

"Yes." She stirred creamer into her coffee, eyes still on the cup and avoiding Val.

Val stared at her, silently. She'd learned several tricks from Powell as well as her own time as an intelligence officer; one of those tricks was that silence invited confessions. Her patience was rewarded when Mandy finally met her eyes as she took her second sip.

Wincing, whether from the bitter coffee or from finally opening up, she continued. "Dad had a cabin out there. I wanted to remember him." She swallowed a sip while Val sat silently. "I wanted to remember the dad I knew. Not this," she waved a hand, "this mad man. The man who had a secret family. The man who had a secret Russian organization at his fingertips." Her face hardened and she stared at Val, something dark and dangerous lurking in her eyes. "The man who shot his own daughter."

"We go to therapy, Mandy." Val stabbed a pile of eggs. "We don't up and disappear with no contact."

Mandy looked away and the feeling of pain and betrayal simmered along their connection.

"And you don't cut your best friend's connection off," Val said heatedly. "I thought you might be dead."

"Best friend? Yeah? Really?" Mandy laughed; a weak and hollow thing. "You might be my best friend, but I don't think I'm yours." Her eyes darted to the ring on Val's hand. "I should have closed the connection after we slept together."

Val leaned back. "What?"

"We shouldn't have done that, Val."

"I know."

"Do you?" Mandy peered at her, searching Val's face. "You were drunk. I was hysterical. Can you really say either of us was in any state to make rational decisions about sex?"

Val's mouth dropped open as she realized what Mandy was implying.

"But then, you seem a little too susceptible to manipulation across bonds." This time she stared directly at Val's hand. "Did you really say yes or did he push you?"

"Amanda!" Val snapped.

"I had some time to think, Val."

Mandy opened her mouth to speak again and Val held her hand up, halting her. "You are overwrought by what's happened. It's a lot to take in and I understand that, but you are out of line, Mandy."

"We shouldn't have let things fester between us, Val. I cut the bond because I didn't want you to feel what I felt and I didn't want to feel what you were feeling. It's as simple as that."

"You need therapy, Mandy."

Mandy shrugged. She took another sip of coffee, ignoring the food on her plate.

"I mean it, I can't leave you in charge of anything when you're in this kind of state."

"So that's it? You don't care about me, you just care about my ability to lead and Jump?"

"No, it's not like that," Val said quickly and stabbed at her food again.

"You've done nothing but push me at this since the first time you saw me Jump. You know I don't want it. You know how it's breaking me inside and yet, you still push me." She shook her head. "I can't believe I ever thought we were friends."

"Mandy," Val pleaded, "we *are* friends. I want to help you. I want to help you heal from this. But you push me away. You don't let me in. You cut me off. How can I help you if you cut me off, push me away, and then run off?"

They stared at each other over a mountain of food and caffeinated beverages. They had sat exactly like this so many times since meeting each other. Something across their connection opened as memories bubbled and boiled across the bond.

Tears slowly started forming in Val's eyes.

"Don't push me away, Mandy. Let me get you help."

A moment passed. Then another. A tear slipped down Val's cheek and finally, Mandy broke.

"Fine, Val," she said quietly. "I'll have Anna set me up with the therapist. But on one condition."

"What?"

"I need to close the bond. It's too much. I can't keep getting flashes of your emotions. Not while Apollo is still here. It's too much."

Val nodded and the connection broke. Its sudden absence again made her gasp.

"We can rebuild a friendship," Mandy told her. "It'll take time."

Val nodded and finally took a sip of her tea.

"Start with that," Mandy told her and pointed at the ring.

Val winced. "Let's start with the fact that I am not actually engaged," she tugged on the ring. "I just can't get the damn thing off."

"He didn't even get the right size? What was he thinking?"

"I know!" Val said and a stressed laugh slipped out. "It was a disaster. I can't believe—"

Val's phone buzzing cut her off.

"Sorry, it's Nurse Sarah," she told Mandy and thumbed the phone on. "Hey Nurse, it's Val. What's up?"

"Sorry to bother you ma'am, but did you authorize Mr. Nelson's release?"

"What? No. Is he gone?"

"Then I'm really sorry, ma'am, I came to his room for a quick round and he's gone," Sarah admitted.

"Sarah, wasn't he ..." Val eyed Mandy and groped for the right way to phrase things. "Wasn't he drugged to the damn teeth? How did he walk out? Jump out?"

"Yes, ma'am, he was under extreme sedation, as you directed."

"Fuck, how did that bastard shake her drugs? Is there really nothing that can keep us from Jumping?"

There was a sigh on the other side of the line. "That's why I called. I don't have a log for it, but I reviewed the CCTV for the clinic, and it was Mr. Powell who removed Mr. Nelson."

Val was silent for a moment. "Damn it, Powell, what did you do?"

TWENTY

RACHEL NG

1049L/1449Z, 31 OCT

"Something splashy and related to international politics? Is she serious with this?" Rachel asked Damarcus. "They just fired the Secretary of State, isn't that enough weird politics for one week?"

"We only have so much intelligence to work with and yes, that means we start with what we know and narrow it down."

"And why us? Why isn't the CIA on this? The FBI? The local neighborhood watch group? Surely even a buncha nosey ass Karens are going to have better tools available to them than us!"

"The CIA and FBI are on this, Rachel. But they don't have our special knowledge and experience with how," he stressed, "*Svoboda* would operate. And while we are known to the world now, we're not exactly ready to share our tactics with everyone who asks." Damarcus's brows pulled together as he frowned.

"You're still worried about those weirdos who want us to register like a draft?"

"I've already registered for a draft, I don't have any intention to register my skills as well. Senator Mitchell has done a decent job so far keeping any proposed legislation from moving forward, but honestly, I think the less they know about us the safer we are."

Rachel shrugged. She'd heard arguments like it before from her former line of work. Register sex workers, make them licensed or something. But she, and many of her sisters still on the streets, knew it for what it was.

"Damn, same shit, different profession. They just want to control and harass us, don't they?"

The two men nodded and she sighed.

"So, we don't know their target and even if we could meet them at that target, we kinda can't stop or hold them?"

"Nope, not really," Murphy answered.

"I thought Val said you could build tactics?" Rachel asked.

"Yes and no. Val said she'd turn a blind eye to me testing certain things, but didn't outright condone what we did figure out."

"Okay, so, now I can do this new thing. We talked about this. Don't you think it's time to politely ask her to look somewhere else while we work things out?" She looked from Damarcus to Murphy. "Something to stop them? Right, like, I can't hold them. So, I dunno, hit them to incapacitate and then inject them with drugs."

Both Murphy and Damarcus locked eyes but didn't speak. Rachel could tell they were hiding something and frowned.

"Right, I could push a blow dart at one of them full of a strong sedative. Or hell, poison. Don't the Russian poison people all the time?"

"Rachel, we don't kill people," Damarcus said, more than a hint of censure in his tone.

"We're the military, the military kills people all the time. Hell, those Russian guys throw people off of buildings and out the window. More to the point, you were allowed to drop guys into open air this summer, letting them splatter on the concrete in broad daylight! You cannot sit here and lecture me about how we're a logistics enterprise when you know damn well, we kill people. If half of what Dee tells me about the original Zeus and Hera, then this organization has killed a lot of people."

Murphy and Damarcus both shifted uncomfortably. Rachel looked from one to the other, waiting for either of them to refute her.

"Well, when you're ready to climb down off those high moral horses, let me know and we can work out more tactics. I guess until then, we're stalking that Russian group," Rachel said with an eye roll.

The entire Pantheon spent the next three days balancing surveillance of the Nation's capital, routine logistics movements, liaising with their contacts at the various three letter Agencies, and providing on-call, emergency extraction for two unlikeable presidential candidates, should the need arise.

"Ugh, she's so bossy," Rachel muttered to Kelly after her latest stint following the Democratic candidate. She stripped her suit coat off as she stomped through the Pantheon's dressing and staging area. "And this coat fits like they found it in a Walmart dumpster."

Kelly laughed, "Sorry, Rach!" She eased the leather shoulder holster off of Rachel's thin shoulder. "Murphy says her opponent loves him. Has 'a real hard on' for military guys." Kelly said with a giggle as she made air quotes with her fingers. "I think Murphy looked a little green around the gills when he said it too."

Rachel snickered. "Why do you put my IVs in a gun holster? I'm not cleared to carry a weapon around her, some kind of Yankee clearance thing? Anyway, wouldn't that holster thing make me look like I'm strapped?"

"Yankee White clearance," Kelly corrected off-handedly as she checked Rachel's harness for signs of wear. "Sorry, Rach. It's that or a fanny pack."

Rachel made a face. "Get me a designer handbag and a pantsuit. She loves pantsuits. I'll be a modern-day lady-in-waiting or some European bullshit."

"Until I can get you measured at Madam Volaire's again, I can't drop a grand on a suit like that. And I definitely can't swing a designer purse right now because do you know how long it takes to work with Hermès to get a Birkin? Besides, between the leather holster and the dark suit, you blend in with the Secret Service. You want a better selection, you'd better get a real handler, who has time for your fashionista dreams, and stop stealing Val's handler!"

Rachel laughed as Val walked in while Kelly was talking.

"Yeah, Rachel. Get your own bestie!" She gave Kelly a half hug. "But seriously, you need to pick a handler."

"I know, I know. I need someone who can cater to my every

whim and make sure my little snack baggie is stocked." Rachel pulled another face. "That sounds to me like a really well-placed minder to keep me out of trouble."

"You are the suspicious type," Val held up a hand to forestall an outburst, "and I understand why. But they do help." She smiled at Kelly. "And you taking Kels means she's got less time to get my things together. I know I don't Jump as often as you, but I'm on the next speaking engagement with Her Highness, and I need my snack holsters set too." It was Val's turn to roll her eyes.

"My God, what are we going to do if she wins?" Kelly asked.

"Oof. What are we going to do if she loses?"

The three gave a collective groan.

Damarcus poked his head around the corner, gave Rachel a quick smile, then addressed his boss. "Val, a word?"

"Ooh, he looks serious, ladies. Give me a few."

"No worries, Val. I'll be stocking your snackle-box until you get back," Kelly said with a light laugh.

Rachel watched them go silently, eyes tracking every movement and smile between the two friends.

"They ever fuck?" she asked as soon as she was sure they were out of earshot.

"Wait. What?" Kelly spluttered.

"Did they have a thing when she got here? She's hot as fuck, so is he. Hot people like to fuck and then be friends later." She started idly looking through the racks of clothing in the staging area. Rows upon rows of boring, bland suits were counter balanced by a small handful of Val's bespoke gowns.

Kelly gave an embarrassed cough. "No. I don't think so, but then I've only been here a little longer than you and even more to the point, it's none of my business. She's your boss and he's your trainer. Geez, Rach, be a professional!"

Rachel frowned at her. "Prude. When do I get my own rack of designer gowns?"

"Once you get your own handler who can coordinate with Madame Volaire. And no, it's really just not my business and I don't see why it's any of yours who's sleeping with who." Kelly glanced at her. "Unless you're worried about butting in on something?"

"What? No," Rachel said quickly.

"Oooh, you like him," Kelly said with a wicked grin. "You do! You're blushing. And you're worried you'll piss off your boss if you snag a former fling. Oh, I get you now."

"Damn it, Kelly, no," Rachel said flatly but even she could tell it sounded forced.

"Yes."

"Fine." Rachel crossed her arms over her chest and avoided Kelly's eyes.

"But, like I said, no. I don't think there was ever anything there. Besides, she's been with Powell for how long? And they're engaged."

"Or not," Rachel said quietly. A silence stretched out between the two women. "He's weird, right? Like, it's not just me?"

"Yeah. There's definitely been something off lately. The proposal was weird. And rushed. Val's pissed at him. Did you see he didn't even get the right ring size for her? What's that about? How could he just buy a ring and not get it sized?"

"That's some phony Tiffany shit too. No reputable jeweler would set a rock that size without a gallery rail. Seems like he was in a rush and didn't want to wait," Rachel told her. "I've seen men do it before. They think they'll lose a girl and would rather rush to lock her down with a shit ring rather than wait to give her what she wants. Those were always the scariest ones. They don't care about their partners."

Kelly nodded and silence fell again, broken only by the sound of her opening and closing drawers as she packed Val's holster.

"Do you think he—" Kelly started but was interrupted by Val's sudden return.

"Kels, you can stop for now. I'm not on the next rotation," she told her in a rush.

"What's up?"

"Metro Police just found Chadwick Nelson dead in Rock Creek Park."

TWENTY-ONE

VALERIE "ATHENA" HALL
1146L/1546Z, 31 OCT

"I don't really owe you any of this Madame Secretary of State, you do know that, right?" Val asked, frustrated.

"No, you don't, but you like having someone on the inside on your side," Maureen told her.

Val sighed. "You're not wrong. Congratulations, by the way."

"Thank you. I knew it was a possibility but I didn't think that Secretary Robertson would have resigned so fast. Nor did I expect to be put in as the interim. I figured they'd waffle on it for a while." She seemed to laugh. "Now, as for you, I may be a burr in your butt, girl, but I'm some help too. You know those scoundrels across the aisle are still calling for you all to be tagged and registered like animals."

"I know, I caught CSPAN yesterday." Val huffed a little at the very thought of registering like some kind of sex offender. "We aren't a publicly traded company so it's not like I have to give reports to shareholders, but anyone with an interest can do a FOIA request on the military members. It's not exactly like we're hiding."

"I've told them as much too, but they want to 'but what if?' me to death. What if one of you is a spy? What is one of you loses your mind? What if one of you goes rogue?"

"Well, you can tell them I have the same fears but making us register isn't like nailing our feet to the floor. Even if they were registered, the person could simply hop, skip, and Jump their way out of captivity." Val sighed again.

"Tell me about the boy," Maureen finally said after a long moment of silence.

"Chadwick?"

"Yes, the unfortunate Mr. Nelson."

"It's been three days since he disappeared and there isn't much we've learned. Metro Police found him and started the case and since he wasn't one of our military members, there wasn't a lot I could do to get him moved to a military forensics team. Metro is okay, but it's not exactly a crack team of detectives that found him. While I certainly have friends in the military medical community who could have performed his autopsy, even I would be charged with some rather heinous crimes if I had Jumped his body to Dover and dropped him with the Armed Forces Institute of Pathology. I certainly wouldn't be helping our cause if I was arrested for desecration of a corpse."

"No, you certainly would not be helping. I've got a lot of pull these days, but I don't think even my considerable resources would have gotten that charge dropped."

Val gave a snort of amusement. "Even the all-powerful Congresswoman, now Secretary Mitchell has limits? Say it ain't so!"

"Trust me, I am working to rectify that in every way possible."

"Oh, I believe you. Anyway, the Medical Examiner's report was less than useful and frankly, I don't trust it. As you might suspect, he had a whole cocktail of party drugs in his system: MDMA, coke, a small amount of heroin, and a blood alcohol level that made him unfit to drive. But, their Medical Examiner said none of it was enough to have killed him. The ME's only note of anything amiss was a fatally low blood sugar level. He can't rule out homicide but says it may have been natural."

"He wasn't a diabetic, was he?" Maureen's question was more of an accusation.

"Not as far as we know."

"How curious," Maureen said, the barest hint of our Missouri drawl coming out.

"Curious and frustrating," Val agreed. "I know how he got out and that he was in no fit mental state to have Jumped, but there's about a twenty-four-hour window where no one can account for him. The ME gave a time of death that indicated he was alive for at least a day before being dumped at Rock Creek Park."

"And just how did he get out of the clinic if he was drunker than a sailor at a port call?"

"First off, don't let my counterparts catch you saying that, a few of them were Navy before joining our ranks. Second, that is a matter internal to my organization right now."

There was a long silence.

"Valerie Hall, how am I supposed to help you if you do not tell me how he got out?"

"Because it's not like he escaped, Maureen. He was walked out the back door. And I need to know why first."

"Who?"

The silence returned.

"Who, Valerie," Maureen demanded.

"Powell."

"Oh child," she sighed. "That is a problem, isn't it?"

"Yes, ma'am, it is."

"I take it you haven't spoken to him?"

"He is remarkably difficult to reach when he doesn't want to be found."

"And you can't just pop into his apartment while he's sleeping? I know that's a huge breach of trust, but so is walking a man out the door who is now dead!"

Val ground her teeth. "While I would like to say that, my morals would not allow me to do that," she sighed. "I tried. He's gone. I've tried twice a day for two days and he's in the wind."

Maureen gave a long 'hmmm' before continuing. "Well, then, I hope you pried that cheap rock off your finger the moment you knew he betrayed you."

Val's mouth dropped open. "Maureen?"

"Oh, girl, you think I didn't know about the proposal? One of my political counterparts was at the table beside you and saw the whole thing. And even if she hadn't, my staff tells me everything about you they find on social media."

"Why would that be on social media?"

"Valerie Hall, I know you are not possibly this dense. You're famous. Rich, beautiful, powerful, and famous. Not to mention that mane of red hair stands out like a beacon. I'm shocked that you don't have paparazzi camped outside the Limitless facility day and night. Of course, your engagement made it to social media. If anyone read newspapers any more they'd have seen you in Page Six!"

Val groaned and dropped her head into her hands. "This is not how I pictured my year going."

"It never is. But you didn't answer my question. You don't consider yourself still engaged to him, correct?"

"I never did," Val said bluntly.

"Oh, now that juicy little morsel was left out of my morning briefing. But I digress. I'm glad you don't consider yourself attached to him because right now, from where I'm sitting, it doesn't look good."

"I know, Maureen."

"You say he walked Chadwick out, under the influence of drugs and alcohol. There's at least a day gap where, apparently, he was still ingesting both, and now he's dead. Not good indeed."

"But we don't know what happened during that day," Val countered.

"Someone kept feeding him his favorite party favors then killed him."

"Or, we didn't know he was diabetic, and while coked out of his mind, he didn't get enough food and died."

"Then why haven't you been able to find your former beau?" Maureen asked gently.

Val let out another sigh. "I know there's a better explanation. There has to be."

"Child, I'm sorry, but I don't think there is. What was the last thing you said to him?"

"Powell?"

"Yes."

"We fought. About the engagement and that he'd been distant since then. He's mad at me for pushing back."

"When was this?"

"Three days ago," Val whispered.

Maureen gave another long 'hmm' before sighing. "I'll give you two days to find him and get it squared away. I think I can squash additional media on this for a while longer."

"Longer?"

"You think that one of the nation's few teleportation specialists turns up dead in a ditch and that stays out of the media? No, we've been sitting on the story."

"You sure have a lot of influence in strange places, Maureen."

"Ha! Don't I? Depending on how this election goes, I might even be able to keep this Cabinet spot."

Val made a rude noise.

"Don't be like that, Valerie. I don't like either of them, but that's politics."

"Well, it's a good thing you're the politician and not me!"

"Oh, watch yourself, girl, you keep working with me and I'll have you on a ballot as fast as you can blink." There was a smile in her voice as she continued, "After all, a worthy adversary often makes a worthy successor in politics."

"You'd have me as a Congresswoman? I run a corporation and a military organization. You'd be hard pressed to sell it to anyone that I'm a politician."

"Oh child," Maureen said in a rush, "aren't all military generals nothing more than politicians in sharper suits?"

"Well, I suppose there's truth to that."

"Think it over," Maureen enjoined.

"It'll be hard not to now," Val laughed.

Maureen's voice turned serious then. "Two days Val, that's all the longer I can hold this story back. Find Powell, get answers, then get your story straight."

"I will, Maureen."

TWENTY-TWO

VALERIE "ATHENA" HALL
1156L/1556Z, 31 OCT

Val leaned in the hallway, discreetly rubbing her stomach, trying to quell a pain that had been bothering her as she waited for Mandy. She knew she should see Nurse Sarah but hadn't found the time yet. She watched Mandy limp out of the locker room and waved her over.

"Mandy, join me for a late lunch," Val's schedule had kept her from her usual early morning workout and she'd spotted Mandy as she left her physical therapy appointment.

"Is that an order or a request?" Mandy said flatly.

Val frowned at her. "I'm asking my best friend to join me for lunch."

Mandy's sharp bark of laughter held a bitter edge that could have cut but she moved out with Val nonetheless. Mandy's cane, the second in two months, was a clear acrylic with pink sparkles mixed in. Unlike its predecessor, it had a rubber tip that no longer clacked on the floor. Even with her fancy new cane, Val found herself slowing every few steps to let Mandy catch up.

"How've you been?" Val asked as they made their way to the Limitless cafeteria. She was glad the café was finally back up and running at full capacity, not just for the Jumpers and their massive calorie requirements, but for the rest of the two companies' teams.

"Physical therapy sucks. I don't like running a company that's primary job is one I don't like. My newly discovered half-brother is a Russian spy allowed to run rampant in the company I hate running. And my supposed best friend doesn't call me."

"You don't call me either," Val huffed, but quickly pushed down that wave of anger. "I'm sorry PT sucks. You doing any other therapy?"

"No," Mandy answered sullenly.

"I thought we agreed you'd get help. Something to help you process this."

"Yeah, I didn't do it."

"Mandy."

"Fine, I'll talk to Anna about scheduling it."

"You said that last time," Val told her, turning to look at her as they walked.

Mandy shrugged.

"You want a best friend to support you but you sure as shit don't listen to anything I have to say to help support you," Val spit at her.

"Where are you going?" Mandy suddenly asked her.

"What?"

Mandy looked at the elevator they were about to pass.

"Oh, sorry, habit," Val said, slightly embarrassed. She typically used the stairs after her workouts to judge how hard she'd worked her legs and how sore she would be the next day.

Mandy gave a humph of disgust and hit the "up" button.

"I'm sorry you don't enjoy running Limitless. I could swap you with Murphy and let you run Spartan Tactical," she said with a smile. A single glance at Mandy let her know the joke fell flat. "Fine. I'm sorry. But James and Walker have emphatically said they won't run Limitless and I need Dee as my number two. You are the next most qualified person to run it."

"Let Jafar have it," Mandy said quietly.

"Mandy, you know very well that Jafar has a great background in program management but he doesn't understand the governmental rules well enough yet. And Rachel, I love her spark, but she'd be even more pissed at me if I saddled her with Limitless." Val shook her head. "If you really hate it that much, start training Jafar in all the inter-governmental stuff, and in six months, I'll swap you out. Does that work?"

"You'd do that?"

The elevator dinged and they stepped in.

"Yes, although I don't love it. You've got more experience in this than almost anyone else in the company."

"True. But I hate it."

"Why?" Val suddenly exploded her voice loud in the enclosed elevator.

Mandy looked at her, face blank. "Have you seen the mural?"

"Mural?"

"Yeah, a whole mural, Val. After the liver transplant run someone painted a mural of me as some kind of angel outside the OU Transplant Center. Right there on the bricks."

"I didn't know that."

The doors opened and they stepped out into the now bustling cafeteria. Val saw Mandy's eyes widen and red flushed her cheeks as she looked out among the pre-lunch throng. One glance showed Val exactly what had Mandy flustered.

"Give me a moment, Mandy," Val told her and set off for a table in the middle of the room.

She approached Murphy and Kelly, clearly mid-meal, trying to think of what to say. Maybe nothing, it wasn't her business, but with Mandy's emotions being so delicate, she at least wanted to show her friend she cared about her feelings.

"Hey, Val!" Kelly called brightly as she approached.

"Kels, Murphy, good morning." Val gave Murphy a quick glance before focusing on Kelly.

"Do you need something, Val? I didn't show you as having a Jump today," Kelly said her happy smile dimming slightly with confusion and anxiety of missing something.

"Oh, no, I was just," Val faltered. This wasn't her business, no matter how Mandy felt. They were all adults and Mandy needed to solve this herself. "I was just coming over to say hey and see if you wanted to hang out and have some wine tonight?"

Kelly glanced at Murphy and bit her lip. "Thank you so much but, uh, we kind of have plans already." She gave Val a sheepish smile.

Val gave her a quick and genuine smile and nodded. "No worries. We'll catch up soon."

"Since Hurlburt," Murphy said quickly as Val started to turn back to Mandy.

"What?" Val turned around again.

"I know you want to ask. We've been together since Hurlburt."

"Oh. Ah …"

"It's okay, Val. I know we probably shouldn't be mixing work and pleasure." The look Murphy shot Kelly made even Val want to blush. "But she doesn't work for me and I only work for her boss. So, I had hoped it wasn't frat."

Val gave a light laugh. "Okay, that's what I was wondering but, hell. I'm the last one to be able to pass judgment on fraternization … dipping your pen in the company ink. Don't cause drama. And," she glanced to where Mandy was trying desperately not to stare, "maybe keep it a little more discreet?"

Murphy gave a little hum of surprise. "I'll talk to her." He eyed Val. "Gently."

She gave a sharp nod. "Enjoy your meal."

She walked back to Mandy, mentally grumbling over the high school-level drama as she watched Mandy's desperate face. Still, she felt for Mandy; unrequited feelings were horrible.

"Before you start, yes, they are together. No, I didn't know until just now. And more importantly, no, I'm not doing anything about it."

"Val!"

Val gave her a hard stare. "What are you going to say, Mandy? They work together and I shouldn't allow it? If you wanted Murphy for yourself, you work together too. I'm sorry it isn't working out for you and that whatever sparked between you has passed, but let it go with grace."

"Yeah, it's always about me just rolling over and letting things go, isn't it, Val?"

"Mandy," Val said with warning in her voice. "That is a personal problem and I'm staying out of it."

"Are we friends or not?"

"We are and I'm supporting my friend as she finds out that her crush doesn't feel the same. But as the head of this organization, I'm not taking any actions."

"So, you're totally fine with your handler dating one of your CEOs?"

"Is that what this is all about?" Val gave Mandy a hard glance. "You're mad that Kelly is my handler now?"

"You of all people know how close Jumpers are to their handlers."

"And you think you're being replaced?"

"Yes."

"You *are* being replaced," Val said sharply. Then she held up her hand to once again forestall an outburst. "You are being replaced as a handler, but not as my friend."

Mandy mumbled something that sounded as lot like, "are you sure?"

"You have skills that I need elsewhere and would be wasted as a handler."

"I don't want to do that job."

"Damn it all to hell, Amanda, I do not care that you don't want it. You are being a petulant child about being able to Jump. I'm sorry, you are my friend and I'm giving it to you bluntly. But you need to grow up and act like an adult. I'm sorry that I can't change what you are, but no one can."

Val set both of their trays down on a table in a secluded corner but realized that half the cafeteria had heard their conversation already. Mandy dropped gracelessly into the seat across from her.

"Pick a handler. Someone. Anyone. We have plenty of people to choose from and it will help ease the burden of Jumping. If they don't fit, we'll find someone else, we have plenty of takers."

"It's not the handler, I don't want to do it," Mandy stabbed her salad.

"We are not discussing this again."

"We are. This isn't me, I don't want this."

"I'm sorry Mandy, but we need you."

Mandy glared at her. "You don't know what it's like being on this side of things. You're 'Athena' everyone knows you are this untouchable warrior. Me? 'Hestia'? They all think I'm this weird goddess. The liver transplant? The mural? I'm no goddess. I'm a Christian, I don't buy into this 'Pantheon of Greek Gods' bullshit. I shouldn't be idolized."

"Then drop the name. Don't be Hestia. Just be Mandy Squires."

"Ha!" she laughed. "Squires? Or Thompson."

"Mandy. Just, Mandy then."

"I don't think a name is going to keep me from feeling like a forgotten outsider on the inside."

"Mandy, I am not forgetting you. You disappeared for a whole day and we couldn't contact you. More than twenty-four hours and I cannot contact someone with whom I shared a mental link."

"It's not just that, Val."

"Then what is it, Mandy?"

Mandy flicked her cane. It made a faint plasticky thump. "It's been two months with this and I haven't seen you change a thing about this place."

"What do you mean?"

"Only two elevators? Stairs everywhere? Do you know how hard it is to get around a building this size?"

"Mandy, you can Jump anywhere you please," Val said, shocked. "Why would we need to accommodate you when you have a built-in accommodation?"

Mandy gave her a filthy look. "I shouldn't have to use superpowers to overcome a disability. What are you going to do when I'm on a 'low power' day after a hard mission? When I'm building up my calories?"

Val hung her head. Mandy was right, Val hadn't even considered it. She felt awful.

"Do you see why I feel like an outsider? An other? One of the few civilians in a quasi-military organization? You say I'm pushing you away but at every turn, you're showing that you only care about what I can do, not who I am."

"You are the one pushing us away," Val said heatedly.

"And you aren't doing anything to make me want to stay! My family is gone, Val."

A twinge of sharp pain hit Val and she groaned.

"What now?" Mandy asked with an eye roll.

"Nothing. Just some stomach pains. Like, bad cramps I think." She rubbed her stomach again. "I may need to see Sarah."

As Val started to rise, every phone and pager in the cafeteria started going off at once. She looked at Kelly and saw her face go pale as she showed her phone to Murphy. Val was reaching for her own phone when she saw Murphy stand up so fast he knocked his chair over. Val made eye contact with Kelly.

"Damn it, that fucker betrayed us," Val said, thinking Apollo let *Svoboda* in. She hit one button on her phone, dialing Anna directly. "Lock it down and prep to Jump to… shit, not Bravo, we have to go to Charlie. Apollo knows Bravo."

Kelly, having bolted to their table snagged Val's arm. "Val, no. It's not that. It's a terrorist attack."

"Standby one, Anna," Val said quickly. "What? Where?"

"They hit our Ambassador to Russia."

"Russia? Why?"

"I don't know. It just happened. They're calling it terrorists. Shot him at an engagement in Moscow. And," Kelly paused, looking around the room, "the shooter was gone instantaneously."

"Fucking hell. They're going to pull us into World War Three." Val said and let out a string of curse words that made even Murphy shift uncomfortably. "Murph, pagers are already off, but get everyone in. And find Apollo. Gods damn it, he's either exactly right or he's with them. Snatch him and pull him back right now."

TWENTY-THREE

VALERIE "ATHENA" HALL

1231L/1631Z, 31 OCT

"Fucking hell," Val muttered as she paced their large mission planning conference room.

"Tea, Val? Snack?" Kelly asked her worriedly and gave Murphy a glance. "Shot of tequila? I don't know, you're freaking me out a bit."

"Sorry, Kels," Val said and stopped. "I'm going to knock that fucker's teeth in if he had a part in it."

"A tranquilizer then, eh?" Kelly asked, face serious except for the tiniest hint of a smile tugging at the corners of her mouth.

Val laughed out loud, her tension starting to break. "Okay, no I will not pummel him. But he'd better have a good excuse or alibi."

Wilson, James, and Walker joined them in the conference room a moment later, each looking as tense as Val felt.

"Anything?" James asked her.

"No new info. Our usual CIA link is ghosting me and, understandably, the rest are a little too busy to answer our calls right now. As soon as Dee gets back, I'll have him wrangle our intel team on getting answers."

James nodded and went to sit with his handler, Chris. They immediately launched into a quiet but intense discussion.

Mandy led in Jafar and Rachel a moment later, giving Val a bare nod as if they hadn't just had an intense conversation of their own moments ago. Val caught herself frowning and turned away.

"Does anyone have contact with Dee?" Val asked, surveying the room and seeing that Dee and Apollo were the only two missing. "Or Apollo?"

"No, Val. No one has seen either of them since this morning," Wilson told her.

Val was reaching for her phone when both Dee and Apollo appeared in the conference room's small Point Zero.

"He's been with me all morning, Val," Damarcus said, preempting Val's angry accusations.

Val snapped her mouth shut and swallowed the line of questions she had been about to hurl at Apollo.

"The two of us have been working on precision Jumps all morning. He hasn't left my sight, so don't pounce all over him." Damarcus gave her a quick smile. "And I can read it on your face, Val, you were about to launch a Spanish Inquisition."

Val huffed a little but smiled. "Then my only question is why does someone who's been teleporting for years need precision practice?"

"Because I can always improve, can I not?" Apollo told her. "I appreciate not being shot upon arrival. This action cannot stand. Pyotr is cold blooded, but I did not think he would risk an assassination that draws our nations closer to war." He frowned. "No, I do. That *is* their plan. But I did not think he would in a way that draws attention and suspicion directly to him."

"They shot the US Ambassador to Russia, that's about as inflammatory as it gets," Val told him. "I can't speak to the political side, but the American people will be outraged. If, no, *when* they find out someone teleported in to do it, those registration assholes will go into overdrive. This was calculated to be visible. It has to be."

Apollo nodded but shrugged as well. "I know Pyotr. He is tactically smart, but I do not know if he understands American politics well enough to understand how this would impact you. *Us,*" he corrected himself.

"Regardless of his intent, he's put our nations at risk for war while putting our freedom in peril." Val shook her head. "What's their next move?"

"They will watch. Observe. See if their action has the intended outcomes."

"How long do we have?"

"Days, maybe." He closed his eyes, appearing deep in thought. "American media is very loud and fast. Pyotr may have his answers faster than he would in Russia where media is more suppressed. You have two days at most before he attacks again."

Val scrubbed her face in frustration. "But where? What? What would he do next?"

Apollo shook his head. "I have no answer. Theories only."

"Your theories are better than the nothing we have right now."

"Attack on American soil. They have proven they are bold enough to attack a high ranking American, they will attack another and the next time it will be on American soil. To make it personal, to make it feel more real."

"It's pretty damn real right now."

"I do not know who, but it will be someone high enough to trigger a war."

Val thought quietly for a moment and looked around the room. "Thoughts?"

"President?" James asked.

"Too hard," Apollo told him. "They have limited access to intelligence to pinpoint his location. And they would not have access to anyone who could give them a visual of his usual locations."

"Fair," James said. "Someone they can readily find and in a location they can access."

"It would have to be a politician with a publicly available schedule or at least a portion," Walker said. "High ranking? So maybe a member of the Cabinet? High ranking military officer?"

"Well, that's all of us, but I doubt that would have the effect they want," Val said with a little laugh.

"Kelly, take those parameters and get the intel nerds on it. I want a list of whoever fits that description in the next two hours."

"Yes, Val," Kelly said and jogged out of the room.

"Apollo, what limits them? Is there something we can leverage against them?"

Apollo made his thoughtful face again, eyes squinting as he stared off into the distance. "They are not good at longer range Jumps. Miller taught them to use IVs for nutrition, but they do not like the needles and have no one to insert them. They tend to stop for longer periods to eat and digest." He squinted again. "Very dangerous, but we could observe their stopover points here."

"Here? Here. Like, in the US?" Val said, voice harsh. "You know of locations they use in the US and you didn't tell us?"

"I did not because I did not think you would seek to meet them in spaces where they would be prepared to fight you."

"Not if they're refueling. But you're right, even with the element of surprise, they could easily have weapons on us before we could Jump back out."

Rachel made a disgusted sound and Val whipped around to face her.

"You have something to say, Rachel?"

"Yeah, I do," she shot back. "But you haven't wanted to listen for the last ten days."

With no warning, Val was knocked to her feet by an unseen force.

"Fucking hell," she shouted as she struggled to rise. An unseen pressure held her whole body down. Arms, legs, head, and hands were neatly immobilized.

The room exploded into shouts and confusion. Several people looked around for what had knocked her over while others rose to assist her. Murphy and Damarcus both turned to Rachel.

"Let her go, Rach, you made your point," Damarcus told her. "Professionalism," he whispered.

Before the pressure could relent, Val Jumped to the room's Point Zero.

"Rachel," Val said quietly. Tension in the room buzzed as Val chose her words very carefully. "That was … extraordinary."

"I know you said we didn't have time to develop anything. And these chuckleheads said we don't kill people," she said, jerking a thumb toward Murphy and Damarcus. "But I wanted to know what I could do, so I practiced. Clearly, I can't stop you from Jumping, but could you have shot me while I held you down?"

"No, not a chance."

"Then I think we have a way in. I go with the team and start suppressing as we Jump in. Hold down anyone in the room so they can't move. *Svoboda* will Jump if they aren't completely tapped out, but maybe they leave clues behind that show their target?" She looked at Apollo.

"This could work."

"But if we catch them in one location, they won't go back to it. If we expose all the ones you know, we may lose the ability to find them as they roll to a backup you don't know, Apollo."

He shrugged. "There are three locations I know of. They have too much difficulty operating outside of Russia and Eastern Europe, they may not be able to create a fourth site before they want to attack again."

"Intel gain versus loss, we play this game every day. Yes, we could arguably lose a place to pin them down but if we find anything that indicates the next attack, it might be worth it." Val nodded, almost to herself. "Give us the locations. Murphy, build your team, with Rachel, of course, and tell me when you're ready to go."

TWENTY-FOUR

MURPHY "ARES" HAWKINS
1252L/1652Z, 31 OCT

"Alright, Val, here's the team run down: me, obviously Rachel, either James or Damarcus for an extra shooter if," Murphy stressed, "and only if something goes really sideways. And you, if you're in?" he asked.

"Pass," Val told him, gently rubbing her side. "I'm not, uh, feeling great right now. And I probably need to stay here and do 'boss things' while you check. Sorry, Murphy. Go be Ares, I gotta do the strategy stuff and be Athena. Take James, he's a better shot, but don't tell Dee I said that."

"I heard that!" Damarcus called from across the room, but he had a slight grin on his face.

"I'm in! Suck it, Dee!" James said gleefully and elbowed Damarcus.

The two launched into manly banter about Damarcus's lack of shooting skills. Murphy let it go on while he finished with Val.

"All three locations Apollo provided are in or around the National Capital Region. We're expecting no more than 200 calories a Jump with no fallback team required. I wouldn't want to put anyone else at risk either." Murphy eyed Val then leaned in. "I see you aren't insisting I take Apollo?" he asked quietly.

"No, I am not," she answered, matching his volume.

"Don't trust him or don't trust me?"

Val looked surprised at the question. "I don't trust him. You know I trust you, right?"

"Hey, just wanted to be sure," he said but grinned. Murphy gave her a roguish smile, but inside he was relieved by her answer. Val had a whole team at her disposal and Murphy was Johnny-Come-Lately by comparison to Damarcus or Wilson. He had deliberately offered either James or Damarcus as party members because they both had been in longer than Val and of the four long timers, they were the best two shots, so he had figured would report to her if they thought he wasn't holding up his end of things.

It was one thing to be the CEO and face of Spartan Tactical, it was another to know he was more than just a pretty, rugged face.

Murphy stepped back from Val and addressed his team. "Rachel, James, work with your handlers to get small tactical bags set. Short jumps, wolf pack tactics, and return to HQ Point Zero if anything goes wrong. Rachel, we've explained the wolf pack tactic to you?"

Rachel's mouth split into a wide grin, echoing the tactic's mascot. "Sure thing, Murph!"

"Tell me what you know and I'll correct you if it's wrong."

She rolled her eyes, but the grin stayed in place. "It's a two-person tactic, A and B. Person A runs at the target directly to get their attention while person B offsets slightly and runs lateral to the target. Before person A can hit the target, they blink through them as person B button hooks to the target and tackles from the side."

"Good. Drawbacks?"

"Uh, it's best if we don't think they're armed or they can Jump, which may not apply today since we expect the *Svoboda* guys to be armed and be able to Jump?" she sounded slightly unsure.

"True, it won't work on the *Svoboda* men. That said, they have to have someone here in the US that is helping keep and maintain their hidey holes," Murphy looked at Apollo who nodded his agreement. "So, if we encounter them, it's a good thing to have ready."

"Who's A and who is B?" she asked.

"James?"

"I think Rachel's smile is more distracting than mine," he said, giving her a grin. "She should be A. Besides, I've got more mass than her, I'm more likely to drop someone to the floor than she is."

Rachel's smile faded and she opened her mouth, but Murphy pinned her with a hard stare to stop whatever outraged response she was going to launch at James.

"Pure physics, Rach. Momentum is speed and mass. He's got you by a solid fifty pounds. Even if you run faster than him, he'll hit harder. Rachel is A and James, you're our B."

"Yeah, B!" Rachel told him with a smirk.

The team dissolved into chuckles.

"Okay, okay, let's pull it together! Joe, Chris, Kelly, front and center!" He called to their respective handlers. The three trooped over. "Sorry Kelly, you may get spread a little thin today because I need you handling Rach but you're on if Val needs you too."

"No problem, Murphy," she said with a quick nod to Rachel.

"Rach, if you're serious about staying under Spartan Tactical, you need your own handler ASAP. And no, you can't poach Kelly, Val will have my head."

"Sorry, Murph, I was kind of waiting for Mandy to have the first pick so I didn't poach someone from her either."

Murphy swallowed several comments about Mandy's obstinate unwillingness to help the team. "Understandable. Let's say I'm assuming that will not happen in the next week. Might as well make your pick when we get back."

Rachel's eyes flicked to where Mandy stood alone at the end of the room but she nodded in silent agreement.

"Right. Three locations, three short Jumps," Murphy told the handlers, "and full door kicker mode."

Joe, Murphy's handler, gave him a grin and a nod. "Quick snacks, no IVs, full guns and ammo?"

"You got it. And body armor. Just in case. Rachel, I trust you, but I don't trust them. It's not a knock of your tender honor. I want all the protection I can manage."

"Tender honor?" she asked icily. The question was asked with the kind of tone that made every man on the team squirm.

"Woman, you are more prickly and faster to flash with anger

than even Val and that's saying something!"

Rachel's mouth dropped open once again and her face pinched with anger until it melted into a laugh. "Yeah, okay. Guilty." She rolled her eyes. "I'll address it in therapy this week."

"Good choice." Murphy slapped her shoulder with a nod. "Handlers, how much time?"

Ryan bobbled his head from side to side. "Draw weapons and ammo then build a fanny pack? Eh, thirty minutes or less."

"Deal. We'll meet you at Point Zero in thirty. Team, you have the next thirty to eat, pull out any more info you need from Apollo and solidify your visuals with him."

The team broke and Murphy approached Apollo. The man sat near the end of the conference room table, the direct overhead lights highlighting his blonde hair like a halo. He was almost opposite to where Mandy stood in the shadowed corner near Point Zero and Murphy couldn't blame him for wanting to keep the girl in his line of sight. Whatever affection Murphy might have once held for her had evaporated over the last few weeks. He had chased women before, but he'd never had one like her. Hot and demanding his attention one moment then cold and distant another. Murphy had admired the grit and determination she had shown until that evaporated into a self-pity party. Maybe she had to right to be upset over how her life was changing, but Murphy didn't think that gave her the right to drag everyone around her into the abyss with her.

He shook his head, fuck her. He had work to do.

"Apollo," he said by way of greeting.

The man gave him a look that said he'd followed his gaze. "You do not like my sister," he said factually, without a hint of accusation.

Murphy gave a grunt and held out his hand, inviting Apollo to grasp it.

"She's changed," he told Apollo as their hands connected. "I don't blame you, you didn't do this to her if that's what worries you."

"It does not."

Murphy jerked in surprise as the emotions that flowed over their touch echoed his statement. There was a hint of hope but mostly a dismissive nothingness.

"Well okay then."

"I did not come to you for her. As I have stated from the beginning, my concern was to escape *Svoboda* and warn you of a threat. If she does not want me I will not force a relationship."

"Same," Murphy said and it was Apollo's turn to look surprised.

"You did like her. That has changed."

"She changed."

"Then I wish I had known her before. I fear she follows my father."

When Apollo didn't elaborate and there was only the vaguest hint of fear in his touch, Murphy pressed on. "Show me the three locations you know."

Murphy's mind was filled with a slew of visuals, smells, and feelings.

"Whoa, whoa, whoa, one at a time."

Apollo nodded and the onslaught focused.

"This is a warehouse in Virginia, I think. My geography of this area is not good."

"Norfolk maybe?"

"Perhaps."

His images showed a stark metal hulk of a building. Murphy got the impression of I-beams, rust, and brackish water. The visual shifted and the memory of rust was replaced with the iron smell of blood. Cold air, glazed tile, and the concrete floors of a small meat processing plant flooded Muphy's mind. He nodded and the visual shifted again. This time Apollo showed him what appeared to be a storage loft in an industrial warehouse. Dust lingered on the round metal railings of a loft overlooking stacks of neatly piled boxes.

"Good enough. The rest of the team will come for their visuals soon."

"You do not take me?"

"No."

"Do you trust me?" His questions were blunt and Murphy appreciated having one person who seemed to be able to keep their emotions and their job separate these days.

Murphy looked at him and considered. "I don't *not* trust you. But, I don't trust that you would be an asset in this situation. How do you think Pyotr would react to seeing you appear with us? How would you react to Pyotr?"

Apollo nodded. "That is reasonable. I wish you good hunting. May you find what you need."

Thirty minutes later the team was assembled with guns and gear. Murphy gave Rachel a searching look. She looked like she was suppressing nerves but seemed steady enough.

"We'll do a count of three then Jump. Flatten them as soon as we Jump, Rach."

She nodded and the three tagged hands.

"In three, two, one ..."

Murphy felt his feet hit the wet concrete floor of the marine warehouse a faction of a second before he was knocked to his ass. His brain went into overdrive as he looked for who had hit him, stunned his attacker could react so quickly to their arrival. However, when he tried to lift his head, he found himself pinned to the floor.

"Rachel!" he managed to roar from where he lay.

"Shit, sorry!"

The pressure holding him down relented and he sat up. "Them, not us."

"There isn't anyone else," Rachel said, gesturing to the empty warehouse.

"Fuck. Dry hole," Murphy said and swore with all the creativity of a United States Marine.

"Sorry, guys," Rachel said. She reached down to help the two men to their feet. "Maybe next time we group tighter and I'll try to, uh, I dunno, think of pushing a hula hoop out with us inside?"

"Whatever works, but my ass is going to be bruised for a week," James said and rubbed his posterior.

"Search the spaces, maybe they've left something behind that gives us a clue as to where they are," Murphy directed.

The suspect corner was damp with seawater or rain that had leaked from the walls and ceiling and they shuffled around pooled water. A pile of musty, molding blankets covered a cache of ammo canisters, a small weapons crate, and a large plastic bin of pre-packaged snacks.

"Tastykakes and Ho Hos? Really?" James said, kicking the tub. "Miller couldn't convince them to use IVs or eat healthy after four years?"

Murphy snorted. "Did you really want them refueling quickly and at full strength?"

"Oh, hell no, Murph. They can have all the junk food they want."

"Nah, let's clean them out." Murphy holstered the gun he had drawn while searching the small space. "Rachel, you grab their snacks, James the ammo cans, I'll get the weapons crate."

"Allow me," Rachel said and made a small gesture with her hand. The supplies rose and drifted gently toward them.

"Do you have to make the hand motion?" Murphy asked with genuine curiosity.

"Nah, it just makes me feel cool. You should see me make dinner these days. Practically a ballet with food whipping around my kitchen," she said with a laugh.

James chuckled and Murphy gave her a quick grin.

"Okay, back in three, two, one …"

The supplies dropped gracelessly onto Point Zero's hard floor.

"Oops. I concentrated too hard on the Jump and lost control of the stuff."

"Let's not be fancy next Jump then," Murphy told her. He spotted Joe and Ryan waiting for them. "Gents, liberated supplies from our Russian friends. We're taking a quick snack break then we'll hit location two. I think that's the butchers."

"Hmm, horror movie vibes. Enjoy that one," Joe said as he hoisted the ammo cases. "We'll get these down to the intel nerds to analyze."

"Wait," Rachel said and popped the lid off the tub of food. "I want one of these." She dug out a cellophane wrapped cake.

"Yo!" James said and raised his hand.

Rachel drifted one to him and turned to look at Murphy. He nodded and she fired one at him as well.

"Okay, now you can take it. I doubt the intel guys will get much out of it other than a fat stomach."

"Second trip. Everyone ready?" Murphy asked when they'd finish the cakes and their usual protein bars. When they both nodded, he held out both hands. "Butcher's work area. We'll group tighter this time. Three, two, one …"

They arrived in a tight group, still holding hands, and were greeted with the loud clatter of cutlery and metal tubs being flung to the floor.

Murphy dropped their hands and drew his weapon, snapping it up as he scanned the room. The room was exactly what he'd seen in Apollo's memories: cold, stinking of blood, with immaculate white tiled walls. Like the first location, it was also empty.

"Dry hole," he said and holstered his gun. "Same thing; search it. We'll take anything we find."

A cursory inspection of the small, cold space found another tub of food, empty ammo canisters, and an empty weapons crate.

"Think they were here recently?" James asked as he peered into the empty cache.

"Yes," Rachel said and pointed at an empty cake wrapper, still smeared with chocolate. "The bugs and rats would have that clean in a day or less."

"We won't wait for them to come back for the rest. Grab it all and we'll haul it back." His face was pinched with frustration. "Damn. Not that I'm spoiling for a fight, but I was hoping for a little more. Apollo seemed confident we'd find something useful."

Their return was smooth, Rachel floated the containers down gently upon arrival.

"How do you feel Rach?" Murphy asked her as they broke out another round of snacks.

"Full," she said and wrinkled her nose at her protein bar.

"You've done the heavy lifting for the last two Jumps. You need the calories. We also don't know what the calorie requirements of telekinesis are yet. We'll hand carry anything we find at the next location. And if you're too full to eat, I can have one of the handlers do an IV."

"I'm fine," she said. A hint of her fire peaked out of her flashing eyes.

"Damn. This must be how Val felt whipping my ass into shape the first month I was here." Murphy laughed. "Don't be like me. Don't be a stubborn ass and end up knocked out on our next Jump. Take the damn line. We're on a time boggle, but not so pressured that you can't get fully refueled. Joe, a hand please?"

Murphy ignored Rachel's baleful stare as Joe swabbed her arm and inserted the IV.

"Fine, I needed this," Rachel said ten minutes later from her spot in one of Point Zero's few padded chairs.

"Wish you could have been there when this guy was earning his stripes," James said. "Val let him run it out with Hank's PJs. Damn fool passed out mid-run and had to be carried back."

"I did not!" Murphy shot back. "I managed to get my ass and my team back to the hangar. Which, coincidentally, is also were I woke up a few minutes later having taken a somewhat unplanned nap." He turned back to Rachel. "Ego is fine but don't let it get you in trouble. Because if you can't make it out of a location, your team can't make it out. You're working for Spartan Tactical now, not this logistics stuff Mandy runs. We work as a team and carry human cargo. And we don't leave people behind."

"Because of our stupidity," James corrected. "We don't leave people behind, especially not because we did something dumb."

"Copy, Murph," Rachel said in as meek a voice as he'd yet heard from her.

"Your bag looks empty. You ready?"

"For another empty room? Sure."

"Prepare for the worst and you'll never be shocked. Assume we're going into an occupied building, no matter what happened at the last two locations."

"Okay, Murph," she said, disbelief evident on her face.

He held out a hand, letting his annoyance leak through the touch. "Same tactic, group tight. In three, two, one …"

They landed in a knot and immediately heard the sound of grunts. The grunts were followed by a yell and a sickening thud.

"Fuck! Hot spot," Murphy yelled. "Are they down, Rach?"

"Well, they aren't moving," she said. "And I think I pushed a guy off a ledge." Her voice was scared.

Murphy had his weapon snapped up and trained on the two men who lay prone on the warehouse's loft floor. He nudged one with his foot but other than his angry eyes tracking him, the man lay still.

"Rach, keep them still. James, zip tie their hands and feet, then you can release them, Rachel." He went to the railing and looked down. He inhaled sharply and turned around.

"They're tight, you can release them, Rachel," James said but he kept his weapon trained on the two men.

Rachel exhaled sharply and the two started to writhe but couldn't move to a sitting position with their hands and feet bound. "What about the other one?" she asked Murphy and stepped toward the railing.

Murphy's hand shot out to stop her from looking over but was too late. She peered over the railing and then gave a strangled gasp.

"Oh, hell," she said quietly. Below them, the man's body lay on the concrete, his right leg twisted at an unnatural angle and his head split open. Until the day she died, Rachel would never be able to unsee his brain matter, like pink scrambled eggs, splattered out behind him.

"I'm sorry, I tried to keep you from seeing that."

"Is he …?" James asked, the question hanging in the air. One look at Rachel's face made him shake his head. "Shit."

Murphy watched Rachel's mouth open and close soundlessly. He maneuvered her gently to a chair and pushed her down. She sat for no more than a second before she began vomiting up her snacks.

"Sit here a second. You need a moment to get over the shock. James, start looking for any clues."

One of the men started muttering in what Murphy assumed was Russian. Murphy turned to him and strode angrily to his spot on the floor.

"What are you doing here? You speak English?" He grabbed the man's shirt and pulled him in close. "You probably want to talk to me, you won't like who I turn you over to for interrogation next."

The man spit in his face in response. Murphy hauled him to his feet and pushed him to the railing, allowing the man to see the mess below.

"You want to end like that? You see him? He's dead, brains splattered on the concrete. Be nice or I'll push you over too. I only need one man to talk."

"I talk! I talk!" the man shrieked in heavily accented English.

"What are you doing here?"

"Supplies. Food. Water. Weapons. Electronics," he spluttered.

"Electronics?"

"For the bomb. I make wires. Wires. Battery."

"Fuck," Murphy said and released him, letting the man slump to the floor. Murphy grabbed his phone and called Val's direct line. "Val, I'm coming back with a party. We've got two for interrogation. We'll need our Agency contact and friends to help. Pyotr and his crew are building bombs."

TWENTY-FIVE

"Rachel's tactic worked well, maybe too well," Murphy told Val in his debriefing.

He had returned to the Limitless Logistic headquarters worse for the wear a half hour prior. They had taken Rachel to the clinic for additional fluid and an emergency counseling session. She had been nearly catatonic when she got back, in shock from having accidentally killed a man by throwing him over a railing.

"I agree with that," Val told him. She was worried for Rachel. For all her bravado, seeing a man dead by her own actions was hitting her hard. "I'll get a cleanup crew in before anyone sees him."

"They mentioned explosives. I didn't see any and there were barely any supplies I would have associated with bomb making there. My assumption is that it's already built and they're getting ready to use it."

"Shit."

"I know."

They gave twin sighs of frustration. Val caught his eye and both burst into laughter.

"I shouldn't laugh, it's not funny," Val said through her giggles. She grabbed her belly, now cramped and aching from laughter as well.

"No. It's stress," Murphy agreed.

She let them wind themselves down before returning to their detainees.

"I need the Agency to interrogate them, this is well outside our wheelhouse." She saw Murphy give her a critical look.

"Powell?"

"I don't have any other contacts on speed dial," she told him.

"Are you sure you want him to do it? I mean," he seemed to cut himself off.

Val gave a deep sigh. "Speak freely, Murph."

"He killed Chad, didn't he?"

Val blinked once, surprised that he had reached the same conclusion. "I don't have any proof of that."

"Rumors move fast, even here, Val. He's on camera removing him from the clinic."

"Yes."

"And then three days later, Chadwick Nelson shows up dead in a park."

"Yes." Tension twisted her belly, making the pain that nagged her worse.

"When was the last time he talked to you?"

"The night he disappeared," Val said quietly.

"Are you suspicious?"

"Of course I am."

"Thank God." He gave her a panicked look. "Sorry. I don't mean it like that!"

"No, you're glad we share the same suspicions," Val said but her stomach roiled.

"He's been manipulating you, Val. Surely you know, or at least, suspect that?"

"It's crossed my mind."

"Is that why you turned him down?" Murphy glanced at her now bare finger.

The swelling from the too small ring had eventually subsided and with soapy water, she'd finally managed to slip it off. The ring was back in its blue box, sitting atop the jewelry box in her walk-in closet.

"You're tiptoeing up to the line between coworkers and friends, Murph."

"Maybe. But when my boss's boyfriend is a major security risk, maybe it's a line I need to fucking pole vault across."

Val held his gaze for a moment.

Then a second moment.

Finally, the dam broke and she sobbed. "Murphy, I know in my gut he killed Chad because I asked him to 'handle the problem.' And I know what he's capable of. I know what he's willing to do on my behalf. He's already had one man killed and not because I wanted it but because he couldn't handle it. Him." She looked Murphy in the eyes. "He had Major Parker killed not because he harmed me, but because he didn't want him triggering me while I was around him. It wasn't even about me," she finished in a whisper.

"Jesus," Murphy said. "I knew he had him killed. He admitted as much to me, but I had hoped he was lying about why."

"I can't even prove it. He's too good. The Agency gives him too much latitude. And Maureen won't be able to hold the story much longer," she said.

"Senator Mitchell?"

"Secretary Mitchell, remember? They just promoted her this week."

"But she's working for us?"

"Not exactly. She had been helping me fend off the national registration assholes and now she's working to sit on Chadwick's death. It will make national news. I have until tomorrow to furnish a believable story."

Murphy shook his head. "Damn, Val. We're in deep."

"I know." She hung her head. "I still need him too. I hate it."

"Let's get this over with then," Murphy said and reached out for her hand.

Val took it and let his support flow over her. "Thank you."

She took out her phone and pulled up Powell's number.

Truce for now. I have three Russian agents we need interrogated ASAP. 99% sure they're connected to the Ambassador's assassination.

She typed and punched the send button. She gave Murphy a nod. "Ball's in his court."

Extraction in 15. The response was terse but almost immediate, indicating he'd been watching his phone for the last three days but chose not to reach out.

Val had no idea how Powell and his team made it to the Limitless headquarters in only fifteen minutes, but they did. She suspected he had been close by but didn't get to ask. Powell and two other Agents met them at the Limitless cargo bay carrying black hoods. Powell looked pale and drawn; he wouldn't meet her eyes and stayed far from her. In moments the two surviving Russians were hooded and extracted, having been whisked away in an unmarked van without a single word exchanged.

TWENTY-SIX

VALERIE "ATHENA" HALL
0945L/1345Z, 01 NOV

Val caught Mandy early the next day. "Mandy. Talk with me." Her voice was terse and sharp, and her mood reflected it.

"And if I decline?" Mandy, who had been slowly trundling down the hall stopped walking, forcing Val to halt her brisk walk or breeze past. "What will you do, Val? Fire the CEO of Limitless Logistics? I doubt it. You sure spent enough on marketing and well-placed ad buys to make me appear friendly and wholesome. People are painting murals of the Angel of Oklahoma still. You wouldn't give that up, would you?" Her eyes narrowed and she looked at Val with cold calculation.

Mandy's saccharine chatter added to the irritation Val already felt at seeing Powell but not hearing a peep.

"I would hate to have to fire a friend—"

Mandy scoffed and turned away.

"But I *will* fire a risk."

Mandy whipped around and pointed a finger at her, almost touching her nose. "Oh? Yeah? Like Chadwick? You going to throw me to the vicious mercy of your little pet Agent?" A strange light flashed in her eyes. Cold. Cruel.

Val rocked back, unprepared for Mandy's icy assault. She was also surprised to hear rumors, that also happened to be truth, come from her mouth so casually.

"What? I," Val spluttered, "that's not …"

Mandy raised an eyebrow over her narrowed eyes. A world of questions in a single movement.

Val steeled herself and then grabbed the pointing hand Mandy had thrust in her face. Without warning she Jumped them both into her office in the C-suite. Val didn't need everyone in the company to hear what happened next.

"Sit," Val commanded. She stood up straight, letting her presence speak volumes. Mandy may have had four inches of height on Val, but Valerie Hall, Athena in name and spirit, held her posture with every ounce of command authority she'd gained since Marco had whispered a change of command into her mind as he died, "*You have the watch now, Athena.*"

Mandy held eye contact but slumped into the seat across Val's desk. When she'd settled herself, Val continued.

"What do you want, Mandy? Truly. You whine and bitch about not wanting to Jump but I know you've made runs. Sloppy. Imprecise. Late even. But you have made runs: organ transplants, humanitarian aid, disaster relief, and Doctors Without Borders. I've given you missions I thought would fulfill you. If you truly hated it, you'd stop altogether. You've made it very clear you aren't in the military and that means I can't fire you. Hell, you don't even have a contract to breach, although I pay you like you do. So, what in the fucking hell do you want?"

"I want out."

"Liar."

It was Mandy's turn to rock back, stunned. She shook her head. "I want a normal life."

"You can have a normal life."

"Now you're the liar. People venerate me like some goddess of old."

"So what? You're an attractive woman. Even if they're just seeing you in the streets, men will fantasize about you. Women will imagine you're a whore if you are single and a saint if you have a passel of children tugging on your apron strings. You will always be something you are not to people who don't know you. Fuck their fantasies. So, I ask you one more time, what do you," Val stabbed her desk with a finger, "want?"

"I've already told you. I want friends."

"So, make and keep them."

"I want a family."

"And? Go make one."

"How?" Mandy exploded finally, coming up out of her chair to tower over Val. "How? I want a child of my own flesh and blood but as soon as I touch the man I want to make that child with, I'll hear and feel everything he thinks of me. If I gain weight? If he thinks the neighbor is pretty? How can I go through with that if I can feel and hear everything that makes me want to shrivel and die."

"Then get fucking therapy like the rest of us. Work through it."

"How do I even date? Who wants me? Not Hestia, the fabulously wealthy CEO of Limitless. Mandy, the disabled and battered woman under the name."

"Make a family." Before Mandy could respond again Val held up a hand. "Adopt children if you think you can't handle a man impregnating you. IVF. A gestational carrier."

"I don't want to adopt, I want children of my own. My own flesh and blood. And I need a husband for that."

"Well," Val drawled, "you don't even need a boyfriend for that."

"I'm not having a child out of wedlock."

"Fine. Keep giving excuses." Val leaned back in her chain. "But you're going on the roster and you're pulling your weight. I'm done giving you a chance to do it of your own accord. We're in the middle of a national crisis, I'm ordering you now."

Mandy huffed and locked eyes with Val. Val stared her down until her nose wrinkled as an all too familiar pain hit her. She clenched her jaw, determined to ignore this until her business with Mandy was done.

"Fine," Mandy said. "Do what you will. Let's see how it works."

TWENTY-SEVEN

MURPHY "ARES" HAWKINS
1250L/1650Z, 01 NOV

"Team, gather round," Murphy called to his assembled group. Rachel, Damarcus, and Jafar stepped closer along with their handlers and intel support. Murphy watched approvingly as Rachel gave Ashley a nod. She had finally settled on Ashley and this was their first operation as a Jumper and handler team. He and Joe exchanged a quick smile. They knew how important a good pairing was to tactical execution.

"Val, are you in or out on this op?" he asked quietly.

Val gave him a pained look. "Sorry, Murphy, I'm falling out for this one. Probably hitting Medical after this briefing." She discreetly rubbed her abdomen.

Murphy, who had no sisters and only a tenuous at best relationship with his mother, simply nodded, not wanting any part of what he assumed were "female problems."

Val took a step back and the team crowded his table to fill her void. Apollo took a position at his right hip. Murphy looked at him, considering, but simply nodded. Apollo let the exposed skin of his left wrist tap Murphy's: gratitude, purpose, and more than a hint of vengeance flowed over the touch. Murphy glanced at him again. Apollo's face was placid, only the tightness at the corner of his eye showed his true feelings.

"Me too, man," Murphy whispered.

"Team, the intel is thin for today's op," Murphy told them soberly. "The Russian stooges we pulled in yesterday didn't give up much, despite the CIA's best efforts. Here's what we know."

Murphy tapped the keyboard in front of him and the conference table lit up. Dossiers, personnel photos, satellite imagery, and the images of gruesomely murdered people projected onto the table's surface. A few people groaned and recoiled at the images. He saw Rachel blink hard and then squint at one of the personnel photos.

"Sorry, it's not ideal, but we're pulling pieces from across the US Intelligence Community as well as Russian open source. The Russian Times doesn't pull punches." Murphy waved his hand and the images of murdered bodies expanded. "Russian media has reported the deaths of several prominent Russian citizens in the last week. Each one was listed as a suicide, but when paired with our intelligence, we know each one was thrown out a window or off a roof. And if you look closely at the proximity of the bodies to the closest building, you may recognize the tactic."

Several folks with stronger stomachs leaned in to look closer. Joe, on Murphy's left, traced distances with his forefinger before glancing up at Murphy and Apollo.

"They weren't thrown from the roof, it's too far. They were released in open air," Joe said bluntly.

"I think so too," Murphy agreed.

"*Svoboda* stole our tactic?" Joe looked at Apollo.

"Yes. I believe that is true," Apollo confirmed.

"Did you hear them discussing this at all before you left?"

Apollo shrugged. "It was tense when I left. Pyotr was starting to leave me out of planning. But I firmly believe this is their work. These deaths destabilize the government. It's an anarchist's dream."

"This means we have high confidence that *Svoboda* is continuing to remove Russian oligarchs as a means of removing the Russian president's power base," Murphy stated. "We also know they are planning to attack a prominent American in the next forty-eight hours and it would follow that they will find the American versions of oligarchs."

"They wouldn't try for someone like the President?" Joe asked.

"We don't think so," Murphy said with a shrug. "The President is too well guarded and too high profile."

"They're pushing for the two countries to come to blows though, right? If they kill the President wouldn't that guarantee conflict?"

"No. We think it would cause the opposite effect. Even Russia would be inclined to denounce a group that assassinated a President. I mean, let's be honest, Putin would be more likely to have everyone in *Svoboda* assassinated rather than leave that option open." Murphy flicked his wrist and the display showed profile photos of three men and a woman. "Based on our intelligence, these are the four most likely candidates. Each is a prominent member of government or has access to the resources to influence the government."

There were murmurs of amusement and concern among the team.

"Him? Really?" Jafar asked.

"Mr. Noel owns the largest social media platform in the United States and we have credible intel that he was backed by several recently deceased Russians."

"Honestly, I believe it." Jafar rolled his eyes. "Are we warning him? If there's a risk it gets back to the Russians?"

"Yes. The risk of it escalating things in the US is a higher priority. While the two stooges didn't give up a target, we know based on the components they purchased and *Svoboda's* current actions, they plan on blowing someone up. After what happened this spring and summer, a third incident would potentially cause nationwide panic. Again." Murphy shook his head. "Two out of four of these folks are slimy as hell, but we can't take that risk."

Jafar nodded and considered the photos again.

"What is the plan, then?"

"Break into four teams. Each team approaches one of these four and provides a warning. Each of them has a very public schedule and if we appear exactly where they are out of nowhere, it further proves our point that they are at risk over the next few days. Hopefully, each team can convince them to lay low until after we can snag Pyotr and his men. Then we stake out their egress point and hope to capture them on their way into or out of the US."

"Hope isn't a course of action, Murphy," Jafar told him.

"True and I'm absolutely open to better ideas based on the intelligence we have available." He stared at him hard.

Jafar held his hands up in surrender. "Do I have to be violent?" He asked, clearly worried about being assigned to Murphy's Spartan Tactical team for the day.

"Nope. In fact, I prefer it if you aren't. Besides, I think your natural reactions will be perfect for your target."

Jafar's brows furrowed. "Murphy?"

"Look, I need you to go to Mr. Noel. We know he's a bigot behind closed doors. Sorry, but you'll be trolling him for a reaction."

"You want me to troll him because I'm brown?" Jafar eyed Damarcus who shifted uncomfortably. "Or something else?"

Murphy inhaled. "Yes. It's dirty and I'm sorry to put you in the position, but hitting him off guard might get more out of him than if I went."

"Murphy," Damarcus said with a warning growl in his voice.

"Dee, you're my boss and you can absolutely veto this if I'm out of line. But if I go, he'll try to 'bro up' with me. If Jafar goes, there's a higher chance he will confirm his Russian ties. I need to know if his ties make him more or less of a target for *Svoboda*."

Damarcus sighed. "You are out of line, but you're also a diabolical bastard. I'm sorry Jafar," Damarcus said to the disgruntled man, "but he's right. We can play off his racism to our advantage. Go in there and lean into it. Hell, if you get anything good, we can find a way to get it on social media and embarrass him over it. Once the current crisis is over. Can you handle that?"

"I'm against revenge like that," he said.

"I'm not," Damarcus said with a wicked grin.

Jafar inhaled and rolled his eyes again. "Fine. If it means we are savings lives."

"Good man."

"Settled then," Murphy said. "Damarcus, your target is Henry Whitney. Nothing cosmic with him. He owns Prospectus Source Energy and, if our sources are correct, as the CEO of a Fortune 500 company he's highly interested in meeting the Vice CEO of the world's most famous logistics corporation. Sorry, but you also have to lean into it."

"Ryan, get the Armani out of storage and steamed," Damarcus said with a laugh.

"I knew you could handle him. Thanks," Murphy gave him a quick fist bump across the table. "Rachel, you have the distinct displeasure of confronting the Secretary of Housing and Urban Development."

Murphy watched her study the photo with a look of disgust twisting her lips into a sneer.

"Rachel?" Murphy prompted.

"Him? Are you serious?" Rachel asked, clearly stunned. "I mean. Uh, why in the hell would they care about the HUD Secretary?"

Murphy wanted to take her hand and feel what she was thinking, but knowing her history and seeing the look on her face, he already knew: the HUD Secretary was no stranger to her.

"He's dirty, a real slimy bastard," Murphy said carefully.

"I know," she said bluntly.

"The best intelligence we can get shows he's already being blackmailed by the Russian oligarchy. If he's on the take with the Russian upper crust, *Svoboda* will hate him. That he's a Cabinet member makes him an even juicier target."

"And you want me to do what? Convince him to stop being blackmailed? Perhaps coerce him?" Rachel's voice was dangerously quiet.

"No," Murphy said, shaking his head. "Well, yes but maybe not what you're thinking. Ideally, he'd stop letting Russian fat cats buy him off, but that's a bridge too far this week. For now, I need him to lay low, stay off a public calendar, and be hard to find for the next three days."

Rachel's face soured. "I can convince a man to stay in bed for three days, but I don't think that's what you're asking for right now. Right?"

"No, Rachel! We don't operate like that and I wouldn't ask that of you!" Murphy scrubbed his face. "Damn, I thought you trusted us."

Rachel regarded him steadily. "And I thought you trusted me. To be a professional. A team player."

"Can you keep your temper in check and your professionalism in place?"

"I won't beat him up or telekinetically throw him against a wall," she said but looked like she was struggling to keep from sneering.

"Do better than that."

"I'm not planning on violence—"

"Thank goodness for that," Jafar muttered.

"And I am planning to be a business professional."

"Then you'll be perfect for this." Murphy smiled at her.

Damarcus reached out and squeezed her hand. Murphy watched her whole demeanor change and wondered what exactly had gone across that touch.

"It's alright, we'll deal with our host of trauma after this," Murphy said and gave Jafar a brief nod. "For now, be strong. Be persuasive and forceful," he emphasized. "Honestly, kidnap him and bring him back here if it keeps him off *Svoboda's* radar for the next three days. I'll take that outcry over his slimy ass being assassinated."

"He's a sleezy bitch who's messing with housing for the lower class during a housing crisis and you want me to go a little feral?" Rachel asked with a wicked grin. "Done."

"Don't hurt him … but don't feel too compelled to hold back."

"And you're going to Maureen?" Damarcus asked. "You don't want Val to take her?"

Murphy shook his head. "No. Val said she was out. I'll work with Secretary Mitchell."

"I'll be mighty curious to hear your take on how she sees us right now," Damarcus said. "I trust Val, but she's been our single point of contact for a while now and I'd like to broaden our perspective a bit." He gave Murphy a significant glance.

"Noted."

"Arm up?" Rachel asked.

"No thank you," Jafar said, raising his hands.

"Take a weapon if you think you need it. Jafar, given your target,

I fully support you going unarmed but take Quincy. Damarcus, you're probably better off unarmed. Rachel, lady's choice—"

"Armed."

"And I will be unarmed. I don't think Secretary Mitchell's security team will appreciate me arriving without warning and I think they would take it personally if I did it armed."

The team nodded at their assignments.

"I'll leave it to each of you to coordinate with your handlers' and targets' schedules for a reasonable departure, but ideally, we'll all be on our way in the next two hours. Check in as soon as your targets are safe, or if something comes up. Good luck and happy hunting."

TWENTY-EIGHT

JAFAR AL RAYYAN
1427L/1827Z, 01 NOV

"Quincy, grab me one of the standard Pantheon polos and a pair of khakis, please," Jafar directed his handler. "Wait. Grab yourself the same thing in your size."

"Jay, I don't think anyone wears khakis anymore," Quincy told him, face earnest.

"Maybe not, but envision an IT professional, what do you see?"

Quincy nodded with a laugh. "Khakis, polo, a clipboard, and some CAT 5 cable thrown over the shoulder."

"Exactly. If Murphy wants us to go hard on the stereotype, let's drive it to the ground. I'm curious to see what Mr. Noel says before he catches on to who we really represent."

"Jafar al Rayyan, are you going black hat on me?" Quincy said with a hint of sass. His ability to follow Jafar's train of thought was what sealed him as a handler.

"Psht, I am above the scheming and machinations of this wild company, but I suppose I do want to know if the rumors are true. About Noel. Don't you?"

Quincy gave him a serious look, his sass abandoned. "Jay, I know. He posts enough things that just skirt around saying the quiet part out loud. He doesn't like me and he doesn't like you. He wouldn't like anything about us." Quincy put a hand on his chest, his dark brown eyes meeting Jafar's.

"I need to know for sure. I can't hate someone without knowing their motives." Jafar took Quincy's hand, giving it a gentle squeeze. "Besides, won't it be such a subversive delight when we save his butt."

An hour later, they had completed their logistics hold in a small conference room Limited Logistics owned in downtown Denver. The pair were dressed in Pantheon logo polos and the only pairs of khaki pants Quincy could find. Jafar's pants hung loosely on his slender hips, held in place with a thin black leather belt. Jafar had a waist bag full of snacks while Quincy's bag held an IV bag and the supplies to insert a line, should Jafar need it. Both carried clipboards with images of Mr. Noel's office and his personal schedule.

"Tag up," Jafar directed and Quincy tapped his hand lightly, nerves and anticipation evident in the touch. Something else lurked just beneath the surface and Jafar suppressed a smile. He glanced at Quincy who avoided his gaze, but his lips tugged upwards with the hint of a smile. "I guess we'll address that later. Jumping in three, two, one!"

On "one" they transferred instantly to a high-end corner office forty-three floors above San Fransisco in the Transamerica Pyramid. In front of them, a lone man yelled into a speaker phone, ignoring the magnificent view of the Bay behind him. Over one shoulder, Jafar could see Alcatraz Island.

"No, Vincent. You're going to launch that ad campaign tonight or your ass is fired and I'll send you back to whatever plantation HR found you on!"

Beside him, Quincy rocked back slightly. For all his boasting that he knew exactly who and what Mr. Noel was, it was difficult to be confronted with such bold racism in person. Jafar swallowed back an old rage and steeled himself.

"Excuse me, Mr. Noel?"

"What?" the man snapped, not bothering to turn toward them.

"Sir, we're here—" Jafar started but was cut off when the man looked up.

"Oh. Yeah. Sure, the computer." He gestured impatiently at his desktop. "Just be quiet about it, I'm on a call."

He then turned away as if neither man existed.

"Mr. Noel, we need to speak to you," Jafar said with as much authority as he could muster.

Mr. Noel's eyes snapped to him, face contorted with anger at having been interrupted. "Look, Raj. Anish. Jayesh. Whatever the fuck your name is, I don't care. Do not speak to me. Get your skinny ass over here and fix this thing. You don't need to speak to work. And you," he pointed at Quincy and snapped his fingers, "I need another coffee. I don't care if you're in IT, go find that blonde piece of ass out front and get a coffee for me. She's an idiot but she can at least get a coffee order right."

"You're going to be murdered," Jafar said with more calm than he felt. The years of racism even in his hometown and homophobia that had driven him from family had made him calloused to Mr. Noel's type of abuse. What was strong enough to trigger Jafar's first Jump had made him strong enough to endure Noel's almost comically bad bigotry.

Something in Jafar's placid delivery that was completely at odds with his words caught Noel's attention.

"I'm going to call you back," he said to whomever he was abusing over the phone. He punched a second button without hesitation. "Security, death threat in the C-suite."

"It won't be me," Jafar said quietly. "You have more enemies than you think and they're coming for you."

"You don't look Russian," Noel said quietly.

"Looks can be deceiving," Jafar said and gestured to his outfit. "For starters, I'm not Indian."

Noel's eyes narrowed. "Maybe, but you are a fucking pillow biter."

Jafar glanced briefly at Quincy and smiled. "Guilty," he all but sang with every ounce of sass he could summon. "And my gay ass is about to save your life, baby."

"Get out of my office!" Noel bellowed.

Jafar Jumped the ten feet to his desk and grabbed the man, pulling Noel into an embrace that brought his ear to Jafar's lips.

"Your Russian friends are coming, Mr. Noel," he whispered. Noel jerked back once but went still at Jafar's words.

"They're pissed about the repayment?" he asked, voice equally quiet.

"You are astute," Jafar cooed and ran his hand down the man's back, hoping to make him as uncomfortable as possible without losing his attention to fear.

"Their funding was locked down. My repayment schedule is on target. Investors and advertisers backing out is all just a rumor."

"Hmm, that last call seems to indicate otherwise." Jafar glanced at Quincy who stood in shock where he'd left him in the middle of the office. If Noel had called security, they only had moments left.

"The repayment will move forward; I'll use my own money if I have to!"

"Noted. I'm not here from the Russians though. I'm here to warn you that you've made too many enemies. Your Russian friends, arguably, remain friends. But you're," he smiled sweetly, "in bed with the wrong men. Pulling them in has angered even more powerful men. Men like me." Jafar Jumped back to where Quincy stood.

Noel's face tightened. "You're one of them," he said with a sneer. "Those fuckers in the so-called 'Pantheon,' aren't you?"

"I am. And I am here to warn you. Our counterparts are coming for you in the next three days. Lay low. Get off the radar. And stop making your schedule public on social media, you idiot."

"And if don't?" Something in Noel's face flickered.

"Then there's nothing further I can do to help you."

The door burst open and security guards rushed the room, yelling at them to drop their clipboards.

"Sorry, boys," Jafar said to the guard. He took Quincy's hand. "Lover's quarrel. Good luck, Mr. Noel," Jafar told him and blew him a kiss with his free hand.

Jafar Jumped them directly back to Point Zero. He slumped to the floor at the loss of nearly over 2,000 calories in an instant from hauling Quincy and himself across the continent.

"Damn it, Jafar. You were supposed to do a logistic hold on the way back too!" Quincy said and pulled him to the side, clearing the way for Damarcus, Rachel, and Murphy in case they came back at the same time.

"Sorry," Jafar slurred out. "He just made me so mad, I lost it."

"You did really well," Quincy said and scrubbed the crook of his arm, prepping him for an IV. "Your double entendres toward that bigot were a master class in trolling."

"Thanks," Jafar said as his vision started to gray out.

"What can I say, Jay, you're a master baiter."

Jafar gave an exhausted giggle as he slipped into unconsciousness.

TWENTY-NINE

DAMARCUS WASHINGTON

1541L/1941Z, 01 NOV

"Do you think Jafar and Quincy can handle Mr. Noel?" Ryan asked, smoothing Damarcus's suit coat over his shoulders. "Also, how does that fit? You've been hitting traps hard in the gym and I'm worried you'll bust a seam."

Damarcus shrugged in the bespoke Armani suit. The fabric pulled at the shoulders and the lapels gapped slightly. "I think you're right, it's too tight."

"Too tight for today or too tight but we can work on another one after this?"

"I'll make it through today. And to your earlier question, I think they'll be fine."

"Really?" Ryan asked.

"Which answer?"

"Either," Ryan told him.

"I'm not giving up on a $5,000 suit so easily, we'll see if the tailor can give me a little ease in the back when I have more time. My other suits are no bigger, so we'll roll with it. And for Jafar, he's stronger than he looks."

Ryan gave a hum of disagreement as he took a note on his tablet.

"You mad Murphy's throwing him to the wolves?"

Ryan gave him a stern look. "You know he's gay, right?"

Damarcus nodded. "I suspected, but since he didn't say it outright, I figured that was his business, not mine. What's your point?"

"Mr. Noel is a raging bigot, he'll eat that boy alive."

"Ryan, you are my brother, but you are not a brother, you get me? Jafar and I? We live with the subtle bigotry every day. It builds up tolerance, like a callous. Do I want to punch assholes like Noel in the face? Sure. But is it worth getting my black ass shot to do it? No. And you know that if we both tried the same thing, you aren't the one the cops shoot. Jafar's lived that life. He knows."

"I'm not invalidating your experience but he's the intersection of two, maybe three minorities. It's exponentially harder."

"I believe you. But," he held out his hand, "I spent two months training him. Feeling his mind, day in and day out. I think I know the steel inside the velvet glove."

"Okay, Dee," Ryan said, accepting. "And what about you? Are you ready for this?"

Damarcus laughed. "Ready to Jump into a Fortune 500 CEO's office like I own it, schmooze him, tell him he's facing assassination, and escape without being arrested? All in a suit that costs more than my first car? Yeah, sure. Born ready."

"Okay then." Ryan laughed and handed him a slim black leather crossbody bag. "You're only going to Atlanta, so no IVs. There are three high density snacks in here. If my sources are correct, Mr. Whitney is a genuine gentleman, meaning he's likely to offer you snacks and a drink. Well, he's curious about you too so he may even offer dinner if it gets you to stay longer so he can pick your brain. That might be enough to fuel your Jump back."

"I'm a long way from the streets of Philly, Ryan. I know how to handle myself around the fat cats. Heck, brother, you've even gotten me to stop drinking martinis with vodka and use gin like a proper gentleman."

"Okay, okay, I know!" Ryan held up his hands defensively.

"Mother hen," Damarcus said with a laugh.

"Guilty."

Ryan held out his hand and Damarcus tapped it lightly. Brotherly love and support flowed across the touch. Damarcus grabbed his hand and pulled him into a hug.

"That scared little kid in foster care never goes away, does he? He just gets taller with a bigger paycheck?" Damarcus gave him a squeeze. "Thanks for always having my back, bro."

"Always," Ryan told him. He released Damarcus and stepped back. "Okay, enough bro-mance. Go do your mission. C-suite, Marquis One Tower. Should be just finishing his last appointment of the day."

Damarcus nodded. "Give me a few minutes to see Rachel off then I'm out."

"Oh, seeing Rachel off?"

"Don't you start with me!" Damarcus said, only half serious. He came back a few moments later with a smile on his face. "I'm ready now. See you in a few."

Damarcus gave himself a silent countdown and Jumped. The executive office was surprisingly understated. A small, sleek metal and glass desk and office chairs dominated the room. Recessed lighting illuminated a single landscape photograph on the wall. The only other piece of furniture was a small side table arranged with crystal decanters and glasses.

Seated at the desk was a middle-aged man of average build. His dark hair was only lightly streaked with gray and his skin showed the subtle hints of a man who took his skincare seriously. He was dressed in a crisp white shirt and a charcoal tie that matched the coat draped on his chair.

"Good afternoon, Mr. Whitney. My name is—"

"Damarcus Washington, what an honor!" Henry Whitney practically bounced from his set and held out a hand to exchange grips.

Damarcus tried to maintain his composure but he was surprised to think this man knew him on sight. He allowed the man to shake his hand, nervous to catch his thoughts.

It was a satisfying surprise to feel the man's genuine pleasure at their meeting. The touch carried the slightest hint of frustration at being interrupted but the feeling was overwhelmed by his delight at seeing a person whose company he'd sought arrive in his office.

"To what do I owe this delightful interruption?" Mr. Whitney gestured to a seat across from his own. "And may I offer you a drink?"

"Please, whatever you're having is fine, as this conversation may be a bit of a shock."

Whitney chuckled. "More of a shock than a fellow executive popping into my office?"

"I'm sorry, but yes."

"Gin martini?"

"Please. Two olives, if I may be so bold."

"My dear fellow, I appreciate your boldness."

"Then I'll continue," Damarcus told him as he watched the man fix their drinks. "There's no easy way to say this, but we have intelligence that indicates you may be the target of an assassination attempt in the next seventy-two hours."

Whitney froze only briefly in pouring their drinks from the stainless-steel shaker. "Russia? Or China?"

"Excuse me?"

"I have my own intelligence team, if you can call it that. Counter industrial espionage, really, but they do unearth some interesting nuggets from time to time. And my personal security team leverages them to ensure I am well defended." He handed Damarcus his martini and settled into his seat. "The Russians have always butted heads over American refined oil exports and with China moving to be a growing influence in the African oil market, I understand they are the two most likely candidates for an assassination attempt."

"You are very well informed," Damarcus said and sipped. He would never admit it to Ryan, but he still preferred vodka martinis.

Whitney nodded to him over his own martini. "I'll give my team a raise then."

"It's not technically either nation. It's an anarchy driven Russian hit squad. You understand what I do, I assume? More than being an executive, you grasp exactly how our logistics organization is unique?"

"You teleport. Am I to assume you have counterparts in Russia?"

"Two, yes. One state sponsored and one that claims to be freedom fighters."

"One man's freedom fighter is another man's terrorist or something very much like that, no?"

"Yes."

"And you believe the terrorists will assassinate me?"

"We have reason to believe you are one of a small group of targets."

"What do they want?"

Damarcus laughed. "Your bluntness is refreshing."

Whitney raised his glass and sipped again. "Oil is and always has been a dirty business. Wars are fought for it. People die for it. And people in my position are always viewed as the bad guy, no matter how they try to spin the business. But I've learned this business is easier when we all cut the bullshit," he gave an unconcerned shrug, "and I appreciate early market guidance."

Damarcus sipped his martini. For all his bluntness, he still didn't know why the man was so keen to meet him. He swallowed the smooth gin and went on. "They wish to destabilize both Russia and the US. They've been targeting the Russian oligarchy and we believe they are looking for an American version to attack next."

Whitney leaned back in his chair, martini sloshing dangerously in its glass. "It won't be me then. Sure, I'm wealthy and I have power, but I've been firmly against Chinese and Russian influence. Hurts the bottom line, you know?"

"Indeed." Damarcus sipped his drink again. "But you are the largest and most notable oil CEO in the US. It does make you a target. Any chance I could convince you to quietly alter your plans for the next few days without making it public? For the sake of safety."

Whitney sipped his drink and considered. "You know, I've never been one to ignore a credible warning, even if I don't think it will impact me. I hear Saint Lucia is nice this time of year. Maybe the missus and I will have an impromptu vacation this week."

"Thank you, Mr. Whitney," Damarcus said. He set the drink down and rose. The man was sharp and straightforward but gave not a hint of what he wanted.

Whitney set his own drink down and rose as well. "Please, call me Henry."

"Thank you, Henry," he said and held out his hand, hoping to finally catch what the man really wanted.

Whitney clasped it. "I'll ask one favor, though. Your background is unique for a CEO at this level ..."

Damarcus tried not to smile, seeing the question before it could be asked.

"My son graduates from business school in the spring. Is there any chance you'd be willing to mentor him? There's only so much he's willing to take from 'the old man' and I think he'd be pleased to have a role model who represents him."

Damarcus's eyes flicked to the only photograph on the man's desk. Henry Whitney and Damarcus presumed his wife, smiling with arms over the shoulders a young man who looked very much like him if Damarcus had grown up in a wealthy Atlanta family and not the Philadelphia foster care system. Across their clasped hands, Damarcus could see a courtroom and feel Whitney's joy as being granted adoption of the small boy beside him.

"If you can see it, you can be it," Damarcus said with a smile. "It would be my pleasure, Henry."

They parted and Damarcus Jumped to DC, pleasantly surprised at the outcome of their meeting.

THIRTY

RACHEL NG

1547L/1947Z, 01 NOV

"Ashley, I need a suit!" Rachel said as she and her handler walked briskly from the conference room.

"Pantsuit or skirt?" Ashely said, her long legs helping her keep up with Rachel's brisk walk.

"Skirt. Short. And I need a blouse I can unbutton a lot or one with a low collar."

Ashley's stride faltered a moment and she had to jog a few steps to catch up again. "Rachel, I thought Murphy said—"

"I know what he said," Rachel snapped. "But I know that man and I need to, hmm, meet certain expectations."

"*Know* him?" The tone of Ashley's question told Rachel she already guessed how Rachel knew the Secretary.

Rachel's guts twisted and she swallowed down bile. "Yes."

They reached the doors to the handler's storeroom and Ashley put her hand on the door, preventing Rachel from entering. "How far are you going to go, Rachel?"

Rachel looked up at her new handler. Ashley was a tall, skinny stick of a blonde with a model's face Rachel had pulled from the secretary pool. Rachel had hated her from the moment she'd seen her and immediately dismissed her from her list of potential candidates. That is until she overheard her in the women's locker room gently talking another woman through recovering after being assaulted. Rachel had lingered in the doorway, out of sight, as Ashely had recommended resources and therapy. The whole conversation was soft and non-judgmental, and it had completely shifted Rachel's opinion of the beautiful woman. Ashley's tone spoke of a survivor and the steel core of someone forged in the deepest hells. Rachel had hired her on the spot.

"As far as I need to go, Ashley."

"Don't, Rach. Please. For your own sake, don't."

"It won't go how you think, Ashley."

Ashley pursed her lips, looking ready to respond, but instead, she stepped back and pulled the door open. Rachel met her eyes and nodded her thanks.

"Black or navy?"

"The suit?"

"Yes."

"Pink." Rachel's smile turned wicked. "Hot pink." She watched Ashley's pursed lips go slack and her jaw dropped. "We're subverting expectations today, aren't we?"

"Yes, ma'am, we are!" Ashley strode forward, delight and purpose etched into her movements.

In under an hour, Rachel stood on a seamstress's fitting stand, considering her look. Her suit's coat fit perfectly. The peak lapels, neat welt pockets, and single button closure spoke of precise tailoring and a professional fit. But unlike the men of the Pantheon, her suit was made of polyester and spandex blend that hugged her figure in a way that was guaranteed to turn heads if the miniskirt and bold pink color didn't already snap necks.

Ashley had ensured their tailor had left just enough ease at the waist to fit Rachel's tiny snub-nosed handgun in a shoulder holster. Rachel would have liked the drama of pulling a gun from her thigh, but her skirt wasn't long enough to cover it.

"What do you think?" Ashley asked as Rachel swung her arms, testing the ease in the shoulders.

"Grab me a big gold necklace and some hoops and it'll be perfect."

"Done. Snacks?"

"I'm Jumping inside the District. I won't need it until I get back. Hell, I don't need the usual tacti-bro bag either. Do we have any Balenciagas? Or a Birkin? Something black with gold accents?" Rachel had a little smile of hope in her heart that just once she could carry the type of bag she'd always dreamt of.

Ashley stared at her. "You think we just keep a Birkin lying around?"

"Yes?" The flutter of hope died but Rachel tried to keep her smile.

"Damn it, I can't pull anything on you. How did you know Madame Volaire pulled strings with every contact she had in Hermès to get us in? There are celebrities who can't get that access!"

"I didn't, I simply assumed this group had the access." She gave a throaty laugh. "After all, what's the point of being fabulously wealthy with access all over the globe if you can't use it for a little fun once in a while?"

Ashley shook her head and walked off, returning a moment later with a paper wrapped bundle. Rachel's grin broadened as Ashley set the parcel down.

"We couldn't get one in black with gold accents, so you'll have to settle for the camel with gold accents." She unwrapped the handbag and Rachel's heart soared.

The bag was more than a fashion accessory. It was a symbol. It was an aspiration. Teenage Rachel had dreamed of wealth and power, spent nights scheming of ways to leave her father's home, go to college, and land a job that gave her the wealth necessary to buy a bag that cost two months' worth of even *her* ridiculously high salary.

But life had happened.

Her father's abuse forced her to run away before she was old enough to drive. She sold stolen goods and drugs before she was finally forced to sell her last shred of dignity to afford food. Six years spent in the dismal hell of selling herself to the men who lived the life she wanted had made her teenage aspirations seem like a cruel joke.

Ashley placed the bag's strap over Rachel's wrist. She looked at herself in the mirror. Tall and lean, she wore her hot pink suit like armor with the Birkin a shield at her side. Years of dreaming manifested in the vision before her. Tears formed in the corners of her eyes.

"I look like Vietnamese Barbie," she told Ashley.

"You do. Now don't cry; you'll get red and it'll clash with the suit." Ashley's words were stern, but her voice was soft. She reached up and squeezed Rachel's hand, sisterly love and support flowing across the touch. Rachel jumped off the dressmaker's stand and hugged her.

"What's this? Is Rachel Ng hugging someone? Willingly?" Damarcus's voice came from behind them.

Rachel turned to see him stepping out of the men's dressing room, his delicious form draped in an Armani suit. She met his eyes and gave him a genuine smile.

Come here and find out, she told him across their open mental link.

Damarcus approached her slowly, waiting for her to spook and step back. Instead, she stepped into him, pulling him into a tight hug and let a hand sneak up to his neck. The touch across bare skin let him feel her happiness. Genuine pleasure in her life flowed to him.

You belong, Rachel, he told her.

I know. I finally know, she said. Before she could get cold feet, she pulled him in for a quick kiss.

Surprise and pleasure bounced between them. Rachel broke the kiss quickly, but the hand on his neck told him she was ready for more if he was willing. He gave her a quick nod.

"I'll see you when this is done, Rach."

"Count on it, Dee."

He stepped back from her embrace but took her hand, kissing the back of it with gentle and courtly grace. "Until then."

She smiled with delight at his actions and that he didn't bother cautioning her to keep her professionalism.

"Ms. Ng goes to Washington," she said to Damarcus and flashed three fingers as a countdown. "Eat your heart out Jimmy Stewart."

Two, she counted across her bond with Damarcus.

Fierce woman, he replied.

"One!" Rachel said and Jumped directly into a Cabinet member's personal office.

She landed neatly on the far side of the room, two plush leather chairs and his desk between them. Rachel's heart smiled and she silently thanked Damarcus for helping her sharpen her accuracy over the last few months.

The Secretary sat at his desk, looking every inch the business professional. He hunched over the desk, papers below his face, and a single cut crystal glass of clear liquid just out of his way. He rested his head against two fingers with his elbow propped on the desk. If Rachel didn't know better, she would have assumed he was actually working.

Sadly, she knew who he was inside.

Fortunately, she also knew exactly how to push his buttons.

"Good evening, Mr. Secretary," she all but purred.

His eyes snapped up and she walked carefully toward him. Each foot was placed precisely, her hips giving the most calculated sway. It was a sway that said as a businesswoman, she was all business, but that anyone daring enough to encounter her in a bar after hours was in for a thrill.

His eyes tracked every movement.

"My dear, it's after business hours and I am due to entertain constituents in an hour," he told her. His words were almost believable if the Secretary's voice wasn't thick with lust.

"Constituents?" she asked, smiling. "Or a girl? A girl like me, David?"

His eyes snapped from her hips to her face. "Diamond? Diamond Steele?"

Rachel looked slowly to the side, ignoring him while giving him a long look at her beautiful profile. "Diamond? Baby, she's dead."

"Dead? What? You're right in front of me," he said, clearly confused. "What do you want?" His voice was a little hiss as if he suspected his office was bugged.

He might have been smarter than he looked.

Rachel tilted her chin up slightly, eyes narrowing, and she stared down at him. This face was true evil, it had never seen toil in the sun. This man's shoulders had never slumped under the heat of a double shift over a minimum wage grill.

No, he'd been given a position of power over some of the most powerless, voiceless people in America and he'd exploited it. He judged the worth of a man by the labor his body provided. He gave housing choices based on the body's ability to produce. He had valued women less, arguing that their lack of strength made them less able to shoulder the rigors of physical labor. And if he saw you as a cripple? You were merely a waste, a drain on resources to him.

While the Administration had mostly kept him in check, the man had privately made it clear he would flip parties to maintain power.

From his dossier, Rachel knew he was also selling his influence to Russian oligarchs.

From her past, she knew almost every dark secret the man had ever whispered across a pillow.

"Justice," she whispered to herself. Rachel inhaled sharply and steeled herself. "I can't believe I am saying this, but I am here to protect you."

He looked panicked for a moment. "You're," he faltered, "you're with them?" The last word was a whisper as if he dreaded the "them" more than her miraculous appearance in his office.

"Them? They?" She smirked at him, trying not to enjoy keeping him on tenterhooks for too long. After all, she'd sworn she would be the Pantheon kind of professional tonight. "Am I one of them, Mr. Secretary?"

"Aren't you?" He stopped, glancing around. "Look, we can't talk here."

Rachel closed the gap between them. "Don't worry, Mr. Secretary, I know what you like." Her hard smile made his face go blank with fear.

She considered Jumping him to one of the many desolate warehouses Limitless Logistics kept in the nation's capital but wanted to play things above board. Spying his minibar, she sauntered to it. Crystal decanters snuggled beside cut crystal glasses that matched the one on his desk.

Rachel selected a decanter, popped the crystal stopper, and sniffing it, decided it would do. "Beluga Gold?" she asked as her hands found a stainless steel shaker.

"Yes? How did you know?"

Rachel turned slightly to smirk at him. "I've had my own dealings with Russians."

The distinct sound of ice hitting steel rang across the room. She poured two capfuls of the pricey vodka into the iced shaker.

"Where are your olives?"

"What?" He pushed the plush executive chair back from the desk as if he wanted to join her but stopped.

"Olives? Where are they? No one keeps cheese stuffed olives on their bartop unless they're an idiot. And while you *are* an idiot," she stressed, "you aren't *that kind* of idiot."

"Fridge under the counter," he choked out.

Rachel got the distinct impression that the more she spoke, the more it solidified in his mind who she was. Good. He should know who his salvation came from tonight. She yanked the bottle of olives from the fridge and plonked them down on the granite countertop with a hollow sound.

"You need more, you're almost out."

"I'll tell my girl," he said.

"Girl? Oh, Davey, baby tell me this one is at least legal to handle alcohol?" She gave him a wolfish smile when he grimaced.

"My staffing issues aren't your problem," he said in an attempt to be stern.

The sound of a shaker filled his office before she poured the drink into a fresh glass. Rachel took a single sip, enjoying the tiny chips of ice that floated in the briny vodka.

"No, you're right, your staff," she glanced at his crotch, "is no longer my problem." She set the Russian vodka laden martini down on his papers. "But unfortunately, you are my problem. Still."

"What do you want? Money? I have money," his eyes flicked to the corner desk that she knew held large sums of cash. Non-sequential and untraceable bills he used to pay women like her.

Rachel gave a throaty laugh and sat down across from him.

The training her one and only madam had instilled in her kicked in. She kicked both feet up on his desk and placed her hands just so, drawing his eyes to the long legs only barely covered by her bright pink business skirt.

"Davey, baby, I have access to more than money now. Why would I need something so," she paused, *"easy?"*

"What do you want?"

"Sadly, to keep your worthless carcass intact."

"What?"

"The Russians who give you that pile of cash," she pointed to his hidden stockpile, "want you dead. Or at least, the people who hate them more than I do want you dead. And lucky for you, I want you dead less than they do. In fact, it's in my best interest to keep you alive."

"What are you talking about you crazy bitch?" His façade of calm broken.

Rachel could have exploded in a rage. She could have given in to her slowly rising blood pressure and the cold fury that was building in her chest being around this slug of a man.

"David, I'm sorry to tell you that your backroom dealing with Russian oligarchs is at an end. Either they or their enemies want you dead. And if I let you die, one of those groups will make my life hell. So, while I would gladly sit back with this drink," she said and sipped, letting the vodka burn pleasantly down her throat, "and watch you fry, it would be inconvenient to me."

He stared at her, jaw on his chest.

"Be a good boy and get your public schedule off the books. Then disappear for the next three days. Hell, I don't even care which woman's legs you end up between, just know that if she isn't legal, I'll end you myself after this."

"You aren't blackmailing me? Over the sex? My," he hesitated, *"preferences?"*

Rachel set the drink down as she laughed until her sides hurt.

"Preferences?" She looked at him. "As if your vanilla ass was unique. You want a quick blowjob until you're ready, holding my hair like you have some power over me, of course. Then you give a cursory flick of my bean to make yourself feel like you did something." She ticked off his desires on her fingers like she was making a grocery list. "Then you give a few quick thrusts in missionary position until you come while grunting in my ear about how powerful you are?" She laughed again as his face fell. "God, men are so pathetic thinking their fantasy is unique."

"But … but …"

"Oh, and liking women who are just this side of eighteen? Oh no. Barely legal." She said flatly. "Yeah, gross, but definitely not unique or blackmailable." She sighed. "Fucking grow up and find a real kink. I hear leather and pegging are all the rage right now," she said, hoping he'd take the bait.

Something in his face flickered but he didn't comment. "You only want me to lay low?"

"Yes. Disappear. Don't be where the Russians, either of them, can find you."

"Thank you. Thank you, Diamond."

"It's Ms. Ng now. A woman has to maintain her standards."

Without another word, she Jumped.

THIRTY-ONE

MURPHY "ARES" HAWKINS
1547L/1947Z, 01 NOV

Murphy's boot heels landed tightly pressed against the wall of the Secretary of State's office. His arrival had been instantaneous and silent. A quick glance around the room showed him no one inside had noticed him yet. Somewhere inside, Murphy's tactical brain smiled at how easily he could infiltrate a location.

"Get me on with the Bulgarian Ambassador this afternoon and follow up directly after with the Jordanian Ambassador," Maureen Mitchell's voice carried to Murphy's spot on the wall. I want a chance to speak with each Ambassador personally before the end of the week. It should help smooth some of the turmoil my predecessor left in his wake."

Their backs to him, two of her staffers diligently noted her directions. Murphy could see her face between them but if she saw him, she said nothing to alert the two staffers.

"That will be all for now, gentlemen," she said in a firm, but polite dismissal. The two men strode out, still oblivious to Murphy's arrival.

He watched Maureen tidy the papers in front of her and turn to a small laptop on the desk. Murphy wondered if she'd truly not noticed him. He started mentally rehearsing how he was going to convince the notoriously prickly woman to lay low for the next three days when her voice carried to his spot on the wall.

"General Murphy, you know it's impolite to lurk in people's offices?"

"Yes, ma'am," he said with a small grin. She was sharper than she looked.

"How long have you been there?"

"How long do you think I've been here?"

"I think you arrived as we were discussing my afternoon agenda."

"You don't miss much do you, ma'am?" The question was rhetorical, he didn't expect an answer as he strode toward her desk. She gestured to the chair across from her for him to sit.

"You're a Southern boy, aren't you?"

"Yes, ma'am. What gave it away? I know I don't have much of an accent anymore."

"You've called me 'ma'am' three times in under two minutes." She gave him a motherly smile. "Where are you from, General Murphy?"

"North Central Florida, Secretary Mitchell."

"Call me Maureen. Val and Dee are both on a first name basis with me."

"What about Marco? Or Mandy?"

Maureen leaned back from the desk. "Mr. Martinez and I had a very different relationship than I do with you younger leaders. It was," she paused, thinking, "not combative. But, more formal. As for Ms. Squires, I like the girl and she did well after the Battle for D.C., but I haven't seen her since. She's even dodged all my offers to attend church. I know the family saga is causing issues, but I thought she was more reasonable."

Murphy nodded. He knew things had gotten tense between Mandy and Val, but didn't realize that Val trusted the Secretary enough to bring her in on such personal Pantheon business.

"Not to be rude, but why are you popping into my office unannounced today?"

"I come with a warning, ma'am," he tried to make himself sound serious but not ominous. Murphy sat up very straight in his chair.

"Oh, dear me, I hope you aren't playing good cop, bad cop with

Val." Maureen shook her head with a little grin.

"Not at all, sorry ma'am. I mean, we've got credible intelligence that you and several other prominent members of American society are at risk. I'm here to request you take the next few days out of the public spotlight. Don't follow your public calendar. Hell, don't be in this office."

"Watch your words, boy." Maureen snapped and leaned forward again. "I'm a good Christian woman."

"Sorry, ma'am."

"But I take your warning. I believe we have some of the same folks giving us threat briefings and I take your words seriously." She leaned all the way back in the chair. "Can I keep my Undersecretaries at their duties?"

"Yes?" Murphy was hesitant. "We believe that anyone in the State building could be at risk, so it may be prudent to have them work elsewhere."

Maureen nodded. "I can't halt the business of the government, son. But I will recommend they alter their public calendars as much as possible to be out of these spaces. When do we think this threat ends?"

"When we catch *Svoboda*."

"Give me a time, I can't be gone forever."

"Three days. Probably two."

"Very well." Maureen eyed him. "You are the CEO of Spartan Tactical, are you not?"

"Yes, ma'am."

"And do you have the personnel and funding you need?"

"I have as many support personnel as I need, yes. But I always need new primary members." He was careful, even now, how he phrased things. The old habits of hiding their organization died hard.

"Tougher when certain members go missing and turn up dead, isn't it?"

Murphy sat bolt upright in his chair. *Fucking politicians, always came at things sideways.*

"No, ma'am, that is certainly a tough spot. Although—" he cut himself off.

"Mr. Nelson was a loose cannon and you aren't terribly put out that he's gone," she stated for him.

"I'd never say I cheer for a man's death but, yes, Chadwick was … difficult."

"He was drugged out of his gourd and was a horse's ass. He put you *all* at risk. He made your job unnecessarily difficult, he put himself at risk, he was uncontrollable, he risked the whole team's missions, and, most importantly, he put national security at risk with his antics."

"Not to put too fine a point on it, but yes, ma'am." Murphy gave her a wry smile which she returned.

"While I will give bashing the not-so-dearly-departed a rest as he is no longer a threat to you, there is a threat that remains." Maureen leaned back in her chair and let the silence between them stretch. When the thread of tension felt like it might snap, she finally relented. "Son, don't make me state the obvious."

"Someone took down a Pantheon member, murdered them, actually, and they have yet to be apprehended," Murphy told her, agitation evident in the set of his shoulders.

"And?" Maureen's tone held the gentle prompting of a teacher pushing their favorite pupil.

"Val said you've been holding the story back from the news media. Chadwick was new enough that he didn't get any fame during the Battle for D.C. and therefore, no one has paired him with us. But if they do …"

"*When* they do, all hell breaks loose. Worse, you have vigilante nut jobs, the same ones that are howling for registration, thinking they can bag a Pantheon member for street cred."

"We call it 'clout,' ma'am," Murphy said with a grim smile.

"For clout then. They will think that taking one of you down means you're vulnerable." She paused and dropped her chin to her chest. "And what's worse is you are vulnerable. Someone did get on the inside."

"They had access," Murphy said tightly.

Maureen's head snapped up. "You know who did it then?"

Murphy's mouth pinched into a thin line. "Not one hundred

percent, but yes."

"They aren't the type to turn themselves in, are they?"

"No, ma'am, as you might be able to conclude, they're the type who thinks they're above the law. They believe their actions are for the greater good. Or that they can avoid the consequences of their actions," Murphy ground out the last words.

Maureen met his eyes. "This isn't the first time?"

Her question was rhetorical. She held his gaze. In an instant, Murphy knew that this whole verbal dance had been just that, a dance around the truth. Maureen already knew who killed Chadwick and if she didn't know for sure, she knew with as much certainty as Murphy.

Powell.

Murphy gave a nod which Maureen returned.

"Find him. We both know his actions can be attributed to the Department of State. Tell him if he sees me, I will find a way to spin the story and find him immunity."

Murphy jerked back. "You really want to give him an out?" Disgust dripped from his question.

"No, son. That's what I'm asking you to tell him."

"What will happen to him?" Murphy asked hesitantly.

"Do you need to know?" Maureen shot back.

Murphy considered it. His mind started spinning down several dark paths. He blinked and cleared his mind. "No. I neither need nor want to know what happens after this."

"Good. He has until tomorrow evening to meet me here." She sighed. "And Murphy?"

"Yes ma'am?"

"Support Valerie, she's going to need it after this."

"Yes ma'am. Now, if you'll excuse me, I need to meet with someone."

"Thank you, General Murphy."

"Ma'am," he said as he stood and Jumped to Point Zero.

He pulled out his phone and punched 'Asshole' on his contact list.

P, you need to meet me in the next hour. I know what you've done but I have an out. He punched the send button, annoyed the touch screen's haptics didn't have the same feel as angrily mashing the old hard key "Send" button on his radios.

Rock Creek Park, 2 hours, was the terse reply a moment later.

"That's fucking rich," Murphy muttered to himself. "At least he's answering me, unlike everyone else."

Agitated, he headed to the headquarters' security office to pull CCTV footage.

It was as Murphy pulled the last videos from the park that he realized Maureen had agreed to avoid the State Department for the next three days.

THIRTY-TWO

MURPHY "ARES" HAWKINS
1759L/2159Z, 01 NOV

Exactly two hours later, Murphy Jumped to Rock Creek Park, landing ten feet from where Chadwick's body had been found.

The yellow tape that had cordoned off his body was gone now and no visible trace of his death remained. Still, parkgoers skirted around the area. Whether they knew a dead man's body lay there or not, they seemed to instinctively avoid even looking at the location.

Murphy looked at the spot, considering how Powell may have killed him. Drugs, certainly. Lots of drugs to incapacitate. The police hadn't said anything about a gunshot wound and he hadn't taken the opportunity to ask Val if she had seen an autopsy report. Murphy's eyes searched the ground for signs of blood but found nothing but verdant grass.

"Did you really think there would be traces of it still?" Powell's voice behind him startled him.

Murphy composed himself and turned to face Powell. "No, I suppose I didn't."

"You know then." It wasn't a question; it was a statement of fact.

"What do I know, Powell?"

"Well, first of all, you know I won't say anything out loud." Powell was on edge. "You know what happened or strongly suspect. And you offered an out. Honestly, I'm a little surprised you would cover for me."

Murphy exploded. Months of pent up anger and frustration at Powell came out in a torrent of words. "Cover for you? Fuck you. I can't say I'll miss Chadwick's loose cannon with powers but fuck you if you think I'm covering for you right now. This is bigger than you, asshole, and all the things you think you're doing to 'help' have only made it worse for us. All of us but most especially Val."

"Fuck you too, you self-righteous prick. I *am* helping. Do you think Val needs a guy like that on your team? Some self-aggrandizing coked out, rich bastard who just happens to realize he can Jump? Do you need a guy like that? Do you really want to spend the first few years as a CEO trying to keep him in check?"

"No, but I didn't want this either. You fucking—"

"Don't say it!" Powell cut him off.

"Why? Why did you do it? And don't fucking tell me it was for us. Don't even try to tell me it was for Val, I've heard that excuse before too!"

"I needed it. Val—"

"Don't lie, Powell!"

Powell tensed. "I needed him to stop. He was messing with Val," Powell emphasized. "It was getting to her and stressing her out."

"So?"

"Her stress is my stress," he said, that stress clear in his tone and the firm set of his jaw. "It's how I work. I couldn't have her coming home every night and bringing her day back with her. It was killing me."

"Then just break it off with her, man. God! Find a woman with a normal job who doesn't deal with stress like this."

"I can't! Don't you see? I can't anymore." Powell sank to the ground, putting his head in his hands. "She's … she's like a drug, Murphy. She's a drug."

Murphy looked down at the man. In an instant, everything he thought he knew about the man unraveled.

"You've been manipulating her emotions for your own gain, haven't you?"

"Yes," he whispered. "It was a little at first. She'd be stressed and

I'd calm her. That calm would come back to me, a little dopamine, you know? But then she got more stressed and I did it more. When she broke it off with me before the Battle for D.C., I thought I might die. I would do anything to make her happy."

"But not like a normal man. A normal man wants to make his partner happy for the sake of their partner's happiness, but you …"

"It was selfish." Powell shook his head. "I needed her happiness. I practically fed on it. I'd push that calm as hard as I could without her noticing." He shook his head again. "And then this asshole comes along and he's worse than that Russian punk. She's so stressed all the time. I thought I could eliminate a threat to the Pantheon and get her back too. I want her. I need her."

"That's why you proposed?"

"That? Yeah. I fucked that up good, didn't I?"

"Shit, you didn't even get the ring right, dude. I mean, geez."

"I bought the biggest rock I could afford. I thought …"

Murphy could see tears starting to course down his cheeks. He wasn't intimately familiar with addicts but he had seen a few meth heads in his hometown. They'd whine, lie, make excuses, then lie again to your face to get their fix. Powell must have realized the futility of lying to someone who could read his thoughts with a touch. Murphy shook his head.

There was no methadone for what Val created in Powell. He was addicted and there was no cure. Powell was as dangerous in his own way as Chadwick had been.

Murphy let his shoulders slump as he realized what he needed to do next. In that moment he hated himself almost as much as he hated Powell. "I think I know someone who can help us," he said quietly.

"You'll help me? You'll actually help cover for me?" Powell's voice was nearly frantic and thick with his tears.

"No. That horrible racist in Alaska was the last time I cover for you. I'm certainly not covering murder for you, Powell," Murphy spit. "But Maureen can help."

"Maureen Mitchell? The Secretary of State?" Powell's voice was incredulous and he stood up, meeting Murphy's eyes.

"She's been sitting on the media, keeping this from exploding, and I think she can help us. I'm not sure what she's really offering, but it sounded like you might avoid jail time."

"And Val?"

Murphy shook his head. "I can't speak for her. Talk to Maureen, be honest, and see what she can do. After all, you work for the State Department, don't you?"

Powell nodded. "Just," he hesitated, "just don't tell Val what you know yet, okay? Let me talk to Maureen first."

"Fine, but this is the last favor you ever get from me, Powell."

THIRTY-THREE

VALERIE "ATHENA" HALL
1255L/1655Z, 01 NOV

"Anna, can you contact Nurse Sarah in the clinic?" Val's knuckles were white as she gripped the chair next to Anna's desk. "I'm not feeling well."

"Ooh, child, yes." Anna grabbed the phone as she gave Val a sympathetic nod, having flipped from the no-nonsense secretary to a concerned mother in half a second. Anna spoke briefly, nodded once, and hung up the phone. "She can see you right now and says Exam Room One is clear."

Val nodded once and Jumped to the clinic. The exam room's harsh fluorescent lighting hit her as hard as the pungent antiseptic odor. Wrinkling her nose in distaste, Val settled herself on the paper lined exam table. The room's door opened as soon as she was settled.

"Good morning, Val. What brings you in today?" Nurse Sarah asked kindly. She moved with brisk efficiency to place a blood pressure cuff on Val's arm but gave every indication she was listening.

"My, uh, cramps right now. My periods have been all messed up and I'm tired as hell, Sarah," Val told her as Sarah placed the cuff on her arm.

Sarah nodded, placing a pulse ox monitor on her finger as well. "Can you be more specific? What does 'all messed up' mean?" She

223

punched a green button on her equipment and the machine began to hum.

"Heavy. Irregular," Val told her, wincing as the cuff reached maximum pressure. "I don't think I'm skipping them, but they aren't regular like they were before. I'm guessing from the extreme weight loss. And I'm tired. More than when I was first losing the weight this spring."

Sarah gave a hum of understanding. "I understand you and Mr. Powell were seeing one another again. Did you use protection?"

Val blushed and looked away. "No."

"Are you trying to conceive?"

"No!"

"You aren't using any protection and my notes say you haven't received any birth control from us. So, that means you're trying to conceive."

"No, I just—" Val started but Sarah cut her off.

"General Valerie Hall, if you are having intercourse without protection then you are trying to conceive. You are smart enough to know better."

Val's head hung. "Yes, Sarah."

"I'll need to check your hormones," Sarah told her. "That means I need blood. Given the fatigue, I'll need blood anyway. We'll do a full CBC, metabolic panel, thyroid, and I'll check your iron to see if that's where the fatigue is coming from." She paused and pinned Val with a hard stare. "But I'm also doing a test for pregnancy hormones, hCG. Go see Tim in the labs and I'll call you when I have something."

Thirty minutes later, Val sat disgruntled and embarrassed in her office when the phone rang. She hated needles and thought the seven vials of blood she'd given were excessive given her fatigue. She punched the line open, "Valerie Hall."

"Ma'am, your bloodwork is done. Come on down to the lab."

"Okay, Sarah."

"And Val," Sarah said gently, "bring a friend." The line clicked off.

Val swore inventively and dialed Powell's desk number. It rang three times before going to voicemail. She called his cellphone from her with the same result. Finally, she shot him a text, indicating she had a matter of some urgency that needed his attention. She realized she didn't really want him there and she'd called by reflex and maybe because she assumed this was a mess they'd created together.

Val pulled out her phone and opened her texts. *Mandy? Sounds like Sarah needs to talk to me and said to bring a friend. You free?*

A friend, really? Was Mandy's terse reply. *Everything okay?* She finally asked.

Honestly? Probably not, Sarah wouldn't tell me to bring someone otherwise. Obviously, Bran's not free. Exam Room One.

Kelly?

I want you, my friend.

Fine. Be right there.

Val Jumped, Mandy appearing beside her. Val was surprised to see Mandy Jump in after the fuss she'd made that last time they spoke. Maybe something in Val's tone told her how scared Val was. Mandy took the hand Val held out, clearly willing to put aside all the pain and friction of the last few weeks, and sighed at the worry that flowed across her touch.

"You'll be okay, Val."

A tendril of hope stretched between them.

"Val, have a seat, please. Hello, Hestia." Nurse Sarah said when she entered.

"Mandy," she corrected, almost absent mindedly.

She took a deep breath. "Valerie, you aren't pregnant."

Mandy's eyebrows shot up.

"Thank goodness," Val sighed in relief. An echo of relief tinged with curiosity bounced back at her through Mandy's hand.

"But you were pregnant," Sarah told her.

Val blinked hard as the words washed over her.

"Your hormone levels indicate you were recently pregnant and are currently having a miscarriage, not a heavy period."

Val stared at her, trying to understand. "I was pregnant?"

"Young, healthy women, of childbearing age who have unprotected intercourse become pregnant, Valerie."

A surprising shot of anger flowed across Mandy and Val's hands. "But I'm not now?"

"No," Sarah's voice held the professional neutrality of someone who spent a long time delivering news, unsure of how it would be taken.

"Is this why I've been fatigued?"

"More than likely. The early stages of pregnancy are usually marked by fatigue."

"This is the third time this has happened," Val said, shocked.

"Third time?" Nurse Sarah asked. She brought her pen back up to her clipboard.

"May, uh, not long after Murphy moved that helicopter I had a really heavy one. Then again in August after—" her voice trailed off.

"After the Battle for D.C.?" Nurse Sarah asked.

Val nodded.

"And now, when we've been in a complete upheaval for what? A week? A month? Then this is likely the third miscarriage you've had in a row. I need to get you on birth control, for your own health." Genuine concern suffused Sarah's face.

"But, Sarah," Val asked softly, "why have they all ended?" Her hand clutched at Mandy's. "I mean, I'm not trying to get pregnant, but three miscarriages seem like a lot for a 'young, healthy woman, of childbearing age who has unprotected intercourse,' right?"

Sarah nodded thoughtfully once. "Many young women do miscarry, we don't talk about it as much as perhaps we should, so it's not surprising you don't know the statistics but—" Sarah's mouth firmed into a thin line as she cut herself off. "You know that Hera and Zeus never had children, right?"

"Yes," Mandy spoke for the first time, a kind of horror tinging her voice.

"I have a theory," Sarah said. She held her hand out for Val and Mandy to touch. "The link? This emotional connection you feel with direct contact?" Sarah's eyes echoed the sadness that flowed across her touch, "I think it keeps the pregnancies from going to full term."

A spike of painful loss crossed the bond and Mandy released both their hands.

"Sarah? Are you," Val swallowed hard and continued, "are you saying that my own emotions are terminating these pregnancies?"

The look Nurse Sarah gave her was tinged with pity. A long silence stretched before she finally answered, "I think so."

"I can't *not* feel for nine months," Val said quietly. She glanced at Mandy, the other woman's face slowly becoming overwhelmed by fear and pain. "Are you saying I'll never carry a child to full term?"

Sarah shook her head slowly. "I'm not sure. It's only a theory and all I have to go on are Hera's old medical records and your current state, but I don't think you will. Either of you. Or Rachel."

Val let her eyes go unfocused, staring somewhere beyond the bland beige wall in front of her. She reached for Mandy's hand again and met only air. Val turned to Mandy and found she was pressing herself against the exam room's wall, almost physically recoiling from Val.

"Hestia? Mandy?" Val asked, feeling for any remnants of their mental bond. Any connection they had ever had was gone.

The missing bond was as painful as a tooth, forcibly pulled, and the void as painful.

"Hestia?" Mandy whispered. "What a joke. Goddess of Hearth and Home? How can I be any of that if I can't have a family? I'll never be a mother, Val." Her face was pale, bloodless, and blank.

"It's only a theory, Mandy. When you're ready, you can try. We talked about this."

Mandy gave a bitter laugh. "With who? Who, Val? Murphy doesn't want me. I hear everything from other men. How will I ever even have a normal relationship?"

"Mandy, you'll find—"

"No, Val, I won't!" Mandy cut her off. "I won't find Mr. Right and even if I did, I can't have children with him."

"There are other options, Amanda. Gestational carriers. Adoption." Nurse Sarah told her. She walked toward Mandy to console her, but Mandy recoiled further.

"No. That's not," she swallowed hard. "I'll never have the experience of carrying my own child. I'll never have a husband.

A family. Even my friends are pushing me away." She shot a dark glance at Val.

"I'm not the one pushing people away," Val snapped.

"I've been replaced in every way, Valerie," Mandy snarled. "As your handler, your friend, and I will be replaced as the CEO of Limitless."

Val watched as Mandy's face changed. The fear and sorrow morphed into anger, hardening her into someone almost unrecognizable. But then Val saw it, the face that peered out from Mandy's angry eyes, it was the same look she had seen cross Miller's face just before she shot him dead.

"My father is gone. Marco is gone. Apollo is not my brother, no matter what blood ties he claims. You've replaced me in every way. I will never bear my own children and build the family that makes me a 'Goddess of Hearth and Home.' I am Hestia no more. And I'm not your friend anymore." She shook her head once. "Goodbye, Valerie."

"Mandy?"

Mandy looked at her sadly.

"Amanda," Val said sharply.

Mandy shook her head.

"Amanda Squires, stop!"

"Squires? Or Thompson?" Mandy gave a mirthless laugh. "Either way, she's dead, Val. Let her go."

Without another word, she Jumped.

THIRTY-FOUR

VALERIE "ATHENA" HALL
0902L/1302Z, 02 NOV

Anticipation.

Research shows that anticipating an event induces stress on the body. In cases of sporting events, this is a positive and performance enhancing stress. But long, persistent stress has the opposite effect. The body can only hold itself in a state of fight readiness for so long before fatigue sets in and it negatively impacts the body's systems.

Since four in the morning, Val's team had endured five false alarms. With each, a credible source had warned them of a potential event matching what they anticipated from *Svoboda*. The team had sprung into action, ready to Jump to the three potential departure sites, only to be pulled back at the last moment.

On top of the rumors of events on US soil, sporadic reports of attacks on Russian soil flowed in as well. The last five hours had seen a list of Russian dead parade across her desk, the most concerning of which was a company of *Spetsnaz* special operations soldiers, eliminated without survivors. Val had asked the intel team to break off two analysts to cross-reference the names of the dead to known *Vmeste* members. Val worried that *Svoboda* was pressing their attack and systematically destroying the Russian oligarchy and their pet Jumpers.

"Apollo, how many?"

"Oligarchs? I do not know, but," he looked over the list, "this is a lot."

"Do you think *Svoboda* can kill them all? And," she hesitated, "then what?"

"Power vacuum?" He shrugged. "Money will always flow but with those who move it gone, the turmoil will make Russian political leadership weak for a time until the dust and money settles."

"How long?" Val's mind churned through possibilities and international security implications.

"If the end of the Cold War is any indication? A few years."

"Years? We don't have years."

"No, we do not, but we also do not have the manpower, or perhaps the willpower, to save Russian oligarchs."

"We?"

"We," he said with finality. "I joined you, Valerie. Am I not one of you?"

Val summoned a smile. "Yes, you have proven that you are trustworthy."

She held out a hand, palm up. He let his own hand rest lightly on it, letting a feeling of acceptance and peace flow between them. Val tried to lock away the broken parts of her heart his sister had left behind but he caught them.

"She may come back," he said quietly.

Val released his hand. "Maybe."

Apollo waited a beat before giving her a quick nod and departing to give her space. As soon as the door closed, she burst into tears again.

Val flipped her phone over, looking for any texts. It was blank. She bit her lip and thumbed the device open. Under Mandy's name, seven unread text messages stared back at her. She closed them and opened Powell's name. She hadn't texted him, waiting and hoping he would reach out first. The last text she'd sent was informing him they had captured Russian assets. The last time she had seen him, he'd rushed away from her after she had admitted she didn't really want to marry him. Surely, that would have merited a call, a text, a carrier pigeon, a smoke signal, something.

She sighed. She knew, or suspected, what he'd done. Every moment he was silent increased her surety. She needed to speak to him. If for no other reason than to tell him about the baby and break things off formally. Stomach turning at the drama of it, she sent the text she knew would draw his attention, even if it was so melodramatic it would be rejected as a soap opera storyline.

Bran, you have to call me. I lost our baby.

If that didn't get his response, she didn't know what would. To ignore that would be the ultimate betrayal and mean he was gone for good. Val put her head in her hands.

Val jerked back in surprise when her desk phone rang. Shock rooted her to her chair, thinking this was finally Powell reaching out. The second ring cut off abruptly and by the time she picked up the handset, the line was dead.

Val dropped the handset back into its cradle and stood, brushing down her pants in frustration. She Jumped to the conference room's small Point Zero.

"Team, status report," she said to the room.

"All previous leads closed out, ma'am," Kelly told her.

"Social media?" She and the team had set triggers to notify them if an event generated social media engagement.

Explosion.

Assassination.

Sabotage.

The list wasn't long, but they were *Svoboda's* favorite ways to attack.

"Cold," Kelly informed Val. "Everything the filters snag is coming from outside the US."

"Can you focus inside the US?" Val asked. She saw Kelly pull a face. "No, no we can't. That would be spying on US citizens, wouldn't it?"

Kelly nodded. "It's already shaky legal ground as we have it set up now, Val."

Val nodded. "Forget I asked." She shook her head in frustration. "We need more contacts inside the FBI to get this stuff."

"I'm working on it, Val. They're trying to set it up, but they don't have access to the same suite of tools as us, even though it's the same software."

"Well, isn't that the most bureaucratic bullshit today?" Val said dryly. Another cramp hit her and she nearly doubled over in pain.

"Val!" Kelly raced to her side. "Do I need to call Sarah?"

Val waved her off with one hand, grasping her belly with the other. "No, I saw her yesterday."

"Are you okay? I mean, I know you aren't but what's wrong?" Kelly leaned over beside her and put a comforting hand on her back.

Val opened her mouth but snapped it shut again. She wasn't upset over the loss of a pregnancy she had neither planned for nor wanted, but something made her hesitate.

"It's nothing," Val told her.

"It's something! You're white as a sheet. I'm calling Sarah."

"It's a miscarriage, Kelly," she whispered to her handler. "So, it's literally nothing. Nothing comes of this."

Val looked up at Kelly who was looking down at her, face drawn with sadness. "I'm so sorry Val. I, uh, I lost one too a few years ago. It wasn't planned, but it hit me hard too."

Val reached for Kelly's other hand and could feel the woman's pain threaded with love and support. "Thank you, Kelly. This wasn't planned either. I'm relieved? I can't imagine having a baby with Powell now! But I'm ashamed of myself for feeling relief? And I'm just plain tired."

"It's okay, Val. You'll recover. And if you want to try again, you can."

Val looked up at her again. She couldn't speak, only slowly shaking her head as emotions bubbled up in her chest, choking off her words.

"Oh, Val!" Kelly scooped her up into a hug and the two cried for everything that would never be.

They broke apart after a long moment, each wiping their own tears away. A glance around the room told her everyone was very careful not to look their way, studiously ignoring her breakdown.

"Look, Val, if you need more time, we can go to your office, close your door, and ask Anna to stonewall everyone for a half hour.

You know she'll guard you better than I could and take no shit about not letting folks through unless the world starts ending."

Val hesitated a moment before letting her better judgment prevail. "Yes, that's probably good. I just need a moment to pull myself together."

"Great. I'll go let—"

Kelly's assurance was cut off by every alarm in the building.

THIRTY-FIVE

BRANDON POWELL
0902L/1302Z, 02 NOV

"I'm here to meet with Secretary Mitchell," Powell's voice was firm even though he felt like his resolve would crumble at the flick of a feather.

"Name?"

"I'll be on the books as Mr. Black," he said quietly. Powell swallowed hard. The consequences his actions were catching up to him. For years he had been accountable only to himself, never questioned by supervisors, and granted autonomy. The Agency had given him a strange sense of power that was now being ripped away by his own choices.

The executive assistant nodded once, unfazed. "She's unavailable today."

"I was told she'd see me. She wanted to see me." Powell shifted, frustration and irritation making him twitch. "I was specifically told to be here today." Sweat was forming all over and he could feel beads of sweat forming under this dress shirt. He tugged at his collar.

The executive assistant gave him a blank look that said he couldn't care less. Powell could feel his anger rising in his chest. He had this one shot. One and only one shot to fix everything. He needed it. He needed to get immunity from Secretary Mitchell. Surely, she'd understand. She wouldn't have asked him here today if she weren't about to offer him some kind of plea deal or immunity. He was protecting Val. Protecting Limitless. Surely, she'd understand.

Powell took a deep breath and had the sudden realization of how chaotic his thoughts were. Like a man suddenly sober and realizing how his mind was swirling in a drunken chaos.

"I'm sorry, perhaps I got my appointment wrong," he said, trying to lace just the right amount of charm into his voice.

The secretary rolled his eyes, just a tiny bit, but nodded. "Look, Mr. Black," he said with a half smile, "She's not in the building today. Short notice schedule change, you know? Do you think you can talk to the Undersecretary instead? He's in."

Powell hesitated. He knew all the Undersecretaries were in the know but wondered if this was a more personal deal with Maureen Mitchell and not the Secretary of State. As he considered it, the Undersecretary emerged from his office.

"Jimmy, get the Ukrainian ambassador please." The man nodded briefly to Powell.

Powell's phone buzzed.

Bran, you have to call me. I lost our baby. The text flashed on his lock screen. Powell's stomach dropped. She couldn't be serious. This couldn't be real. Powell started sweating in earnest. He opened the text and smashed the call button for Val's direct line.

"Sir, you know you can buzz me to make these kinds of requests," his executive assistant said with a halfhearted laugh.

"Sure, but then how am I supposed to get my steps in?" He turned to Powell and gave him a smile. "They tell me 10,000 a day is good for me. Can you believe that?"

Before Powell could respond, a man appeared in front of them. Powell's long-standing relationship with Limitless Logistics made him familiar with that type of entrance. The Secretary and his assistant, however, rocked back with surprise. Doing a double take, Powell took a step back as well, hitting the end button on his phone.

"Pyotr!"

The man's face was haggard. Thoughts of IV nutrition flitted in Powell's chaotic brain before he registered what Pyotr held.

"Bomb! Bomb! Bomb!" Powell shouted drawing his gun and

shooting Pyotr in the chest. The man staggered back a step, blood appearing at the bottom of his ribcage, and two more men appeared beside him. Without hesitation, Powell shot each neatly through the head.

Powell realized too late that each had held a Deadman switch. A bloodied Pyotr Jumped away as the two others fell, their hands going slack.

Powell's last thought was that perhaps, by shooting Pyotr, he'd defended Val once last time.

THIRTY-SIX

VALERIE "ATHENA" HALL

0923L/1323Z, 02 NOV

"Sitrep!" Val barked.

"Social media is reporting an explosion at the Department of State," Joe told her from a bank of computers along the wall.

"News media?"

"They're not on it yet."

"Can you pull CCTV of the exterior?"

"No," Joe told her, "but I don't need to." A few taps on the keyboard brought up shaky video from a social media stream on the room's main screen. Several other videos popped up beside it as the team narrowed their filters to the State Department building. Each video showed the pale stone building framed in smoke, with debris littering the sidewalks below.

"Anyone know State well enough to know where that is?" Damarcus asked from beside Val, having Jumped in silently when the alarm sounded.

Joe squinted at it but stayed silent.

"It's the executive suite, Dee," Kelly told him. "I've been there before, that's their corner."

"Fuck," Val whispered. "Get Maureen on the phone. Murphy, she agreed to be out of the building, right?" Val watched something flicker across his face. "Murphy? She agreed, right?"

"Yeah," Murphy told her and gave a little shudder.

Val's narrowed her eyes and he gave his head a quick shake.

"Later, Val. It's gotta wait right now," Murphy told her. "We need to move out."

Val frowned but accepted it. She turned back to Damarcus, "We've got to check the others, ensure they're safe."

"No, Valerie," Apollo cut her off. "We can check them later. Pyotr and the rest of them will be at their hold point prepping to leave. We have an opportunity to catch them now."

"I can't stop them from Jumping," Val told him.

"Rachel," he turned to her. Like Damarcus, she'd Jumped in silently and was listening to the conversation. "Dart them. Drug them and keep them down. You had suggested that to Murphy and Damarcus, yes?"

Val frowned as Rachel nodded. She closed her eyes, dreading what she would say next, but she knew that like with Chadwick, there was no other choice.

"No," Val said quietly. "No darts."

"Val—" Murphy started but she cut him off.

"Extreme prejudice."

The room went silent. Murphy and Damarcus both stared at her, but Apollo nodded.

"Rachel, suppress them on arrival. Dee, Murphy, me."

"And me," Apollo spoke up.

Val nodded. "You deserve the opportunity. Anyone disagree? I won't hold it against you and you can be dismissed from this mission, but say it now. Murphy's right, we have to go."

She looked at Damarcus who looked conflicted but nodded. Murphy gave one quick nod as well. Val looked at Rachel who gave her a thumbs up, a grim look on her face.

"Warehouse in three, two, one."

They landed on the loft platform and were knocked to the ground.

"Rachel!" Val could hear Murphy groan out from his place on the floor.

A second groan came from beside her and she saw a bloodied Pyotr beside her. "Here! Keep him down, Rach!"

Val rolled away and stood up. The other four came up beside her.

"It's just him," Murphy told her, his weapon up and ready.

Apollo kicked Pyotr in the ribs before Val could stop him. He yelled something in what she assumed was Russian. Pyotr spat something back at him with equal ferocity, blood coming from his mouth.

"Apollo!" Val brought her gun up on the man. "Don't make me regret trusting you."

Apollo stepped back, hands up. "I apologize Valerie. I asked him where Alexei and Yuri were. They are dead."

"Good," Val told him. She turned to Pyotr. "You blew the building, didn't you?"

"Fuck you," he spit the words at her. More blood bubbled at the corner of his mouth and he laughed.

"Why are you laughing asshole? You're dying," Murphy told him.

"You bring your own doom," he responded. "We killed *Vmeste*. We kill the leaders. There is nothing to stop war now."

Apollo knelt down swiftly, putting his gun to Pyotr's shoulder. "This is for Adam. You killed my lover, I will make your death extra painful." Apollo pulled the trigger, destroying Pyotr's shoulder.

Pyotr howled in pain, incoherent screams fading into a choked sob.

"Not just *your* lover," Pyotr finally ground out.

"Don't," Murphy warned him.

"What?" Val asked him.

Pyotr gave a choked laugh, blood streaming from his mouth. "I killed your man on the way out," he said, looking Val dead in the eyes.

"No!" Val yelled. "Liar! Fucking liar!" She lunged at the man, shaking his one remaining shoulder, hands brushing the exposed skin of his neck. She locked eyes with him and watched the life fade from them. But, as his mind faded into death, she could see the image of Powell shooting him in the Secretary of State's front office.

THIRTY-SEVEN

VALERIE "ATHENA" HALL
0929L/1329Z, 02 NOV

Val's head reeled and she staggered against Murphy. Hands caught her and eased her to the ground.

Val tried to shut out the image of Powell shooting Pyotr. Powell in the State Department. In the leadership's front office. The front office that was now blown to pieces.

"We've got to get rid of the body, Dee," Murphy's voice broke through her shock.

Val shook off the hands that were keeping her upright and stood back up. Val waved away help.

"I'll be fine. Let's get to work," she told them. "Dee! You, Rachel, and Apollo take him to spot Bravo. That should be remote enough to keep any unfortunate hikers from stumbling on him."

Damarcus nodded and Rachel looked like she would protest but Val's face silenced her protests.

"Murphy, we need to tell Maureen."

"I'm sure she'd been informed by now."

"About the explosion, sure. But she needs to know what he said, about *Vmeste* and the oligarchs. We need to be ready. She needs to be ready."

Murphy nodded. "Do you think she'll still be on our side?"

"What do you mean?"

"Someone just teleported into the State Department and assassinated anyone who was in there. It'll be hard for her to publicly back us when undoubtedly this will further turn America's opinion of us."

Val sighed. He was probably right. "We'll just have to see. Did she say where she would be if she was staying out of the State building?"

"No," Murphy told her.

Val held her hand out. "Okay, she's probably in her home then."

Murphy eyed her hand, hesitating before finally touching her hand to get the visual. The brief contact pushed agitation, fear, and guilt.

"Murphy?" Val asked once he had the visual.

He shook his head. "Let's go."

They landed in Maureen's plush living room, startling a Diplomatic Security Service agent. He drew his weapon and had it trained on the two of them before they could identify themselves.

"It's alright, Chuck, I was expecting them," Maureen's voice came from the doorway to her dining room. "Come in here you two. And kick off your shoes please, I can only imagine where you've just been."

Maureen's eyes settled on Val's torso. Val followed her gaze, suddenly embarrassed to see blood smeared across her shirt. She brought her hands up and saw they were also coated in blood.

No wonder the agent had reacted so strongly.

"I'm sorry, Maureen. May I use your washroom?"

"First door on the left, down that hall," she pointed. "You know the rules, no blood on the nice towels."

"Yes, ma'am."

As Val washed with the door cracked open, she could barely hear Murphy speaking to Maureen.

"Does she know?" Maureen asked quietly.

"I think she's connected the dots, but you'll have to confirm it," Murphy told her.

Val took one deep breath in to settle herself. "Strength," she whispered to her reflection in the mirror. Steeling herself to face hearing what she already knew, she walked to Maureen's dining room.

The woman's elegant dining room was strewn with computers, reminiscent of the Limitless Logistics conference room right now. Men and women who Val assumed were Diplomatic Security Service agents manned computers, seeking updates on the situation in the State Department building.

"Trevor, give them your report, please," Maureen directed a young man sitting at the head of the dining table.

"News media is classifying it as a terror attack and word has already gotten out from survivors that someone teleported in. They have CCTV footage of a man appearing in the front office who is then shot by someone they haven't identified before two more arrive. The first man disappears but the other two are fatally shot. Unfortunately, it would appear their bombs were wired to Deadman switches and the footage stops then."

Val absorbed his words, thinking of Pyotr lying mortally wounded in the warehouse loft. The last image from his mind played in her head.

Val looked up to Maureen and Murphy staring at her. Murphy opened his mouth to speak when a commotion in the living room halted him. It took a moment to settle the Diplomatic Security Service agents again when Rachel, Damarcus, and Apollo appeared in the living room.

"Secretary Mitchell," Damarcus said by way of greeting.

"General Washington," she acknowledged him. "Ms. Ng. And you are Apollo, I presume?"

"Indeed, ma'am." He offered his hand, but Maureen ignored it.

"News already has it," Damarcus said.

"We were just discussing that," Maureen told him.

"Those registration twits are already howling for a way to track us," Rachel said with a grim look on her face.

Val caught Murphy's eye and sighed. "We can't let them tag us like animals, Maureen."

"I know," Maureen's voice was firm but tired.

"It means we can't do our job."

"I know."

Val looked at her. "You know, but you are no longer in a position to stop them from introducing legislation, are you?"

"I am not, sadly," she said and looked genuinely remorseful. "And we have a bigger problem growing too. I can spin the narrative that they were terrorists, and they are, but even from the State Department, I don't know if I can halt what is coming."

"The power vacuum?" Val asked and looked at Apollo.

"Yes, mostly. They took out almost every oligarch that held power. Without them, there will be social infighting." Maureen said and looked at Apollo, who nodded.

"Yes, she says it well."

"One person could easily push them into destabilization. His assessment was overly simply, but still accurate. They will start the propaganda machine now and I have almost no one to liaise with now that I trust," Maureen confirmed. "Oh, I have some back channels I can work, but no direct diplomatic links until they settle their top leadership." She shook her head.

"Two years," Apollo said.

"To settle down? Yes." Maureen agreed, finally looking at Apollo. "You lived through it, didn't you?"

"Yes, to a degree." Apollo's answer was stiff, conveying the two years of turmoil he lived through upon his return.

The room was quiet as they took in the enormity of what was about to happen.

"Ma'am, I have access to the CCTV footage. Do you wish to view it?" Trevor told Maureen.

Maureen shot Val a glance. "No, Trevor, not yet."

Val held Maureen's gaze. She had no desire to see Powell's demise on a screen. Remnants of Pyotr's memories flittered past her eyes. In an instant, she felt numb. No pain. No sadness. Just calm detachment from her world.

"Valerie?" Maureen's voice was calm.

"I know Maureen. He's gone, isn't he?"

"He was supposed to be seeking asylum from me today," Maureen told her.

"I'm sorry, Val. It's my fault," Murphy said. "I'm so sorry. I'm why he was there."

"No," Val choked out. Powell's actions hit her full force and the emotions washed over her again. "No, Murphy. He wouldn't have been there if he hadn't murdered a man and been looking for a way out of his troubles."

Val shook her head and went silent. The world was about to ignite into war and all she could focus on was her own loss. Mandy's face suddenly crossed her mind.

Mandy who had loved and lost. Mandy whose fear drove her away. Mandy who couldn't accept changes to her dreams and work to find a way still seek happiness. She would rather irreparably break a friendship rather than accept help. The loss of a dear friend echoed in Val's heart.

"If we are the Pantheon, then we're descending into Tartarus right now," Val said, pulling on her deep well of Greek mythology.

"Are we descending into Tartarus or is Tartarus rising?" Damarcus asked quietly, eyeing Murphy, and clearly worried about what would happen in the next few moments.

***

Valerie Hall had been the victim of a horrific crime. A child who lost her mother. A friend who lost a near sister. A leader who lost her mentor. Now, a woman who had lost her second love. Val had stood by as her best friend lost those she loved the most, sinking into the abyss and choosing to descend deeper. Val knew no one would blame her for following Mandy down into the cold and comforting darkness. It would be so easy.

Sink?

Rise?

Val took a deep breath, deciding in that moment how she would live her life.

As always, Val chose to rise.

Acknowledgements

Dear Readers,

First and foremost, I did not think it would take me this long to get Pantheon 3 published, so my very first "thank you" is to the readers who stuck with me. When Pantheon 2: Ares & Athena was published in September of 2021, I had every intention of finishing Pantheon 3 by the next September and having it out in the Spring of 2022.

But life happens.

And for those of you who follow me on any form of social media, a lot of life happened to me. Enough life that I eventually stopped giving updates because it all seemed so melodramatic I didn't think anyone would believe it. You see, in May of 2021 I was elevated into my dream job. The job I had been chasing for fifteen years. But by January of 2022 my health was in shambles. Sure, the new position was stressful, but not that stressful! In March of 2022 I had surgery that diagnosed me in with my chronic illness. I spent the summer desperately battling for my health, right up to the brink. Apparently, when you tell ER personnel, "I feel like I'm dying," you are either a wimpy loser or you are actively attempting to shuffle yourself loose the mortal coil. Imagine my surprise when the ER nurse agreed with me rather than telling me to suck it up.

November of 2022 unfortunately marked my eighth month without working on the Pantheon series but a turning point in my health. This acknowledgment section wouldn't be complete without thanking the fabulous medical care team at Walter Reed for quite literally saving my live, even if they took a few organs in the process!

I got back on my feet and my fingers back on the keyboard while I recovered and have been writing ever since. But while my heath declined and then recovered, I learned who my true supporters were. My biggest thanks to everyone who stuck with me, who listened to me sob over everything that happened, and chose to be there when it looked like it was the end. Like Frodo of the Shire, I found my

Fellowship.

I also need to thank all the folks who helped me with specific portions of Pantheon 3:

To Doc Andy, thank you for the in depth knowledge of the endocrine system and telling me that in fact, my method of murder was more plausible than I thought. I swear to only use this knowledge for good.

To Doc "Darth" who helped me work out how to depict the effects of Alcohol Use Disorder and cocaine without having to make a very, very suspicious Google search history.

To Jade, thank you for your encouragement and letting me use your likeness for Kelly's replacement, a very "jaded" Naval Officer.

To Marcus, thank you for being a shoulder to cry on, a void to hear my screams of futile rage, and my staunch supporter.

And to the rest of the "Olds" and my girlies with "Tilted Crowns," thank you for being there for me on my very best and worst days.

To Dr. Tracey K. who lent her expertise and likeness for the engagement scene, thank you!

To Daniel C. Ross, who first believed in the Pantheon series. Through it all, you've encouraged and mentored me. I cannot thank you enough for giving my story the wings to fly and the support to keep the dream going.

To James Young who has been both a mentor and co-conspirator in equal measures. Thank you for all the memes and advice.

To my fabulous editor Donna who is both cheerleader and drill sergeant and whose comments never fail to make me giggle. I'd be "ass deep in alligators" without your help!

To my favorite Agency friend, who wishes to remain anonymous, but has helped me understand some of the bureaucracy associated with the Agency and get a very, very close look at the Oval Office. (I'm sure that will come out in the next book!)

As always, a thank you to my Beta Squad: KGB, Thunder, Kevin, Newt, and DCR. You all help me smooth out the rough edges, challenge my errors, and keep the Pantheon grounded. Thank you all!

A big thank you and hug to my daughter, my sweet pumpkin,

who weathered a few very long years with grace. One day I hope you are able to look back on this time and remember a mother who loves you so much and fought to live.

Finally, as I mentioned, like Frodo of the Shire, I found my Fellowship in the last few years. Like Frodo, I also found my Sam. My best friend, my love, my calm, and my ride-or-die bestie. From a casual friend to play games with to my best friend and now my husband. Thank you for being by my side, "here at the end of all things" as well as now that our season of life has moved to a happier one. It took 350 steps to get to this moment and I'm glad to have had you there by my side. Thank you for your unwavering support and love.

KR Paul
FL Panhandle
November 2024

This narrative is a work of fiction. Nothing in this work constitutes an official release of U.S. Government information. Any discussions or depictions of methods, tactics, equipment, fact or opinion are solely the product of the author's imagination. Nothing in this work reflects nor should be construed as any official position or view of the U.S. Government, nor any of its departments, policies, or personnel.

Nothing in this work of fiction should be construed as asserting or implying a U.S. Government authentication or confirmation of information presented herein, nor any endorsement whatsoever of the author's views, which are and remain her own.

This material has been reviewed for classification because the author is smarter than a Navy Seal.

About the author

KR Paul was born in California but moved to North Carolina as a child. She grew up rock climbing, horseback riding, and writing fan-fiction like so many other 90s kids. Her love of adventure took her into the US Air Force where her love of writing grew.

She has written non-fiction for business, industry, academia, and leadership education. Through it all, she kept her love of writing and continued to write fiction in her free time.

Today, KR still works her military day job but writes short and novel-length fiction when not being an absolute jock or absolute nerd. When not at work, her hobbies include competitive bodybuilding, video gaming, kayaking, cosplay, skydiving, and playing with light sabers.

Her work serves up a blend of powerful action and the vivid world of urban fantasy. She draws from her own life experiences to fuel the emotionally charged, fast-paced plots found in the Pantheon series.

For more information on this and other exciting new authors, please see KRPPublishing.com

EMAIL

WEBSITE